The Interview Room

Also by Roderick Anscombe

Shank
The Secret Life of Laszlo, Count Dracula

The Interview Room

[•]

Roderick Anscombe

St. Martin's Press ❧ New York

www.stmartins.com

Library of Congress Cataloging-in-Publication Data

Anscombe, Roderick.
The interview room / Roderick Anscombe—1st U.S. ed.
p. cm
ISBN 0-312-32399-9
EAN 978-0312-32399-8
1. Psychotherapist and patient—Fiction. 2. Childern of the rich—Fiction. 3. Prison psychologists—Fiction. 4. Prisoners—Fiction. 5. Stalkers—Fiction. I. Title.

PS3551.N67I57 2005
813'.54—dc22   2004065831

First Edition: May 2005

10 9 8 7 6 5 4 3 2 1

The Interview Room

one

I dreaded the dream. I lay awake beside my wife and each time I started to nod off, I'd jerk myself back from the brink. It wasn't even a real dream. It was a memory that possessed me while I lay trapped in sleep, the sequence playing out time and again.

The dream begins slowly, with a vague unease, as Abby and I drive in the car with Adrian. Gradually, like a whistle rising in pitch, the anxiety increases. When I recognize what is about to happen, the fear intensifies quickly. We approach the traffic lights. The emotion is unbearable—not just fear, but anguish at what I can't prevent.

Sometimes I cry out at this point and wake, but not this night.

It's almost a relief when the real danger emerges—a flinching awareness, just before the moment of impact, of the pickup truck barreling through the red light.

The dream doesn't bother with dazed confusion, pain, vision obscured by blood, helpers who gathered outside the crushed car, frantic efforts to free us. It goes straight to the heart of the matter. Abby, in the passenger seat, turns to me. My mind is working effectively in trauma-center mode, ticking off the pallor of her skin and the sheen of sweat on her forehead that indicate impending shock from internal bleeding. But she's trapped by the twisted metal of what was the passenger door. She's asking for Adrian. I can't turn my head to see him. With terrible dream prescience, I already know of the horror in the back, where our two-year-old son is strapped in his car seat.

I stand outside the car. I have to hide Adrian's injuries from Abby. She reaches out her hands to take him from me, but I make a show of cuddling the body and rocking him in my arms as if to comfort him, as if he's still alive. I have his good side facing her. His eyes are closed. He might be asleep. I show her how my fingers trace the nebular spiral of his fine, blond hair.

I was sitting bolt upright in bed. Abby was shaking my shoulder. She was telling me to wake up.

"What happened?" I asked, dazed by the horror.

"You were dreaming," Abby said. "You screamed."

"Sorry."

I put my hand to my face and found it wet with tears. Adrian had died a year ago, but it felt like yesterday.

Abby stroked my back rhythmically, and with each motion of her hand I felt some of the dread melt away.

"Try to sleep," she said.

We lay together with our arms around one another, but it wasn't working, and after a few minutes we rolled apart. Our separate griefs combined like the feedback when you bring a microphone so close to a loudspeaker that it shrieks. Some couples fake orgasms. We faked sleep. We lay close and tried to breathe with the profound regularity of sleepers while our minds worked over memories of Adrian and came to the dead end of his loss.

When the call came early that morning, I'd been up for several hours.

retiremen
long w
sho
p

I don't like being called at home. C
forensic psychiatrist is that my pat
where they can't do any harm. It's n
ered. I work long hours. Sometim
Abby has given up on me and I f
book. I put myself into my work,
experience that I investigate at the Sanders
emotion has to stay there; perhaps because I'm able to
two worlds separate, I rarely connect the violent crimes of my patients with the accident that killed my son. I can tolerate the de-
scent into barbarism precisely because I can leave it behind. I can
bear almost anything—heartrending sorrow, manic rage, the re-
counting of evil acts that cause me to question the very nature of
humanity—but at the end of the day I have to be sure that it's
sealed off by the heavy steel doors that slam shut after me. I'm uneasy when it leaks into my home along a telephone wire.

I'd told the people at Sanders I was going to write up some reports and would be in late. I was in the kitchen, filling the pot of
the coffeemaker at the faucet and gazing through the window at
waves breaking on the rocks where our property meets the At-
lantic. No one but Sanders would call me at seven in the morning,
and I let the phone ring a couple of times while debating whether
to ignore it. Then, above me, I heard the thump of the shower
door thrown back and the pad of bare feet.

"I'll get it," I called.

But right after I answered the phone, I heard the click as Abby
picked up. The person at the other end was already talking. Abby
didn't say anything. Out of context, I didn't at first recognize the
voice of Larry Shapiro.

"You have a 401(k), right, Paul?" he asked.

"Sure," I said.

It seemed like a strange time for my boss to inquire about my

t. I'm forty-one, and always assumed that that day was a

ay off. In the years I'd worked under him, Larry hadn't

vn much solicitude for my welfare. I wondered if he was

eparing to tell me I was being let go.

"Who's it with?" he asked.

In the background, I heard the soft click of Abby hanging up, and a few seconds later the slide of the glass door as she returned to the shower.

"Cavanaugh, I think."

"Exactly!" Larry exclaimed.

Larry is chairman of the psychiatry department at New England Methodist Hospital and full professor at Harvard Medical School. He isn't given to business calls before the workday begins. They're not his style. Early rising, missed lunches, working late—this kind of striving smacks of a materialism that offends Larry's sixties sensibility. The ponytail is gone and the raven black hair is graying; the brown corduroy jacket with the leather elbow patches was long ago recycled through the Salvation Army. Larry no longer calls you "man." His genial, spacey manner encourages the impression that he simply floated down into his position atop the medical school pinnacle, instead of winning it through a mixture of shrewd choice of research focus, a politician's sharp elbows, and plain old hard work.

"He's the only male of his generation," Larry was saying. "He's the prince. You see what I'm saying, Paul?"

Conversation with Larry is like playing in a baseball game in which the first baseman might be the one to throw the pitch. Or the umpire.

"What I'm having difficulty with, Larry," I said, "is figuring out how this ties in to me."

He sighed with impatience. "The Cavanaugh Mutual Fund Family! Cavanaugh Wealth Management! Okay? That's who the kid is. Prince Cavanaugh. They're sending him to your place for a period of observation."

"What's his crime?"

"That's the point, Paul. It's nothing. Some bullshit charge. Violation of a restraining order on a girlfriend. Jesus! If they'd had laws like this when I was dating, I'd have spent my whole frigging adolescence in the slammer. But there it is. The family's freaking out. The prince is going to prison and he hasn't even been found guilty. They're real upset. Obviously."

The Cavanaughs are the kind of family whose upset sends tremors through their immediate surroundings. Their upset is measured on the Richter scale. They are major donors to the New England Methodist Hospital. When the hospital was on the brink of bankruptcy during the Medicare cutbacks ten years ago, it was John Cavanaugh who personally shepherded the hospital's bond issue to market. In fact, the psychiatry department occupies three floors of the Cavanaugh Pavilion.

"We wanted him here," Larry was saying. "At the Methodist. Judy O'Donnell was all set to do the evaluation. The lawyer told the judge, 'Hey, if it's a question of security, the family will spring for a private duty cop twenty-four/seven outside the kid's door.' But the DA objected on some technicality—the Cavanaughs are paying for the cop so there's a conflict of interest. I don't see it myself. Maybe you have to be a lawyer. The judge wavered. As soon as he started fussing with papers you could tell he wasn't going to buy it."

"You were there," I said.

Even Larry was momentarily at a loss to explain why the chief of psychiatry of a Harvard teaching hospital would attend this arraignment. "As an observer," he allowed. "Lending support to the family. The New England Methodist community reaching out. You know how it is. Politics. Anyway, the judge went with the DA."

"Brenda Gorn," I told him.

"I'll tell you, she was one tough mama."

"She's very good. I work with her quite a bit."

"But hell, Paul, the kid's a senior at Harvard. All but graduated. His whole life's in front of him. A place in the Cavanaugh Family of Funds. Starting at the top. What's he going to do to jeopardize that?"

People who don't know crime, even well-versed psychiatrists like Larry, have no appreciation of the truly trivial motivations that impel people to murder.

"And this is a kid who needs to be locked up?" Larry asked. "In your place?"

"Brenda's a stickler," I said lamely.

"Anyway, the judge went with her." He sighed. "And I got a call from John Cavanaugh."

From the moment I'd recognized his voice on the phone I'd been asking him silently, "Why are you calling me, Larry? What's the message?" Now I prepared myself to receive the pitch, though I knew well enough what it would be: Tread carefully. Do nothing to antagonize the Cavanaughs. Nothing that would jeopardize their generosity to the New England Methodist Hospital.

None of this would be stated. It couldn't be. Larry had simply called to tell me what time it was. It was payback time. I was to cut the kid some princely slack.

"Look," he said, the way that salesmen do when they've decided the moment has come to close the deal, the voice dropping in pitch, the vocal cords relaxing to increase the degree of aeration so that the tone takes on a slight huskiness that's often associated with sincerity. "Paul. Do the right thing. No one wants you to pull your punches. I want to tell you personally you have a free hand in this."

He'd mentioned "your place" twice to contrast it with "here" at the center of things at New England Methodist. There was no mention of my request to renew the funding for my research or the new proposal that had been sitting on his desk for the last two months. There was no mention of a quid pro quo.

"No one here's going to be looking over your shoulder," he insisted. "Call it as you see it. We're not going to second-guess you. And if it doesn't come out the way the Cavanaughs want . . . ," Larry ventured, teasing me with a vision of disaster.

He let the sentence hang. For someone like myself who has a professional interest in deception, who has been lied to by the very best, it was a pause of exquisite artistry, as poised and confident as a rest in a Mozart violin concerto.

He broke the spell. "In fact," he said, laughing, "screw him." Larry chuckled as if at the pleasure of trying on some relic of a misspent youth, an old pair of Frye boots, perhaps, discovered at the back of a closet, that still fit perfectly. "Fuck him, man! Fuck old John Cavanaugh and his money!"

two

Larry's threat in itself didn't bother me so much as the fact that he'd interfered in a finely tuned process. I'd be fair in evaluating the Cavanaugh boy, but impartiality is a delicate balancing act. My father was a judge, an imposing figure in my childhood, and a stickler for accuracy. His eagle eye detected the slightest shading of the truth. Though he's been dead five years, I still feel his presence, that eagle eye, and I think that's why I pursue the ideal of fairness with such discipline, with his severity. That's also why lying—the unattainable hiding place—holds such fascination for me.

You assume the patient will lie to you; the bigger the charge, the more at stake, the bigger the lie. That's a given. And lying—or, its euphemism in academic circles, declarative deception—is my area of expertise. I accept deception. But it means that you approach the truth as though you're walking a tightrope. When someone who isn't even part of the process, like Larry, tries to influence you, you adjust by bending over backward so that you're not influenced. You start to second-guess yourself. You compensate by going against your tendency to react in certain ways to certain kinds of people. You adjust to your adjustment.

I was brooding on this, struggling to regain my clinical equilibrium, and I didn't hear the first ring of the phone over the whine of the coffee grinder in my hands. When I turned, I saw that Abby had come down and already picked it up.

"It's for you," she said.

I reached for the phone, but Abby had already laid it down on the counter. She was dressed and ready to go, distracted by her hurried inventory of what she needed to take with her to work.

I hoped she wouldn't rush off. I wanted to tell her I was sorry I woke her. I felt we had to grab hold of each moment we were together, however fleeting, before the centrifugal forces in our marriage spun us apart. For a moment in the darkness of the night, as I struggled to wake from the nightmare, she'd comforted me, but now that seemed part of the dream world. In daylight, we were like people riding on roundabouts set side by side, revolving in opposite directions, at speed, so that we flashed by one another, carried away into our separate days.

As I came to the counter for the phone, Abby crossed to the fridge to pick out a bottle of water. Abby has startling blue eyes that still made my heart miss a beat when her gaze came up to mine, but she wasn't meeting my gaze. She was unusually scattered, abstracted.

Her eyes moved across my face with scarcely a pause. She was wearing a new lipstick, I noticed, a bold red that was very striking with her fair complexion and blond hair. And she had more makeup around the eyes than usual; it was subtle, and I couldn't at a glance make out what she'd done differently. I wanted to tell her how terrific she looked, but then I remembered the phone.

Abby closed the door of the fridge, turned to me, and half-mouthed, half-whispered, "Got to run."

I picked up the phone and covered the mouthpiece with my hand. "Wait," I asked her.

I'm late for work, she pantomimed, fluttering her hands in mock panic; then she set her head to one side and puckered her lips in regret.

I waved the phone in my hand as though I might toss it away. "This is just going to take a minute."

But Abby seemed not to hear me. She was already moving toward the door. She turned to mime a kiss in her radiant new lipstick across six feet of empty air. Seven. Eight. Waving. She was gone.

"Hullo? Hullo?"

I put the phone to my ear. "Brenda?" I asked.

"Sorry to bother you at home, Paul, but the people at Sanders said you weren't coming in till the afternoon and they gave me this number."

"They did?" I knew Sanders wouldn't give out my unlisted number.

"Well, anyway," Brenda rushed on, "I'm glad I reached you."

Brenda Gorn, the deputy district attorney for Exeter County, is nothing if not straightforward, which is why she's the deputy DA and not the district attorney. There isn't a political bone in her body. When I first started at Sanders, Brenda and I had our share of disagreements over the not-guilty-by-reason-of-insanity pleas, but the fact that I stood my ground gave her confidence in my clinical acumen, though through a prejudice endemic to law-enforcement types, she still sees me as part of that sorry tribe of starry-eyed liberals.

"Calling to give you a heads-up, Paul."

"I think I already had one. You're calling about Cavanaugh."

"Right. Craig Cavanaugh. But the people from the Methodist already got to you, I guess."

"They didn't get to me, Brenda. They called to let me know the kid was coming my way."

"Ah. That would be a professional courtesy. He's not a kid, by the way. He's twenty-two going on forty-five. He's smooth as silk. Slick as a lizard's tongue."

"But he's a Harvard man," I protested. Brenda doesn't respect a man who can't find a way to needle her. It had come to be a sign of something like affection in our relationship.

"Not if these charges stick."

"Violation of a restraining order?"

"Oh, no. That was last time. That must be what the Methodist people told you. No, Mr. Cavanaugh is moving up in the world. He's charged with stalking. He could do time."

"That's a bit of a stretch, isn't it?"

"Maybe you should talk to the victim before you decide on that."

"Alleged victim," I corrected her.

"Right," she said wearily.

"I'll speak to her," I promised.

"Look, Paul, I'm not trying to influence your professional opinion or anything, but you should be absolutely clear that Craig Cavanaugh is an evil shit."

"Right," I sighed.

I took the flask of coffee upstairs to my office, fully intending to put the Cavanaugh case aside until I'd finished the reports. I arranged the folders of the cases I was going to work on in a line across the sturdy oak desk I'd inherited from my father. The high-backed, leather-covered chair I settled into had been passed down with the desk and had once graced my father's chambers. When he retired from the bench, the court bailiffs had been more than ready to carry it out the back door for him, but he had insisted on first writing a check to the Commonwealth. It showed its age somewhat; the leather was a bit rubbed at the edges, and there was a dark stain in one corner of the seat from the time the lid had come off my son's sippy cup and the milk had spilled. I had brought the chair up to my office out of a misguided sense of loyalty to my father, but the truth was that I had never felt comfortable sitting in his place until the milk stain, proof of the joyous presence of my son, had served to counteract his stern influence.

I clearly remembered the day of the spill—for me, memory had become a process largely outside my control. Abby had brought Adrian upstairs so that he could show off his stuff. He was one year old and could totter several paces from one parent to the other, with a kind of dive at the furthest extent of his range. He was very pleased with himself. He was bringing his daddy some milk, the cup held with deep concentration in both hands before him, and as he half-jumped, half-fell toward me I went to catch him and let the sippy cup land where it might. The recollection had come unbidden, but now I made myself remember it again as an active, willed process: finding Adrian's exact starting point on the rug, counting the steps, measuring my outstretched hands, imagining the dual trajectories of child and cup, blinking away tears, until I felt I'd reclaimed the memory and made it my own once more. Then I felt freed to work.

I was halfway into the first report when the fax machine sprang to life and the cover sheet of the police report from Brenda dropped into the tray. I continued typing, but the hum of the fax machine was a powerful distraction that increasingly piqued my curiosity. It was old history I was working on, and the future was spooling into my office one page at a time. After fifteen minutes, I saved what I'd typed and reached for the police report.

The victim's name was Natalie Davis, and most of the report consisted of her statement: a long, dry litany of times and dates and places drawn from her during the detectives' interview. Police reports aren't intended to convey the passion that drives a crime, and this one was no exception. I learned that Natalie was twenty-nine years old and a teaching assistant for one of the courses Craig had taken at Harvard. They'd been in frequent contact for several weeks, and then she'd rebuffed him. But he'd continued to harass her. There'd been the usual notes, hang-up phone calls, messages on the answering machine, impromptu encounters in which Craig pleaded for reconciliation, bouquets of roses, and then the violation of a restraining order. No threats that I could see. No overt threats, anyway.

I could have interviewed Natalie Davis on the phone. There are some forensic psychiatrists—Judy O'Donnell at the Methodist would be the first if this evaluation went awry—who would say I should have taken Craig's story first. I suppose part of why I wanted to interview Natalie first, and in person, was that I wanted to prove I wasn't going to be pushed around by Larry Shapiro and the Cavanaughs.

But there was another reason closer to home: Abby's social work agency was fifteen minutes from Harvard Yard. I thought that af-ter I'd gotten Natalie's story I'd surprise Abby by taking her to lunch: We'd sit outside at one of our favorite bistros in the Square. We surprised each other too seldom. In fact, it seemed we'd ceased being surprising to one another altogether, in the parts of our lives that were visible. We knew what there was to know, it seemed. What was made available to be known.

I was looking for a new start. I'd just turn up at her work. To-tally out of character. Then, partners in crime, we'd steal some time together. That's why I didn't call Abby first.

three

I couldn't get hold of Natalie Davis. Her home number was un-listed, of course. I got the runaround from the English depart-ment. But I was determined this interview would go through, as if it were the one thing that stood between Abby and me. When I did finally get Natalie's office number, an answering machine picked up on the first ring and I listened to a recording of a forbidding man's voice that seemed designed to discourage messages. I started to explain who I was, and halfway through, Natalie herself picked up. She seemed mightily relieved that I'd called.

"Yes, of course," she said when I suggested a meeting. She began to tell me what she had scheduled that morning, information I hadn't asked her. "But I'll tell them they'll just have to wait."

She was at first gushing and unguarded in a way that seemed slightly girlish, and I sensed her good nature and vulnerability. She trusted too quickly. She was so pleased to hear from me—a perfect stranger until ten seconds ago—that I felt I was stepping into a role that had been prepared for me, a knight on a white charger, her long-awaited deliverer. Then she seemed to catch herself, and her tone took on a new wariness.

"You'll never find my office," she said, with an embarrassed laugh.

She spoke in a clipped, precise, academic accent that I sensed was recently acquired. The cadence of her speech was staccato, with rushes of words followed by pauses, as though she needed to check what she'd just let loose for a faux pas. She seemed brittle now, on edge, while excited by my attention.

"It's an absolute rabbit warren," she told me. "And even if you did find it, I'm not sure we'd both manage to fit into it comfortably."

We agreed to meet at the top of the steps of Widener Library.

It wasn't until I parked the car that I realized we hadn't talked about how we'd recognize each other. I got to Harvard Yard early and climbed the library's broad steps, making eye contact with any young woman who looked likely. At the top, I leaned against one of the pediments and watched for her among the people exiting the library. I was curious to know if I'd pick her out before she caught sight of me: a man in a summer suit, out of place among students with backpacks and the occasional frumpy professor. Maybe I would be able to recognize her simply from our phone conversation.

I lounged in the shadows and watched the possible Natalies pass by. I was starting to suspect that I'd missed her altogether and that she'd started down the steps without noticing me when I saw her. I knew at once it was her. In fact, I was entirely unprepared for the feeling of utter certainty that took hold of me.

Natalie had glanced left in my direction when she came through the library doors, but her eyes hadn't adapted to the glare of sunlight and she'd missed me. Yet I knew her, although that recognition had nothing to do with the sound of her voice, so much as the sudden pang I felt on glimpsing a vision of a younger Abby.

It must have been the color of her hair—blond with the same hint of red as Abby's—that convinced me. Her hair was shorter than the way Abby wore hers now, curling at the level of the jaw and the nape of the neck, but it was just as Abby's had been when I first set eyes on her as an attending on the ward at City when she was a younger—far younger—social work intern. Natalie hugged the books she carried, arms folded across her chest, swiveling left and right as she looked for me. Even before she turned a second time in my direction, Natalie was beginning to assert her independence from my vision. She was smaller than Abby and thinner, and her movements were more abrupt, with sudden turns of her head as she cast about, like a bird. And then she turned to face me directly, and the vision was gone.

She saw me staring. "Dr. Lucas?"

She held her hand straight out, arm stiff, and when I took it I was aware of every bone. She looked me in the eye, then glanced away shyly, then looked back again.

"It was good of you to make time for me," I told her.

"Oh, no—thank you, Doctor. I can't tell you how glad I am to see you." She put the flat of her hand to her heart in a gesture that in someone else might have appeared histrionic, but from her it was ingenuous and somehow endearing. "I've been waiting—" She had to catch her breath. "It seems forever."

"I read what you told the detectives," I said. "It's been a long time coming."

She nodded, biting her lower lip. She looked at me in gratitude and there were tears in her eyes.

"Too long," I murmured.

She nodded her head quickly, silently, close to losing control and unwilling to risk undoing herself by putting what she felt into words.

"Look," I said. "I've got a lot of questions to ask you."

"Good."

I gestured to the expanse of grass below the steps, where groups of students sat in the shade of trees. A languid, stylish Frisbee game was in progress.

"I'm not sure this is going to be the best place for us to talk."

All of a sudden, coming to the Yard didn't seem like such a good idea. I like to keep these interviews formal, with the loyalties explicit, and already she was looking at me as though I might be her friend, therapist, comforter. Against all my training, I was feeling chivalrous and protective.

"There's a bench over there." She pointed to where one of the paths curved from view. "It's pretty private."

"Behind the Henry Moore statue."

She seemed surprised. "Did you go to undergrad here?" she asked as we descended the steps.

You don't answer personal questions. It's poor technique. In answering the first, innocuous inquiry, you encourage the misconception that an interview is something like a conversation. Instead, you hope your manner communicates that questions about who you are simply aren't on the agenda.

"Yes," I said. "Though sometimes it seems like it was in another life. How about you?"

"B.U."

"But you're from around here—am I right? The Boston area?"

"I grew up right next door, in Somerville."

Fashionable now. But I figured Natalie would have lived in Somerville before gentrification, when Somerville was on the wrong side of the tracks.

We followed the path that skirted the reclining mass of bronze and found the bench behind a group of dogwoods, whose foliage screened us from the more heavily traveled path. Natalie settled herself on the other end of the bench and fixed me with an alert, expectant look.

"You know you don't have to do this," I said. "You don't have to talk to me if you don't want to."

"I want to," she said. "I've got nothing to hide."

"I know that," I replied, more hastily than I intended, and with an apologetic tone that surprised me. Already, I was concerned about her fragility, afraid my questions would hurt her, losing objectivity.

"You can ask me anything you like," she said. "Really."

She had been a teaching assistant for Professor Kennedy's creative writing class. She didn't recall noticing Craig Cavanaugh until he turned in one particular assignment.

"He'd written a piece about the last words of a dying soldier." She paused, remembering. "It was really quite good," she said, judicious and fair, even about the work of a man who had made her life a misery.

She became excited telling me about the challenge and the gratification of turning around a skeptical student, and I let her go on, even though it probably wasn't relevant to my inquiry. I sat back and enjoyed her. She was young, idealistic, and full of zeal. For a few minutes, even I forgot that she was talking about her stalker, a man who, as we basked in the early summer sunshine on this bench in Harvard Yard, sat less than fifteen miles away in a maximum security prison.

"There came a point, I expect, when you realized he had feelings for you over and above those of a highly motivated student."

"Well, you know."

She was looking down, picking a thread from her denim skirt. She'd been flattered by his attention.

"No," I said laughing, "I don't. Spell it out for me."

She was coy, perhaps even a little flirtatious, glancing sideways at me. "It's not uncommon for undergraduates to get a crush on the professor or the teaching assistant." She shrugged. "You know—the older woman thing."

"Okay. Sure. It happens all the time."

"Actually, it had been going on for quite a while before I realized."

"You were focused on Craig Cavanaugh the student. On the assignments he handed in."

"He's really quite talented."

She put all the emphasis on "quite," tilting her head as she said it, as academics do to mean "very." She was a strange mix of affectation and vivacious impulse, and I wondered who she'd end up as, which one would win out.

"Once he got going, once he understood what the class was all about, he just blossomed." She stopped and frowned. "Then he handed in an assignment that was overwritten. It was just over the top, and I told him so. He got very upset."

"He didn't take criticism well."

"It was more than that. He took it extremely personally. He was outraged."

"What was the assignment?"

"They were to take two people out to dinner. Each person from a different era."

"Who did he choose?"

"Lord Byron and Catwoman. You know, from *Batman.*"

"Some date."

"Well, it was imaginative."

"But there was something off-kilter? Something that made you feel uncomfortable?"

"Byron was too intense. Even for Byron. He was promising

undying love before they'd finished the appetizers. Craig came up to me at the end of the class. He managed to time it so that everyone else had left. He kept saying, 'I did it for you. I did it for you.' I was shocked. I thought he'd lost his mind. The doors were closed. I couldn't hear any sounds in the corridor. Just Craig and myself."

"It was good you kept your wits about you."

"Do you think so? Sometimes I'm not sure whether I should be afraid or not. I am. Then I think I'm exaggerating, and I try to talk myself out of it. Then I think I'm in denial, and I try to talk myself back into it again."

"I think in these kinds of situations your gut instinct is usually right."

"It's not easy to live that way, always afraid."

"Especially if you live alone."

"Which I do."

"No pets?"

I'd slipped the question in casually, on a hunch, and I saw her balk.

"No."

I let it ride, waiting her out. There was something she was holding back. She was a fundamentally truthful soul, and I knew she'd be uncomfortable with it, like a tiny pebble in her shoe, and she'd tell me if I was patient.

"I used to," she confessed. "I used to have a cat."

I didn't like the sound of this. I didn't like her uncertainty about whether to tell me about the cat, and I didn't like the fact that there'd been no mention of it in the police report.

"He disappeared. He was an outside cat and he liked to roam. I put him out one evening . . ." She shrugged helplessly. "And he just didn't come back."

"You never found out what happened to him?" I asked.

I didn't have the heart to ask her if she had recovered the body.

If she had come upon it "accidentally." If it had been mailed to her. I was assailed by horrible images from crime scene photos: mutilated cats, flayed cats, a cat nailed spread-eagled to a bathroom door. Virtual cruelty. Death by proxy. I blinked to come back. I looked up; I searched the blue sky for the dazzle of sunlight.

"I scoured the neighborhood for half the night," Natalie was saying. "I couldn't sleep, anyway." She gave me a wry smile. "I know it sounds a bit neurotic. If you're not a cat person, it's hard to understand. I stapled flyers to utility poles. I offered a reward."

"But nothing?" I hoped for nothing. No body. No sending of a message. "No sign of him?"

"He just didn't come back." She was thoughtful, considering how much she'd share with me. She must have gone over it a hundred times, trying to figure out the possibilities, narrowing it down to probabilities. "He got run over, I guess."

She looked for me to confirm her conjecture, to give my professional imprimatur, but I couldn't meet her eye. I believe in the truth. I see the truth as a patient, irresistible force in the universe that, in time, will permeate all lies, all self-deception, all denial. It will soak through. In my mind I heard the slow, inexorable drip of truth, and I wanted to cup it in my hands, to keep it from her.

"Don't you think?" she insisted.

I shrugged, indicating lack of interest as much as ignorance. "I don't think there's any way of knowing."

She laughed nervously. "It's crossed my mind . . ." She looked to me for encouragement.

I headed her off. "Of course it has," I assured her. "It's a reasonable speculation that Craig might have had something to do with it. Anything's possible." I raised my hand in a gesture that could have meant, "But so what?" A gesture to ridicule danger.

"I don't think he's capable of anything like that," she said without much conviction. She waited for me to contradict her. "Do you? Do you think he could do something like that? Kill a living thing?"

"Cats do fall out of trees. Or choose a bad time to cross the road," I said. "Even street-smart cats."

She thought this over. She wanted to be reassured, only, it wasn't quite working.

"But you've seen him, haven't you?" she asked. "You've assessed him? You've done tests?"

"He's safely locked away; and, yes, we're going to assess him very carefully."

"Sometimes I think this is all my fault."

"I think that's very unlikely," I said. "You have to keep in mind: Craig's the one on trial."

"Well, I blame myself." She shut her eyes tight and raised her fists in a gesture of exasperation. "Oh, God! How stupid can you be?"

"Look," I demanded. I touched her, another no-no. I touched her upper arm, and she flinched. "Don't go there," I told her. Then, more softly, "Why don't you tell me about it. We can look at it together."

"I said I'd go out with him. There! Was that dumb, or what?"

"I don't think so," I said. "You don't know who someone is until you go out with them."

"I never went out with him."

"There was no—"

"Affair? No."

"No—"

"No," she said abruptly, as though slamming a door. "Nothing."

"I see. You only said you'd go out with him."

"He pestered me until I gave in. This was during the course. He'd complete the assignments and hand them in, and he'd have found some way to make them about me. It sounds crazy. I showed one to Professor Kennedy and he gave me a look. He said, 'This could be addressed to anyone.' Craig's pieces were really good. When I praised him he took this as my response, not to his work, but to him. He thought I'd been encouraging him. When he asked me out, I realized what I'd done. I put him off. But he wouldn't let it go. I felt responsible. I said yes, just to get some breathing space."

"Then, when the course came to an end . . ."

"It was awful. I said, 'Look, I'm sorry, this isn't going to work.'"

"But he wouldn't take no for an answer."

"Thank God, there was a security guy passing outside the classroom. Craig was ranting. The security man poked his head in and asked us, 'Is everything okay in here?' I felt like a hostage. I thought I'd have to give some kind of secret sign to the guard to get me out of there. But Craig didn't bat an eyelid. It was spooky, really. One minute he'd been on the verge of—I don't know what. The next, he was calm, personable. He told the man, 'Yeah, we're fine.' And he turned to me and said, 'Got to be going. I'll see you later,' as if nothing had happened."

"Then we get all the incidents in the police report: harassing telephone calls to your apartment at all hours, cards slipped under your office door, the face-to-face encounters."

"I never knew when he'd pop up. He could be behind that tree over there—I know he's locked up, but I still have that reaction, because that's the kind of thing he'd do. If I talked to a man— anybody—there'd be a denunciation the next day. As if he owned me."

"Did you think about leaving?" I asked. Craig, even if convicted, wouldn't be locked up for long. And there was a chance, with a full-court press from the kind of heavy hitters the Cavanaughs could hire, that he'd beat the charges.

"I thought about it, but I haven't finished my dissertation, so I'm kind of stuck. I'd look into other jobs—I even set a date for defending my thesis—and then weeks would go by without hearing from Craig, and I kind of hoped maybe he'd turned his attention to somebody else." She gave me a guilty glance. "Then it would start up again. So I got the restraining order."

"And he violated it."

"Even that's touch and go," she said. "I have an apartment in a triple-decker. There's a lobby. The street door's kept locked. He came in and went up the stairs and put a dozen roses outside the door to my apartment."

"But insofar as you know, he never entered your apartment."

"I'm not sure."

I went on quickly, brightly, as if this were just another piece of the puzzle. "Something happened, though, that makes you wonder?"

"I came home one day, and the furniture had been moved. But very slightly. The sofa was angled. A table was turned around. Nothing was missing. Some books on a shelf had been rearranged. Not that it mattered."

"Not in any practical sense," I said. I wanted to tell her: "Defend your thesis. Get out of Massachusetts. Move on!"

"It's only a matter of time before he loses interest," she was saying.

It was almost noon when I left Natalie on the bench. I was afraid I'd undone her illusion of safety. I tried to reassure her about the long reach of the law, but we both knew the law isn't much good at protecting people before the fact.

Abby's agency is in East Cambridge in a rehabbed Victorian on an iffy street. A couple of blocks in the direction away from Harvard Yard, the neighborhood takes an even steeper dive and there is an all-but-abandoned apartment building that I suspect is being used as a crack house. Abby's oblivious to this. When I tell her my concerns ("Honey, I know these people"), she points out that it's exactly the kind of neighborhood where there's truly a need for an agency for troubled teenaged girls ("Honey, I know these people," she counters).

She doesn't have to work there. If she wanted, she could have a psychotherapy practice in an affluent suburb. But after her father left, Abby's family lived hand to mouth, and I think it's because we live in a big house on the ocean that Abby feels compelled to serve those who don't have much. To her way of thinking, it balances, and so makes our lifestyle permissible.

At the front desk I recognized from holiday parties the formidable lady who served as the receptionist-cum-bouncer, and in a moment of inspiration remembered her name.

"Nan, hi," I said, but she looked at me blankly. "Paul Lucas." Then I added, "Abby's husband."

"Oh," she said without much friendliness, "yes."

I thought she'd at least go through the ritual of small talk, and then after a couple of minutes' chat offer to call Abby to let her know I was here. I was feeling pleased with myself. I was looking forward to seeing the look of surprise on Abby's face.

"I happened to be in the neighborhood," I told Nan.

"Nice of you to drop by." She looked slightly puzzled. "So how's Abby?"

"Bored out of her mind," I said. "She asked me to pick up a book from her office."

It wasn't bad, as impromptu lies go. The words were pretty good: adequate, without saying too much. I hadn't gabbed. I'd learned enough from the inmates at Sanders to resist the temptation to offer more explanation than the situation demanded. When you lie, you don't want to overshoot the other person's curiosity. The composition of the words themselves was at the level of a competent sociopath. But the timing was off. I'd let a gap open up between Nan's question and my response. An entire second. An eternity in social intercourse. Though I'm an expert on lying and a researcher in the field, I lack the temperament to lie well. The part you can't fake, the part that gives you away unless you're really, really good, is the hesitation, the blink, the eye slide.

I looked at Nan and she looked at me, and in that gap it was clear that Nan knew that I had been totally unaware that Abby had called in sick. That I hadn't the slightest idea where my wife was.

four

On the drive to the Sanders Institute I replayed the events leading
up to Abby's leaving for work. The new lipstick: That was nothing.
Abby changed colors all the time. But how could she have heard
the phone when she'd been in the shower? By leaving the bathroom door partly open, which she never did. Abby is a very private
person. But if today she had left the door ajar, she must have been
expecting a call. Not from Larry, obviously, or Brenda. Some other
call. At a time when usually I would have been driving to work.

Or it could be much ado about nothing. Just because Abby
didn't show up at work, there wasn't any reason to question a new
shade of lipstick. But this is what I do. This is my job. I look for
patterns in scattered, insignificant, unrelated actions. Apparently
unrelated actions. It's taken years of training to bring me to this
pinnacle of finely tuned paranoia. You can't just turn it off when
you want to.

It was a coincidence, I told myself. Abby had gotten out of the
shower to fetch the shampoo, when the telephone rang.

But then . . . But then . . .

I despise jealousy. Simply letting these doubts about Abby enter my head made me feel petty and disloyal. Yet the eight-year difference in our ages did make me slightly insecure. That, and the chill that had entered our marriage after Adrian died.

I was nearing my destination. Abby had taken the day off. So what? So she hadn't told me? Big deal. She didn't need my permission. I was going in too deep, as usual. Over-psyching. Now I had to pull myself together.

I'd driven through the industrial park, past the screen of pine trees. Ahead of me, the razor wire strung along the fences sparkled prettily in the midday sun. It was time for closure. You can't walk into Sanders with open wounds.

From the parking lot, the Sanders Institute is a low, dispersed collection of buildings surrounded by a double perimeter fence, within which is a barren strip containing motion detectors set in the dirt. Guard towers sit at each of the four corners. I rang the bell at the chain-link gate that led through the perimeter fence and waited patiently in view of the correctional officers in the bullet-proof front control booth. They would buzz open the gate so that I could proceed to the next layer of security.

A certain wait after you ring the bell is obligatory. You do not ring the bell a second time on the off chance they might have forgotten you, however long you have waited. If they have forgotten you, they will not have forgotten that you already rang the bell once. We clinicians have a precarious relationship with the officers. When push comes to shove—and it does several times a day in the Sanders Institute—they will restore order, without our help. Though they have high-school diplomas and we are graduate-school professionals, though we may think we make the important decisions, this is their house.

My wait at the gate was less than thirty seconds. In the shadows of front control, behind the thick glass, Lieutenant Kovacs gave me an impassive, professional stare as I passed; and I did not venture so much as a nod in his direction. Any gesture of greeting on my part would have been a sign of weakness, a noncombatant's need for affiliation, an inability to leave outside the social niceties of my world. Especially with Lieutenant Kovacs. After five years I still had no sense of the man. He was polite, curt, and utterly self-contained, as befits the lead sniper on the tactical operations team. Sometimes, when I walked past the front trap, I felt the itch of the red dot of a laser sight dancing on my forehead, and, though I knew it was only my imagination, I was reassured by the bullet-proof glass that stood between us.

Kovacs buzzed open the first door of the entry trap and I presented my ID to the officer inside the small space. He checked the seal on my bottle of water to make sure I wasn't smuggling vodka and then nodded to Kovacs that I was cleared to proceed. The opposite door opened, and I exited to the main corridor of the administration building. A second trap let me out onto the Sanders campus.

Surveyed from the steps leading from the administration building, the Sanders Institute resembles a down-at-the-heels state college built during the sixties. Two-story buildings of cinder block painted a light tan form three sides of a square surrounding a three-acre expanse of dry brown grass crossed by concrete paths. The fourth side of the rectangle extends like an afterthought, with a jumble of one-story buildings in the same cinder block and clusters of prefabricated offices, each contained by its own fence.

I paused a moment on the top step to prepare myself for Admissions. In a sense, you enter the prison twice. There's the journey of your body through the traps and searches, and a psychological movement that runs parallel to the physical process. You must leave home. You have to cover your soft, civilian sensitivities with an emotional body armor. You toughen up. You make yourself hard and cynical. But this presents a problem. When I interview someone, I rely on hunches, twinges of feeling, gut responses to guide me to the emotional truth of the person: If I don't let him affect me, I can't sense him. But I have to look out for myself, too. This is the dilemma: How can I tune myself to detect the infinitesimal, the vanishing humanity of a child killer, and at the same time protect myself from his inhumanity? How to be there and not be there?

You do it because, mixed in amongst the monsters, the wife beaters who never laid a finger on her, the addicts who want to con me out of Klonopin, and the fakers after an insanity plea, are lost souls: the impulse-ridden kid with ADHD; the psychotic man who extinguished the robots who were impersonating his parents; the manic who robbed a bank of money he knew was his own; the despairing mother who almost euthanized her children to spare them the suffering of earthly existence. These people can be salvaged. They're not rare at all. People like this enter Sanders every day. But so too do the scammers and the predators who must be culled before they can damage those who are truly ill. It's not at all obvious which is which. The only way you can make the distinction is up close and personal.

Sanders sits on the edge of a cliff with a deep drop into the abyss: natural life in the state prison system, madness, suicide. I believe my job is to yank people back from the brink. When I hit it right, it's the greatest altruistic buzz you can imagine. But to get it right, I first have to separate my true patients from the liars. And to do that, to go among them, I must also protect myself.

As I passed through the traps, I also moved through this hardening process, and by the time I'd crossed the yard, I was prepared, more or less, for what awaited me at Admissions. The single steel door rumbled back and I waited a couple of beats, checking to the right and left to make sure none of the patients milling about was lying in wait for me. Our sergeant, George Ramirez, sat watchfully behind the steel grille of the control center. In what was a morning ritual, I passed my brass chit through the mesh in return for the body alarm that George pushed through the opening below.

"Just one, Doc," he said.

"I heard," I said. "I've had two calls already."

"Tell me about it. I've had calls from everyone from the superintendent down."

My way forward was blocked by a clamoring throng of patients and I took a few minutes to sort out what they wanted—telephone calls, medication changes, postage stamps, the number of their attorney. They were scared and needy, and they caught me on the way in, before my transformation was complete.

The staff room during afternoon rounds resembles a commodity trading pit, everyone calling at once to get their deals done. The action appears chaotic to outsiders, but in fact it's every bit as efficient as the Chicago Merc. Presiding over this outcry, closing three-way deals, umpiring disputes, levering stuck negotiations back onto the tracks, was the imperturbable Maria Baldini, who should have been making real money selling BMWs instead of running Admissions for a social worker's pay. With her sharp intelligence and dark good looks, it seems like Maria should be happier. She's not in a relationship, pushing forty, and lives with an ailing mother. But Maria's like many of us at Sanders: We've adapted to the pungent reality of the Institute. If you don't watch out, it can become a more powerful reality—more intense and elemental—than the world outside the razor wire.

As I came in, Maria was in animated negotiations with the directors of two other units about transferring a patient. She looked up long enough only to give me the telephone sign, jerk her thumb in the direction of the patients, and roll her eyes heavenward.

I gave a shrug of resignation. *I know,* I mouthed.

I checked the status board to see that there had been no important changes in my patients overnight, quickly riffled through the memos and glossy junk mail from drug companies in my pigeonhole, and was out of the room and starting down the corridor before anyone could engage me.

For my first encounter with Craig Cavanaugh, I selected Interview Room One: four walls of cinder block, painted pale blue, growing steadily hotter as the summer sun beat down on them, a window rusted closed, and a concrete floor. The acoustics are terrible, but I gladly trade the tinny echo for space. The attraction of Interview Room One is that it's large and uncluttered, with lots of room in which to maneuver.

Of the four pieces of furniture in the room, three are mismatched chairs. I placed the one with the broken back against the wall behind me so that it would be out of play. The one on the patient's side of the desk is a special item, the modular frame cast from four-inch tubular steel filled with concrete. A strong man could heave it off the floor; an immensely strong, enraged man might manage to swing it above his head—but only very slowly, with a lot of puffing and grunting.

The desk in Interview Room One has always bothered me. It's a steel office desk in olive green. Its one good feature is the modesty partition in the leg space, which now serves the function of protecting the interviewer if the patient lashes out with his feet. The dilapidated state of the desk's frame spooks me: its sagging drawers and broken struts. If I'm assaulted, I move away from trouble. No heroics. I don't know how to fight—I'm a doctor, for goodness sake. All I know is how to kill people.

The last thing I want is to engage the patient in physical terms, so if he looks like he's about to get out of hand, I press the button on the personal body alarm. In ten seconds, a gang of correctional officers, fired up and ready to go, will burst into the room and flatten every human being in their path. That's reassuring. Then again, ten seconds is a long time, if someone's managed to get hold of you. That's why you have to react by anticipating. All you have to do is dance around the room for one, Mississippi, two, Mississippi . . . When you count it out all the way to ten, like a soundtrack to imagined action, you realize how much can happen in ten seconds. You have to be realistic about this. You must come to terms with it—as much as this is possible—in advance, because if you're unprepared, it's devastating.

The vital thing is, you must stay on your feet. If things go wrong, you can take a couple of licks—a split lip, a torn ear, a broken nose, bruised dignity—all this can be repaired. But if you go down, if your head reaches foot level, or—God forbid—concrete floor level, irremediable things happen. There's an apocryphal story of a psychiatrist who was pushed by a patient and fell backward; the patient didn't even hit him, but he went down and whacked his head, and now somewhere in a nursing home in Massachusetts an aide feeds him lunch with a spoon. He's one of those people everybody in the sanity business has heard of but no one actually knows firsthand. A powerful myth.

The trouble with the green desk is that it's already falling apart, and it wouldn't take much effort to rip out some jagged piece of metal. My fear is intricately choreographed.

One, Mississippi: He comes out of his seat. I come out of my seat. At the same time I hit the button on the body alarm.

Two, Mississippi: I move left. He tips the desk right. The file drawer that sags on the broken runner falls out.

Three and four, Mississippi: He grabs the drawer. I circle round, thinking I might make it to the door.

Five, Mississippi: I'm not going to make the door. Three fingers in the handle, he swings the drawer at my head. I backtrack, away from the door, unexpectedly into the direction of the blow. I'm backed up against the wall, but I duck just in time.

Six, Mississippi: The drawer disintegrates against the wall. His fingers that are caught in the handle break.

Seven, Mississippi: We both look at his broken fingers, still gripping the shard of steel drawer.

Eight, Mississippi: Footsteps, many, running, in the corridor. He's looking at his wrecked hand. We both know who he blames for this. I realize that I've let him get too close to me.

Nine, Mississippi: The cavalry, when it charges, is indiscriminate, friend or foe. I don't want to get trampled in the stampede. The door is opening. My head is turned to see. My neck exposed. I make a mistake. I go right. Into his backhand.

Mississippi infinity. End of story. Nothing. Not even lunch from a spoon.

I rehearse these horror-movie scenarios all the time. Strangely, I find the procedure comforting. It helps me believe I'm gaining familiarity with a future that—precisely because I'm familiar with it and therefore prepared not to repeat my mistake—I can prevent. The sense of mastery these rehearsals confer is illusory, of course. It's all part of the hardening process.

"Sergeant Ramirez," I called along the corridor. "Would you send Cavanaugh down?"

I checked the room one last time, and had just sat down behind the green desk and was giving the file drawer an extra shove with my foot when Craig Cavanaugh came into the room.

I thought, "Jeez, what is Brenda thinking? What am I getting all worked up about? He's just a kid."

five

I glanced up when Craig Cavanaugh first came to the doorway, then let him stand at the threshold while I struggled to ease the broken file drawer back along its runner into the desk. I kept at it for two beats, then decided to let it go to three, giving him time to take his measure of me: a forty-something psychiatrist who worked in an office little better than a jail cell, no air conditioning, furniture that was truly pitiful. I looked like a bumbler to him. And that was how I wanted it.

An interview is combat by other means. Privileged people who find themselves, for the first time in their lives, at the receiving end of the law will go out of their way to demonstrate their superiority by engaging me in intellectual arm wrestling. I am at times sorely tempted. But I have nothing to gain from these wrangles—especially from winning them—and so I try to convince the patient that I'm simply not worth one-upping. With these patients I plead no contest and prepare my ambush.

So when Craig Cavanaugh came into the room, I paused for a moment before looking up from my defeat at the hands of the file drawer. "Mr. Cavanaugh," I said. I held out an open hand to invite him to take the concrete-upholstered seat on the other side of the desk. "Come in."

He closed the door precisely, then turned and paused with his back against it for two seconds until he was sure he had my attention. He wore standard issue gray cotton scrubs, but they might have been tailored for him, and in spite of his twelve hours in an institution where the only mirrors are indestructible plates of polished steel, he managed to appear perfectly groomed: long black hair swept back around his ears, unblemished skin, a straight, delicate nose, full eyebrows, dazzling teeth. I noted the perfect left-right symmetry of his face, unusual among patients in my practice. No genetic defects on display there. Craig had been brought into the world from an optimal uterine environment—privileged even before he was born.

He looked younger than his twenty-two years, slender of build, and with refined good looks that made him almost pretty. For a moment, I was distracted by a protective impulse. But he didn't look like a victim. Victims give off vibes. Their body language advertises submission. If danger lurked out there in the wilds of the TV room, he wasn't giving any sign that he acknowledged it. He carried himself with a self-assurance that, in this place, was extraordinary. There was in his posture, in the tilt of his chin, a seignorial bearing that allowed that perhaps, temporarily, this was the correctional officers' house, but it was the Cavanaughs' world, and if the Department of Correction enjoyed possession of Sanders, it was only because his people presently had no use for it.

He was used to being looked at. When he felt my eyes on him he blinked, two beats, as if batting down my inquisitive stare. He had long dark lashes, and when he lowered his head slightly as he did at that moment, he seemed to look through them so that his gaze was veiled, and I wasn't so sure that I had him tabbed. Then he came forward with his hand held out, gaze fixed in man-to-man eye contact.

"Craig Cavanaugh," he announced. The way he spoke his name, giving each syllable its own special weight, seemed to draw it out forever. Perhaps it was the tone of his voice, somewhere between a purr and a drawl, that brought about this effect. His presumption was as arrogant as all hell, but I found myself not resenting him, as though his status were part of the natural order of things.

I took his hand, although I prefer not to shake hands with patients in maximum security. I don't want people getting a grip on me. But the basic personal affront of refusing a man's hand is not without danger either. He gave me a firm handshake, a somewhat overdone, no-bull handshake.

"Dr. Lucas," I said. "Sit down."

I noticed a slight unease, like a ripple passing over his face, with this last interaction, but it was gone in an instant. He'd expected the concession of a first name from me and he hadn't gotten it. We could shake hands, but we weren't really man-to-man at all. He was who he was, naked of any role, while I wouldn't easily be coaxed out from behind my professional title. And I'd given him an order.

"They told me it would be you," he said. He may have been naked, but he wasn't alone. He had *Them* on his side. Whatever I might manage to find out about him in the next few minutes, *They* had already given him the jump on me. "They speak highly of you."

Not the bland, conventional "very highly," but a notch below. Plus, he'd inserted a slight pause before the "highly" that negated whatever shred of respect the phrase might have conveyed. But this subtlety was for his private amusement. It was my impression he thought I wouldn't get it. He gave me a patronizing smile. His eyes, veiled by lashes, studied my hands. I was pleased with the progress we were making.

"That was nice of them," I allowed. Perhaps, a slight frown of concentration suggested, if I'd been speedier, I'd have found a way to ask which *They* they were.

I cleared my throat as hack interviewers do when they want to indicate the beginning of a new paragraph. "Well," I said, "I should tell you the ground rules."

"The so-called Lamb warning," he said promptly. Perhaps a little too quickly, too impatiently.

"Exactly. The Lamb warning. Very good. Your people already briefed you."

"My attorney is Ross Hamilton."

He spoke the name as if it were a threat, as primitive tribes place juju dolls at the boundaries of their territory to scare off intruders. Ross Hamilton III was a criminal attorney with Sutton, Baumeister, and Malan—certainly a force to be reckoned with, an intelligent and ruthless lawyer—but he was by no means as daunting as Craig would have liked.

"You're in good hands," I acknowledged. "Look, just so we're on the same page, why don't you tell me the main points of the Lamb warning, so that I know you know."

He spoke quickly, like a prize student who knows what he knows and doesn't want the professor interfering with his demonstration. "You're going to file a report with the court, so what I say isn't confidential. I don't have to participate in the evaluation if I don't want to. I don't have to answer any question I don't want to."

When he'd finished, he let go a little sigh of impatience and at once sensed he'd gone too far. "How am I doing?" he asked, boyish and appealing, taking on the part of the good kid who only wants to do well. It was a good recovery, the faux ingénue, and well executed.

"I don't know," I told him. I thought it was time to give a small tug on his chain to remind him it was there. "It all depends on what you're trying to do."

I flipped a couple of pages of the chart, avoiding any eye contact that could have suggested a confrontation. I was impressed. He'd been deprived of the educational benefits of formative years spent in a juvenile detention center, and yet he had an intuitive sense of institutions, rules, legalities. Even leaving his age and what I supposed was a lack of criminal experience out of the equation, Craig was quick and admirably adaptable, sensing my moves and shifting his responses rapidly. If he'd been a medical student, I'd have relished teaching him.

"What the court wants to know," I began, "is whether you're competent to stand trial—"

"I really don't think that's a serious issue."

I pursed my lips in polite skepticism. "Well, the judge does."

"What the court wants to know is whether I'm criminally insane."

He couldn't resist grinning at the grotesque application of the term to himself. The Prince of Cavanaugh mad as Hamlet. He shook his head, on the verge of hysterical laughter, in disbelief. This was the first opening he'd given me, and I let him go with it. I like to run these interviews hot. Emotion degrades processing power. If Craig got a little giddy, it would loosen him up. If he got giggly at the thought of being criminally insane, he'd start blurting stuff out. I pulled my notebook out from under the chart.

"I know," I agreed. "It's a weird notion."

"You have no idea!"

He looked at me directly, head up, eye to eye, and I felt an intensity of emotion that seemed real and that I couldn't identify. I'd thought I had him figured out—a talented, though amateur, sociopath—but for the second time I felt a pang of uncertainty.

"Tell me," I suggested.

He'd found a blemish where the Formica of the desktop had chipped, and he worried the edge of it with the nail of his left thumb as he appeared to weigh my proposal. He glanced up, a sly, sideways look as if to catch me unprepared and so gauge my trustworthiness. He looked down again and seemed to think hard. I was disappointed to see that he'd mastered his emotions and now feigned a hesitant, calculating sincerity.

"Sooner or later, I guess," he began, with a show of reluctance, as though tracing in his mind a slow inward spiral toward the place where truth lay, "I'll have to tell you."

His nail scraped audibly at the crater in the Formica as though cleaning out the bed of a pressure sore—so many elbows had rested there—and I felt an odd twinge for the old green desk.

I said nothing, waiting for him. When it was clear that I didn't feel the need to encourage him to tell his story, he looked up again. He saw the notepad for the first time, and the pen in my hand, and he took those to indicate that I'd listen to him adequately.

But to his way of thinking the moment wasn't right. It didn't have the drama he wanted for his disclosure. He laughed. Not a chuckle. Not for my benefit. A gust of contemplation.

"Shall I tell you the truth?"

I shrugged. "What difference does it make?"

He waited for me to smile, to signal I'd made a joke, and when I didn't, he gave me a look that suggested uncertainty. I wasn't living up to his expectations of me, but I saw that he wasn't a person who placed any value on doubt, and it passed in an instant.

"Don't you trust me?" he asked.

"Of course not."

It's always a revelation to me how much this response, delivered with no trace of animus, delights habitual liars. Sociopaths, people who lie so pervasively and with such facility that they've lost all notion of what truth is, use the "Don't you trust me?" line as a challenge to get the rest of the population to back off. Harvard has its fair share of sociopaths—more, probably—but on campus the students obey the taboo against calling someone a liar to his face, so the ploy probably worked well enough among his peers.

"I'm going to tell you the truth," he insisted.

"What for?"

"Because I love her." I thought he might genuinely be searching for an adequate answer. "Because I owe it to her."

"You're talking about—"

He rushed me. He snatched the words from my lips, another man's lips, before I could mouth her name. "Natalie," he said. "Natalie Davis."

I breathed the victim's name, "Natalie Davis," as though it were a line of poetry fondly recalled. I watched his face, how he was overpowered by a flush of tenderness. The power she—oblivious—had over him! He was Othello, not Hamlet. I thought of Abby's scarlet lips and crushed out the thought before it could take possession of me.

"This is crazy!" he said.

"Love is strange."

"You think I'm crazy, don't you?"

"You haven't said anything crazy so far. But then you haven't told me much, either."

He took his hands off the desk and pushed them together in his lap as he wrestled with the idea of disclosure; then he seemed to steel himself to the task, though I was sure the telling of the story, in some version or another, was a pleasure impossible to resist. I was curious to see how much he'd risk, how closely he'd skirt the truth.

"Natalie was a teaching assistant for one of my courses. Kennedy's creative writing. Usually, it wouldn't be my kind of thing, but I needed some quick credits and Professor Kennedy has a reputation for easy grading. Basically, he'll give you an A if you turn in work that's half decent. It was just a means to an end."

"And then you noticed Natalie."

"No. She noticed me."

"How was that?"

"It was one of the writing assignments. I've still got it, what I wrote, as a matter of fact. I read it sometimes to go back, to try to understand how it happened."

"How you fell for her."

"You might say it was love on the rebound, but it had to be more than that. I'd broken up with a girl, Angie, some time before. My roommates tried to get me to go out. I just wasn't interested. I went to lectures, but I didn't work very hard. I got a couple of incompletes. That's why I'm not graduating. I didn't really do much of anything."

"So you were discouraged, lonely—"

"Not lonely. I could have been with anyone I wanted."

"I'm talking about a special kind of loneliness. An emptiness that only one particular person can fill. And she wasn't there for you anymore. So you closed yourself off from the world. But then you found that you were locked in with this feeling."

He didn't disagree. He'd forgotten me, as I hoped he would. There comes a moment when all the fakery drops away and the interview takes on a life of its own.

"And then," I prompted him, coaxing him from his silent reverie into speech, "along came this assignment. And somehow, it unlocked you and you opened up in a way that was totally unexpected and perhaps a little bit strange to you."

"I kept putting it off. I'd gotten pretty good at procrastination. I was sitting at my desk, staring out the window. You know, thinking about doing what I had to do, instead of doing it. I'd written something. Not much. I couldn't take it any further. The radio station was playing some old thing, a Rolling Stones song with Angie's name in it. It was very repetitive. They kept singing her name, and every time there was this sizzling sound from the cymbal. And then I was writing. I didn't even have to think about it."

I heard the words, but I couldn't make sense of what he was saying. There was something missing, an undercurrent that I wasn't tapping into. I tried to keep him going. "Something changed," I said.

"I don't want to say it was sudden. But it was a turning point. It wasn't the assignment. That had nothing to do with it."

"What was it?"

"We had to write a dying soldier's farewell. A Civil War soldier. North or South. You could choose. The letter could be to his wife, or his girlfriend. Whoever."

He hesitated. I waited for him to come to me. But he wouldn't.

"Anyone you wanted," I cajoled. "Anyone you had something to say to."

"As long as it was from the soldier's point of view."

"Of course."

"So I wrote to his grandfather."

To the patriarch. To old John Cavanaugh. "Not to the girl he was going to leave behind?" I asked. He'd lost me. He'd made a turn I hadn't expected, and I didn't know where this was going. "Not to Angie?" I asked.

"No," he said quietly. "I'd already said all I had to say to her. I'd said it to her and I'd said it in my head. I'd thought myself to a standstill."

He was pensive and somber. The charming smile had disappeared, because he wasn't looking for advantage. He was balanced precariously, and I'd already taken one wrong turn. It was time to draw back and to phrase my questions in a way that would allow him to put himself at a distance from what we were really talking about, the topic I couldn't see.

"Your soldier," I said, "had something to say to his grandfather. Something only for his grandfather." I was groping, flying on instruments, blind intuition. "A message his grandfather was entitled to receive. Perhaps, a summing up?"

"That he'd been a disappointment."

"Already? He was young. He'd scarcely begun."

"All the same."

"No second chance?"

"He was dying—remember?"

I was being too oblique and it wasn't working. The rapport was gone. I was missing something big; that was why he'd pulled away from me. It was time to loop back into the center of it all. "And did you have a feeling your life was coming to an end, too?" I asked him.

He sighed, as though a burden had lifted from his chest. The truth is not heavy. Truth is buoyant. "Kind of," he said, not looking up.

"You were wondering whether you might kill yourself," I said, as one would glimpse the landing strip, rearing up, rushing perilously, through a gap in fog.

"It didn't work, though."

"What did you do?"

He looked up now so that he could see my reaction to what he was going to tell me. "What did I do?" He wore a goofy grin. The kind of grisly smile kids put on when they're relishing the thought of shocking you with something really gross. "I put a gun to my head and pulled the trigger," he said.

When he didn't get the reaction he wanted, he looked aside and shrugged as though it weren't anything much. But I was troubled by the disconnect, his lack of authenticity when it came to life and death.

"What happened?"

"It was a handgun someone in the house had. It wasn't anything cool, like a semiautomatic. Some old thing with chambers you put the bullets into. A revolver. He'd take it out after he'd been drinking and show off with it and poke it in peoples' faces. It wasn't loaded. In fact, when I went looking through his stuff for the gun, he didn't have any ammo for it. I had to go out and buy some shells."

"So this wasn't some sudden impulse."

"Oh, no." He sighed. "That's not my style."

"Had you been drinking?"

"No. I told you: I was sitting at my desk, staring out the window, listening to some Rolling Stones number, thinking about doing the assignment.

"And thinking about killing yourself."

"Right."

"So the assignment, the dying soldier, was also a suicide note to your grandfather."

"Now you're getting it."

He was a little smug. As though risking death gave him a moral edge over me.

"No wonder it was difficult to write."

"I'd gone as far as I wanted to go, when that song came on the radio. That was it."

"You put one bullet in the weapon," I continued. "Is that right? And you spun the chamber."

"That was the idea. But the gun hadn't been looked after, so it wouldn't spin like they do in the movies. Just one or two clicks and then it would stop. So I had to improvise. What I did was, every time Angie's name came up, with the sizzling sound of the cymbal,

I turned it one click. I'd already tried to spin it several times and I hadn't kept track. But even if I'd known the bullet was coming up, I wouldn't have changed it."

He glanced up to see if I believed what he said. I nodded my acceptance.

"Were you afraid?" I was afraid I already knew the answer.

He looked at me intently. "That's an interesting question." He studied me, measuring me, feeling for what might distinguish us here. "The short answer," he said, "is no."

"Then the song ended."

"And I put the gun to my head. And I pulled the fucking trigger."

We both waited, staring at one another across the desk. He for effect, I because there wasn't anything more to ask until the echo of the action had died away. We waited for the other one to break the silence. His breathing had increased during the last ten seconds, and I was certain that if I'd had him wired up in the lab his heart rate and blood pressure would be rising. He used the respite to reestablish control over his emotions, to re-center.

"You don't need to worry about the gun," he said, matter-of-fact. "It's at the bottom of the Charles."

"You know, don't you, that we're going to have to follow up on that?"

"But I've already told you. It's disposed of. It's at the bottom of the river. Isn't that enough?"

"No."

"You don't trust me."

"We've been there already," I said with a weary smile, as one sophisticate to another. He was going to balk, but he was proud of his act of bravado, and I thought he could be deflected from what would be an utterly useless confrontation, so I asked him, "Why don't you tell me where the bullet was."

"It was in the chamber that had just passed the firing position."

"Close." I raised my eyebrows and pursed my lips in what I intended as a salute to his sangfroid. I suppose, in one way or another, I'm a connoisseur of suicide attempts. I shrugged and said, "One Angie, more or less . . ."

He was flattered that I'd treated him semi-tough. He tried to hide his pleasure, but I saw him blink, and he looked away so that his eyes wouldn't betray him. He allowed a low chuckle, a Confederate buck whose hat had been plucked off by a minié ball. He was telling a war story to someone who knew about such things, who'd seen battles himself. He was with me. Now that I had him back I moved quickly, pushing him harder. If there was any craziness in his thinking about Natalie, now was the time to flush it out.

"So what was it?" I asked him. "Providence? Blind luck? Something that wasn't meant to be?"

"You're looking for me to say something psychotic, aren't you?"

"Not especially."

"I don't know what it meant."

"That's pretty safe."

"At the time . . ."

He looked to me as though he thought I should be able to finish the sentence. I held out my hands, palms up, in a gesture of ignorance.

"You don't trust me," he said accusingly.

"Right," I told him.

"Then why should I trust you?"

"I haven't asked you to. Actually, I don't think you should."

He sensed a trap. Some obtuse, verbal trap. Some lawyerly cleverness that dealt with problems by defining them out of existence. "Why not?" he asked.

"I don't think trust is a good idea."

He was wary, looking for the punch line to the joke. "Are you supposed to be saying things like that to patients?"

He'd slipped away from me again, and now I had to win him back. He'd gone cool and thoughtful, and I had to raise the emotional temperature back up, get him moving faster, more spontaneously, so that if there was some delusional thinking propelling this crush on Natalie Davis, he'd blurt it out. If he was crazy, I had to jazz him so much he wouldn't be able to resist telling me what really made the world go round.

"Isn't it true?" I asked him with the sharpest tone I'd used so far. "Trust isn't going to get you and me anywhere. All it does is set people up for disappointment. Look at what's going on here—right here and now." I was wagging a finger at him like a pistol. "You tell me a story about Russian roulette." I proffered an even-handed gesture of skepticism. "This is what you told me. You put a gun up to your head. You hold it there. You don't pull the trigger right off. You have to hold it there against your head for a second, because you can't do it all at once: You can't raise the gun up there and pull the trigger all in one go. I've talked to fifty people who've done this. And I know you can't do it all in one go because it's too much for a man to bear. One, Mississippi. 'I'm going to die.' Two, Mississippi. 'This is it, for God's sakes! The Big It!' Three, Mississippi. Now you pull the trigger. Click. Except, it's not really a click, is it? There's actually a bit of a jolt, when the hammer comes down, that you feel—you definitely feel it—on the side of your head. But there you are. There you still are. Maybe you pissed yourself. Or maybe you've got a hard-on. It doesn't matter, because the hammer's come down on an empty chamber. And the chamber is empty purely and simply because the song you're listening to is one word longer than it might otherwise have been. Your life hangs on one word in a Rolling Stones song. Of all the takes in the studio that day, they decided to use this one. Not the one with one fewer Angies in it. Not the lethal version. The death-dealer. And when it's over, all you say—this is what you're telling me, right?—all you have to say for yourself is: 'Gee, what do you know? This must be my lucky day! Oh, well—back to that class assignment.' Is that it? Is that the subtext? You're telling me that's all that went through your head?" I rested my case. "Now you see why I don't put any trust in trust."

"Why's that?"

"'Why?' You don't know what bullshit is?"

"I'm not bullshitting you." He was as aggrieved as if I'd called him a cheat.

"Oh."

I flicked through the chart, turning pages impatiently, to advertise my displeasure—I was, I suggested, a victim of trust, in spite of my better judgment—and waited for him to come to me.

"As a matter of fact," he offered.

I looked up expectantly.

"I did go on with my assignment."

I nodded reluctantly, with nothing more than a concession to politeness, to indicate he'd have to do better.

"But it wasn't me anymore," he said. "I mean, I wasn't writing about myself. The first part, before the song, was, but then I wrote about this farm boy saying good-bye to his grandfather. It was easy. It just came to me, effortlessly. All I had to do was write it out."

"Because you knew what you were writing about."

"I got an A."

"But that was automatic, wasn't it? In Professor Kennedy's course? Isn't that what you said? And that, in a way, must have been disappointing, because you'd put yourself into the paper, and it would have meant something to have had an honest response to it."

"But this was real. Natalie said so. She loved it."

"She said that?"

"She said . . ." His eyes misted with the recollection and his lips curved in a secret smile. Then he wised up. However I seduced him, he was still in hostile territory. "She said I was pretty gifted."

"And although this wasn't a course that you'd cared much about in the beginning, it came to really matter that your work was valued."

"It took on a new meaning."

"The work itself? Or Natalie's responses to it?"

"It was Natalie. I did it for her. I would do these writing assignments, but really I was writing . . . to her."

"And this was a new feeling. A new purpose that began with the Civil War soldier assignment."

"Right."

"Up until then you'd hardly noticed her."

"But then, I suppose she noticed me first."

"And then?"

"And then—" He put his head back and laughed with the craziness of it, the helpless craziness of love. "Then I couldn't stop thinking about her. Then I couldn't think about anything else."

"You liked that?"

"I loved it."

"It didn't bother you that you weren't thinking of other girls? Other interests?"

"I loved loving her. I was content with that being my purpose in life. It was all I wanted to do."

"You told her this?"

"Sure. All the time."

"How did she take it?"

He shrugged: It was self-evident. "What woman doesn't like to be adored? Absolute adoration?"

He laughed, snickering in a slightly unhinged way that disturbed me.

"You know what I mean?" he persisted.

I thought I didn't. "Tell me," I suggested.

He snorted and rolled his eyes as though there was someone else in the room who might appreciate how slow I was. "I've been talking to you all this time, and you don't know what I'm talking about?"

"You put her up on a pedestal."

"Pedestal!" He shook his head at my bloodlessness. "I worshipped her!"

He was getting overheated. He was giving me a glimpse of his secret passion, but I didn't want him to unravel here and now. You take them to the edge. Anyone can do that. The real expertise lies in knowing where the edge is.

"You're a pretty intense kind of guy," I said to draw his attention to the emotion, to make him mindful.

"I know."

"You don't mind me saying it?"

"No. It's okay."

"And that's the way you loved Natalie."

"Of course."

"When you say you loved her—"

"I didn't 'say' I loved her."

"I'm sorry. I thought that's what you said."

"I didn't 'say' I loved her, okay? I loved her."

"Isn't that the same thing?"

"You think I don't know what you're doing?"

"It's not something I'm doing on purpose," I said. "I think we have a misunderstanding."

"It's not some wordplay. I loved her, pure and simple. Okay?"

"Sure."

"It's not some sneering wordplay, like: 'You "say" you loved her, but really . . .'"

"Look," I said, calmly and slowly, "I think we're getting jammed up on this. Maybe we should move on."

"You think it wasn't real!"

"I don't know," I said. "How can I know?"

"Because I say it is." Then he remembered and turned his head away in disgust. "Ah, yes," he said with a bitter chuckle. "I forgot. You don't believe what people say."

"I believe in your passion," I said.

"Then what's the part you don't believe?"

"I believe you truly love Natalie."

"Then what's missing?"

He was close to shouting. As if, in convincing me, he could snuff out the flame of uncertainty that lay within, beyond his reach.

I should have ended the interview there. We'd lurched closer to the edge than I'd realized. But I thought, "What the heck? He's hot. Let it run."

I said, "Why don't you tell me the part I'm missing?"

"We love each other!"

He was shouting now. He sat forward; his face was red and the veins of his neck were swollen with the pent-up pressure in his chest. I thought I could control him. I thought, "Let's see how crazy this guy is."

"These charges . . . ," I ventured, delicately, hesitantly. I knew what I was doing: jabbing him with a sharp object.

"Wake up, Doc!"

"Help me out here."

"Come on! She would never initiate anything like that. Someone put her up to it. Someone pressured her."

"Who?"

He spread his hands in exasperation, as if the answer were too obvious, too all-encompassing, too implicit to allow for words.

"Who knows?" he said.

He was still angry and he glowered at me, scanning my face, my hands, much more closely than he had done before. The reality of the charges didn't cut any ice with him. It was a dead end, and I thought I'd change tack.

"You said I'm missing something," I began. "Why don't you tell me more about the affair with Natalie."

"What do you want to know?"

"Well, I suppose there was a physical side to it?"

He didn't respond. He looked away. He could have been fuming mad. He could have been simply switched off, emptied, waiting me out. Either way, without eye contact, I couldn't read him.

"Is that right?" I asked.

His head swiveled slowly and he regarded me through veiled eyes. The corners of his mouth were turned down in contempt. "Is this the lead-in to some tacky question about sex?"

I started to answer, but he cut me off.

"Is that what everything boils down to? Sex? Is that what life is to you—cheap and tawdry? Doesn't your question say more about you, Doctor, than it could possibly reveal about me? Did we have sex? How did we have sex? How often? Don't you ever worry, Dr. Lucas, that you're becoming a cliché?"

"I was going to ask if you shared a kiss."

He was on his feet. I had no idea he'd be so fast, that he was so close to action. But this was no time for thinking. Reflexively, I stood up too, as I always do when a patient gets up. Not to do so would be like giving away a move in chess, and in this endgame you would never catch up.

He stood, glaring at me, and I was careful to keep my gaze moving, passing over his face, not lingering in any eyeball-to-eyeball confrontation. He wanted to lunge at me. I had a hunch he wanted to strangle me. My remark had defiled his sacred love. His hands were clenched at his sides, empty.

He weighed in at one-seventy against my two hundred. He had an inch on me, an inch in reach—you assess these things without thinking about them when the person first walks into your space. But he wasn't strongly developed, while I have good upper body strength.

I thought, "Screw the body alarm. I'm not calling for help every time someone goes off." Then I tensed behind the green desk, strong side forward, left foot back, legs bent slightly to unlock the knees so that I'd be flexible and ready to take him down. If he came across the desk, I'd go with the momentum and twist him, using my weight to drop him to the concrete. Then I'd press the button.

All this passed through my mind in two seconds.

I looked up to his face and stared at him levelly. If you're going to do it, you're going to do it in the first three seconds. At four seconds, the air starts to leak out of a confrontation.

I told him, "I think that's about it for today."

six

One thing I learned at Sanders is that when it comes to knives, amateurs tend to be underpowered. In cooking, as in murder, you should always use the biggest blade you can handle. That evening in my kitchen, I sliced mushrooms with eight inches of honed French steel, a present from Abby. Grimly, unheeding, I sliced shiitake mushrooms into smaller and smaller particles until I had a pile the texture of gravel.

I didn't want to think about Abby's absence from work, but I couldn't come up with an explanation that would let me set it aside. Had she, that morning, already called in sick when she told me she was late for work? Had she actually told me she was going to be late for work? Or just late?

The oil in the wok was smoking when I dumped in a slithering handful of raw chicken, oblivious to the small explosion as the moist flesh hit the hot oil. I stirred to distribute the meat and watched morosely as the flesh turned from living pink to mere opaque matter.

I didn't want a fight with Abby. I wanted to handle this in a reasonable, mature way. At the same time, I was furious at being trapped by the moral dictates of maturity. I struggled to convince myself that there was an innocent or, at worst, a mischievous purpose—a misdemeanor, not a felony—behind her absence.

As I took the rice off the stove, I heard the sound of Abby's SUV in the driveway, and then the thud of its door closing. It was odd that Abby, even though she hadn't been to work, would arrive home at exactly the usual time. I set the thought aside and composed myself, determined to be open to the best interpretation.

But I'm a trained observer, and, in spite of myself, I watched Abby for telltale signs as she came into the kitchen. She has an athletic fluidity of movement. She walks briskly, with a long-legged stride; she has an assertive, sexy roll of her body; she's given to spontaneous gestures of her arms and hands: These are things you can't fake if you're self-conscious. So I was glad when she came into the kitchen with a rush, pocketbook swinging, without any of the deliberate quality that betrays simulation.

"The traffic was awful!" she said. With a heave of her shoulder that began low in her hips, she shrugged off her heavy pocketbook, then dropped her keys with a clatter onto the counter opposite me. A piece of the day's mail caught her eye. She started to pick it up for a closer look, and I was pleased when she changed her mind and came to me.

She put her arms around my neck and looked into my eyes. I held her waist. Now that I had her close, I wanted to talk. But Abby wanted to keep it light. She pouted humorously, inviting me to kiss her. When I touched my lips to hers I felt her respond, and I closed my eyes and tried not to evaluate what was happening, to hear the music, not the notes. I let myself go in the moment, and the doubt that had held me in its grip began to loosen, and as the flush of relief came over me, Abby pulled away.

When you live together, comfortably together, as we did with Adrian, you don't think about it. You don't analyze happiness—you live without questions. Then, suddenly, when Adrian was killed in the accident, we had this gaping hole in our life where he'd been. All the hundred routines involved in caring for a two-year-old that had occupied our waking moments were canceled. When Adrian came into the world, he filled our lives, and, in a sense, pushed other parts of the relationship out of the way to make room for himself between us. Abby and I were still in love, but the relationship was changed. It's inevitable. You can't continue at the passionate intensity of your first kiss. If all you have is passion, it will burn out.

I loved Abby. I loved Adrian. I loved being Adrian's father. More than that, I loved being the father of my wife's son. I loved being the husband of Adrian's mother. Love was a matrix: We three. You take out one part and the whole thing collapses. It's meaningless—until you find a new meaning.

When a two-year-old dies, you don't simply revert to husband and wife. After Adrian died, Abby and I didn't know how to go on. The grief you share binds you for a while. But later, when you come face to face with what remains and try to move on, you can't simply continue the way you were when it was just the two of you, because you're different. You're no longer the same people you were before this wonderful being came into your life. Before you both fell in love with this little boy. Before.

We no longer knew what we were to each other. I was afraid we'd fly apart at the slightest provocation. I'd reached such a point of sensitivity that I hesitated even to say Adrian's name. Driving by the playground where we'd played or seeing another child would trigger a memory; I'd learned not to share these moments with Abby. My grief, added to hers, was enough to tip her; it overwhelmed her. A month before, I'd dug out a small bear who, one day, long, long ago, had gotten jammed down the back of the sofa. Without thinking, I put him to my face and nuzzled the little fellow. Crazy as it seems, I swear I could smell Adrian in the fur of that bear. I held him out to Abby so that she could experience the same magical evocation of our son, but she ran crying from the room.

Abby was on the move. Our kitchen is centered around a large island that contains the stove top, counter space where I'd been slicing the mushrooms, a small sink, then more counter space which we use as a drop-off point for mail, keys, messages to one another, or groceries that require a temporary staging area. Abby was circling the island, heading for the pile of letters and a couple of magazines that I'd brought in from the mailbox.

"How was your day?" I asked her, busy adding mushrooms and snow peas to the wok, stirring, intent.

I could have asked her, "How was work?" but the last thing I wanted was to trap her in a lie. I didn't want to use my professional expertise on my wife, to bring the deviousness I needed to outwit expert liars to bear on Abby. I hoped she would come to me, tell me where she'd been without my asking.

"Okay."

"Busy?"

"So-so."

The thing is, Abby is careless with the truth. It's one of the quirks that attracted me to her, strangely enough. She's not inherently deceptive; she simply doesn't value truthfulness as an abstract quality. I remember the first time I became aware of this: She had turned up late for a date and told me she'd been doing paperwork at the hospital and lost track of the time. But I hadn't been able to reach her at the hospital to tell her I'd gotten reservations at the restaurant later than we'd planned. I hadn't asked her why she was late. She had volunteered the excuse to smooth the waters, as she thought necessary. I was still getting to know her.

Haltingly, I asked her about the discrepancy. She'd had coffee with a friend and they'd gotten to talking; then she hadn't wanted to hurt my feelings. She smiled. I smiled back, in amazement and confusion. She'd taken my breath away—such facility, such ease of conscience. More than that, absence of conscience. Conscience didn't come into it. Either the truth was convenient, which kept things simple, or it wasn't, in which case, Abby had to help things along. "See?" she'd asked, reassuringly. "It worked out perfectly: They couldn't seat us anyway. So it's really like I turned up on time."

To Abby's way of thinking, a little white lie doesn't hurt anybody when it's for a good cause. She's single-minded, which is why she's such an effective advocate for her girls. When she goes to bat for funding at city hall, she's oblivious to the other side of the equation. There's no room for argument; in her mind, feeling is conviction. And conviction is simple. Which is why Abby is a person of decided convictions, while I am handicapped by a need for nuance, balance, fairness.

Who wants those nasty, jagged edges of the truth, which you know will only hurt someone sooner or later, when you can ease things with the social lubrication of a little white lie? It was a flash of insight for me, the stickler. For someone brought up under the judge's gaze, who had internalized the imperious discipline of the finder of fact, such insouciance was liberating. Not that it was easy to throw off my burden. Not that I can ever throw it off, really. But under her influence I felt I could occasionally play hooky from myself. Abby's freedom to indulge conviction gave me a counterweight, and I think it helped make durable a love affair that, in the natural course of such things, would have soon burned up in its own sexual incandescence.

Abby was picking through the pile of mail with two fingers. She stopped at an envelope I'd opened.

"That's our car insurance," I said. "They jacked it up."

"That smells good," she said. "What is it?"

She was walking again, stripping off a light linen jacket, her arms bare. She tossed it in the direction of a chair by the breakfast table, not looking to see if it landed safely.

"Chicken in a strange stir-fry oil I found in Chinatown."

The jacket made the chair, but not with enough overlap for the weight of the fabric to hold it there; it flopped over the back of the chair and then slowly slid to the floor. Abby had already forgotten it.

And if someone had been playing Abby, if Abby were playing herself, that's what they'd have done. Maybe it was a little overstated, I thought, the carelessness, but it was authentic. It was in character. I didn't want to think like this. I wanted to stop analyzing.

She was restless. I moved back and forth from the cutting board to the wok, while Abby always seemed to be at the opposite side of the island. If I shifted to two o'clock, she'd be at eight. She was back now at the pile of mail. She picked up the bill from the insurance company, then tossed it away again.

"You never told me you got a speeding ticket," I said. I tried to make light of it, to keep from my voice any note of accusation that would put her on the defensive. The emotional current kept pushing me toward confrontation.

"It was a while ago," she said.

Several weeks ago. Ancient history. Except, just as years are dated from the birth of Christ, it didn't take any arithmetic for me to see—my mind simply jumped out and grabbed the date—that the ticket was issued a week before the first anniversary of Adrian's death. We'd decided, on that day, to light a candle. It was a ritual that Ellen Hollenburg, Abby's therapist, had suggested, and I dutifully went along with it. We had waited in silent vigil for almost an hour for the candle to burn itself out. It was not helpful.

"That's why they raised the insurance," I said.

"How much?"

"Three hundred bucks."

"For speeding? Give me a break!"

"It's a moving violation."

"Well, I paid the ticket. You'd think that would be enough."

"You never told me."

She glanced at me quickly, and I saw a flash of anger. I was intruding; I expected too much. Then she shrugged. "It's not a big deal, is it? A speeding ticket?"

She came around the island to peer into the wok, then suddenly plucked out a piece of chicken. She held it suspended between her fingertips, blew on it, and smiled at me mischievously.

"Do you tell me every time you pick up a ticket?" She nibbled the chicken, testing the temperature. "Do you?" she teased me. She dropped the piece of chicken into her mouth as though it proved her point.

"Not the felonies," I said. "I only tell you about misdemeanors."

"Mm, that chicken's delicious."

In this brief instant of contact, which I knew she'd deflect at any moment, I was done with subterfuge. I wanted us to be straightforward, with everything laid out in view.

"I missed you," I told her.

She had retreated back to the other side of the island to pick up her jacket, and when I spoke she glanced up, surprised and wondering.

"I know," she said. She looked down at the jacket on the chair as her hands smoothed the shoulders. "I miss you, too."

She hadn't understood that I was referring to this morning, but

I liked her misunderstanding better. From the other side of the island, I reached across the pile of mail to take her hand.

"I don't feel we're making contact like we used to," I told her. "And I miss you."

She nodded in agreement, still not looking at me.

"We're drifting apart," I said.

"I know."

"I'm afraid I'll lose you."

"I don't like it, either."

"I don't think we can just tough it out and hope everything sooner or later will fall in place. We're changed. What I mean is, we can't just assume that we know each other."

"Sometimes I don't think I even know who I am."

"That's what I'm saying. We have to start over. It's not going to happen on its own."

"Is that what you want?"

"That's why I wanted to take you out to lunch today."

"I would have loved that!" She was taken unawares, charmed, smiling. "Why didn't you call me?"

Somehow, I'd blundered into the very spot that I'd been trying to avoid. But it didn't matter now. Abby had nothing to hide. We'd settle this.

"Why not?" she asked again, mistaking my hesitation.

"I did."

"I didn't get it."

"You weren't there."

I waited. I'd given her the opening. I hadn't meant to set a test for her. Certainly not a trap.

"I was in and out all day," she said.

There it was: the little white lie, to spare my feelings, or the whopper—no knowing which. I felt betrayed.

"Busy day, huh?" I asked.

She must have sensed the bitterness in my voice, because she put down the mail. I became aware I had the big kitchen knife clenched tight in my fist. I laid it down on the chopping board.

"Yes. Pretty busy."

Now that we'd passed the point of no return, I didn't see any reason to hold back. "You saw a lot of clients?"

Her eyes narrowed. She turned to face me, feet planted apart, chin up. "What is this?"

I made a shrug of faux-incomprehension, hands up, empty. "I don't know," I said, far angrier than I had expected, than I wanted to be. "What is it? You tell me."

"Tell you what?"

"Well, let's see." I searched, it seemed, for possibilities. "How about: Did you see a lot of clients?"

She was angry, too. She stared at me, hands on hips, trying to figure me out. "No," she said finally. "Actually I didn't see a lot of clients."

I felt the pressure released. I was being a jerk. That was the best of all possible worlds: that I was a jerk for thinking Abby had something going. There was nothing going on. "Look," I said. I let out a sigh of concession.

Then Abby said, gratuitously, "I've been in a lot of stupid meetings all day."

Back to square one. Little white, or whopper. I wanted out. "Look," I told her, "I went to the agency. They said you called in sick."

"What did you do that for?"

"I happened to be in the neighborhood."

"Oh, yes?" She was dealing from the stack of junk mail, flipping and tossing, like someone cheating at solitaire.

She looked up. Her eyes were fierce. "So you stopped by."

"I was there. I thought we could take some time together. That's all."

"If you'd called first, you would have found out I wasn't there."

I was in too deep to pull back. "If it isn't a problem," I said, setting the challenge against all my better judgment, "why don't you tell me where you were?"

Abby regarded me with something I feared was dislike. This was the centrifugal force in our relationship: Every time she set eyes on me, I reminded her of Adrian. If, in moments of anger, she was inclined to see it this way, my very presence was a cause of pain. We were mirrors to each other, infinitely reflecting the same pain, each presence a reminder of Adrian's absence.

Finally, she said, "I went shopping, as a matter of fact."

"Okay." I looked down at the food I'd prepared. "You called in sick and you went shopping. Good for you. End of story."

Some of the tension escaped from the scene, but not all of it. This was the closest we came, these days, to making up: a face-saving concession, an unstated agreement not to pursue an issue further, to pull back before we went over the brink for good.

"Are you ready to eat?" I asked. "The food's ready."

With her fingers, she plucked a snow pea from the wok and bit it in half. I served the rice onto the plates.

"So really," she asked, "what were you doing slumming in East Cambridge?"

She seemed to be making small talk, but to me the fact that she couldn't let it go was not a good sign.

"I had to see this woman over at Harvard. I thought how great it would be to have lunch with you."

"Really?"

"Really." I was at a loss to explain to her my uncharacteristic behavior. "It was a spur-of-the-moment thing."

"If only you'd told me this morning."

"Then it wouldn't have been a surprise."

She looked uncertain, as though she'd lost her taste for surprises.

"Remember when we were dating," I reminded her, "and I'd call you on the ward, and we'd sneak away for lunch at the Patagonia Café?"

But it did no good now to evoke a past that lay on the other side of the accident. Adrian's death loomed so large it obscured our view of what had gone before.

"I'm trying," I said. "I really want—"

"I know," she said, cutting me off. Not abruptly. Or unkindly. But quickly, as you would close a door in order to prevent a troublesome dog from getting loose. "I know you do." She took an uncertain step toward me, but it didn't seem to close the distance. "It takes time."

I put my arms around her and held her. Abby was still in my embrace; she rested her head on my shoulder. But even though my arms encircled her, I sensed she was elsewhere, that she had left her body for me to hold as a temporary measure, a marker, as one leaves an old letter in a book to mark the place where you intend to resume.

"It just takes time." She sighed.

We both knew this wasn't true. Time wasn't helping. Time was running out.

"I know," I said.

seven

The next time I interviewed Craig Cavanaugh, a week after our first meeting, he came briskly into Interview Room One, closed the door behind him, and sat down as though he'd been looking forward to the encounter. With a winning smile, he asked me how I'd been.

"You know, this is a really interesting place," he told me. He might have been talking about Kandahar.

"I suppose it depends on what you're interested in," I replied.

"Human nature, for example. Don't you think this is a wonderful place to study human nature?"

"From where I sit, it is."

"On one side of the desk, or the other, there's one of everything here. It's a human zoo."

I paid out rope, waiting for him to show me a glimpse of his agenda. "I suppose it is," I agreed.

"And people are helpful. They're willing to help you out, if you really need it."

While I could see Sanders as a kind of zoo, the last thing the other patients could be called was helpful. Exploitive, yes. Preda-tory, of course. Craig was dangling bait in front of me, and I didn't know what the hook was. At an opportune moment, at a time of my choosing, I'd come back to it.

I asked him to paraphrase the Lamb warning I'd given him be-fore, which he did, quickly and succinctly, then he sat forward in his chair with all the tensed alertness of a seal ready to snap up the herring that the keeper would at any moment toss into the air. He was ready for me, in a way that made me slightly uneasy. I hadn't intended to toss him anything.

"Last week," I began, "you told me about your feelings for Na-talie."

"You've talked to her."

"Of course. She's a witness."

"She has a lovely voice, doesn't she?"

I sighed and looked away. I started to remind him that an inter-view is different from a conversation, that this was a one-way street, but he wasn't listening. He'd caught sight of something in my expression, or he'd detected some quality in my voice that sud-denly tipped him off.

"You've seen her," he interrupted excitedly, "haven't you?"

"You know I'm not going to answer that."

He sat forward, over the green Formica of the desk, as if he might sniff some of her scent on me. I had brushed against her. I had touched her. I had smuggled some element of her, a miasma, an essence, back with me into maximum security. But if I had done that, the thought that another male had had contact—perhaps, in his overheated imagination, I'd had carnal relations with her—stirred his jealousy.

"You've seen her—it's okay." He waved away any denial I might try to palm him off with. "Now you know what I'm talking about."

His face was rapturous. He scrutinized my face for signs of the encounter with Natalie. I wasn't sure what he was looking for. An afterglow, perhaps. Or a guilty flinch of my eyes from his gaze. He looked away, dissatisfied.

"I talked with Natalie," I said, voice neutral, emphasis evenly distributed. "One of the things we have to do in this kind of examination for the courts is to check what the accused says with the witness's accounts."

"To see whether I made stuff up."

"Right."

"To see whether it only happened in my imagination."

"Exactly."

"Did you tell her what I said about us?"

"About you and Natalie? No."

He was visibly disappointed. Then challenging: "Then what was the point of seeing her?"

"I said I talked to her."

He settled back in his chair. "And what did she say?"

"She said you attended Professor Kennedy's creative writing class; that you submitted a number of pieces that she critiqued; that you approached her several times at the end of class to ask her out; but that you never actually went out on a date."

He spread his hands with a rhetorical shrug. "So what?"

"I know that you had feelings for her."

"More than that."

"That you loved her."

"I still love her."

There's no graceful turn at this point. No nifty verbal pirouette that lets you finesse the collision between your patient's beliefs and stone cold reality.

"This is what I'm trying to understand," I began hesitantly. I wanted to suggest that there might be a compromise with reality, that the apparent circle could be squared, if he could help me grope my way toward it. "But—and this is the part I have difficulty with—it seems like the two of you never actually got together."

I waited. Craig stared at me coldly.

"Is that right?" I insisted. "Is that how you understand it?"

"Of course we were together. We didn't always see eye to eye, if that's what you're talking about. Do you always see eye to eye with your wife?"

"We're talking about you."

"I am talking about me. And I'm also talking about Natalie, and you, and your wife."

"That's out of bounds."

"Says who?"

"I do."

"You're wearing a wedding ring. Right? Isn't that what it is?"

He reached across the desk as if he might put a finger on it. Even if he'd lunged, he'd have been six inches short, but all the same I pulled my hand back. I'd flinched, and I cursed myself for reacting to his feint.

"Isn't that a statement?" he demanded. "Aren't you advertising you're married? Doesn't that put you and your wife, both of you, in the public domain?"

"We're getting off the subject."

"No, we're getting into the subject. Except not in the way you want. Not in the way you feel comfortable with: you the spectator, me the specimen in the zoo."

"That was your choice of words."

"And I'm not objecting to it. This place is a zoo. But I'm saying this desk doesn't change anything. You're on that side; I'm on this side, but it doesn't make us different."

He rested his case. He sat back. He seemed to have accomplished what he set out to do. If all he wanted was to demonstrate that he could get to me, that he wasn't entirely powerless, I'd accede to that.

"That's not in question," I said. "We're essentially the same. We're both men. We have the same kinds of feelings."

I heard myself getting preachy and I stopped. But Craig had already pulled out of this argument. There was no resistance. I was pushing on empty air. Craig lounged in the concrete chair and regarded me with a sardonic tilt of an eyebrow.

"We were talking about the sense in which you and Natalie were together," I resumed.

"You were talking about it."

"All right, I'll talk about it. You didn't go out on dates. Right?"

He shrugged indifference.

"You didn't have any physical contact. You never met by mutual agreement."

"She said we'd go out when the course finished. The college has regulations about relationships between faculty and students." And he added, with a wolfish grin, "To prevent people like me from being exploited."

"But then the course ended and Natalie changed her mind."

"Or had it changed for her."

"Who by?"

"She was under a lot of pressure."

"What kind of pressure?"

"You know: older woman, younger guy. She was getting the message not to get involved with an undergraduate. Subtle pressure. There's nothing to stop students going out with instructors after a course is over. It's permitted, but it's frowned on."

"But if you never on any occasion had a meeting that you both wanted, how can you say you had a real relationship?"

"Is that what she said? That it wasn't real?"

"That's what I gather, given what everyone's told me about it."

"Well, that's all it is: your opinion."

"Then tell me what kind of relationship you think it was."

"I don't have to answer that question."

I nodded. I was resigned to the dead end. "No," I agreed, "you don't." I reached for the folder on the desk, cleaning up, ready to end the interview.

"But I will," Craig said.

I waited while he sorted through what he'd toss out to me from what he'd retain, secret and inviolate, within himself. But once he got going on the subject of Natalie, he wouldn't be able to censor himself.

"Do you believe in love at first sight?" he asked.

"Yes, I do."

"Well, this wasn't quite love at first sight. I'd seen Natalie several times before. But it was as sudden as love at first sight."

"What was it you felt?"

He looked at me appraisingly for a moment. In someone else I would have thought he wanted to gauge whether he could trust me with what he was about to disclose. In Craig's case, I thought he was estimating what effect his words would have on me.

"It took me by surprise. It seemed like I'd never really seen her before, and then, all of a sudden, my eyes opened and I saw her. I really saw her. I can tell you the exact instant I fell in love with Natalie. I remember she'd turned, with a smile, and it wasn't even for me. It didn't matter. Something happened to me. I had to look at her. I didn't want to do anything else. She noticed I was staring, so I looked away. I got back into the discussion. And in between, when someone else was talking, I'd steal looks at her face. I thought she was the loveliest woman in the world. I'd glance at her secretly. My eyes would slide across her face as though I was thinking about something else. It was like I was dying of thirst and Natalie was the most delicious drink you can imagine, but I could only take tiny little sips of her.

"From then on, I started thinking about her all the time. I couldn't get her out of my mind. I tried to understand her. I tried to guess what she might be thinking. But mainly I was happy that she existed. Everything she did, every turn of her head, every word she uttered, was a delight to me."

"After that moment, you couldn't stop thinking about her."

"I didn't want to stop. It was all I wanted to do, except to be with her. All the class assignments, I wrote for her. I found out her weekly schedule. It wasn't difficult. I'd arrange it so that I happened to be walking down a path in the Yard that intersected the path she was on. Sometimes I'd pretend I hadn't noticed her when I'd be coming up the steps of Widener Library and she'd be on the way down and she'd say hi to me and we'd have this surprise encounter, as though destiny had made our paths cross."

"And soon your thoughts of Natalie pretty much pushed everything else out."

He stopped. At some point, I realized, we'd parted company. He was staring away from me, in a reverie, and now he collected himself as if recalling that I was present and might pose a threat.

"I know where you're going," he said. "You want me to say I was obsessed with Natalie. You're working your way around to getting me to say I'm crazy."

"I only want you to tell me the way it was."

"I looked up 'obsession' in a psychiatric dictionary."

"So you must have wondered yourself whether the way you were thinking might be extreme."

He ignored this point. "An obsession is a repetitive thought that the thinker actively resists. He doesn't want to think it, but it keeps coming back. That wasn't me. I could take some small thing that I'd noticed about Natalie and think about it all day. Happily."

"Do you think there's anything unusual in that?" I asked him.

"No."

"To think of nothing else?" I pressed him. "To the exclusion of all else? You don't think that's extreme?"

"Yes, it's extreme. What's wrong with that? Love is extreme. If you're in love with someone, you don't want to think about anything else. That's what love is. You don't consider the cost. You don't add it up. You don't try to make sense of it. If you did, it wouldn't be love."

He waited for my reaction, and when I didn't respond, he asked, "Don't you think so? Isn't that your experience? Didn't you feel that way when you were in love?"

I gave him my best poker face.

He leaned over the desk and dropped his voice to a confidential murmur. "Dr. Lucas, didn't you feel that way when you married your wife?"

I had scarcely opened my mouth before he wearily waved away my protest.

"Love isn't calculating. Love isn't reasonable. Love is crazy." He moved his hand in a shoveling gesture toward me. "There you are," he said contemptuously. "Isn't that what you wanted?"

"It's love that got you put away," I reminded him.

"Do you think I care about this?" He scoffed. He waved his hand to encompass the cinderblock walls, the stark, empty room. "To me, this is a test. If I can't endure a little hardship, what's my love worth? If I give up so easily, how can it be real?"

He was leaning in toward me again; his jaw was clenched and there was a strange, intense light in his eyes: a zealot of love. He caught himself. Then he leaned back, making a show of calm, smoothing his hair, stretching and relaxing the muscles around his neck and shoulders.

"Anyway," he said, "I won't be here long."

But he'd shown me his true colors, and now he scrutinized me, a rapid scan of my upper face to see what I'd detected.

He hurried on, to put what he'd just let slip into a context of his own choosing before I could come at him with my questions. "Think about this," he said. "It used to be that people would die for love. No one said it was crazy. It was heroic. It was tragic. Think about Romeo and Juliet. He thinks she's dead, so he stabs himself. Not some pathetic overdose. Not some halfhearted wrist-scratching. The guy kills himself for love. It's one of the great stories. No one said Romeo was mentally ill. Now they'd pin some psychiatric label on him. What's your diagnosis, Doctor?" he taunted me.

I sighed in regret. "Something like, 'Adjustment disorder with mixed emotional features,' " I told him.

"Adjustment disorder!" He shook his head in disgust. "It's soul-less."

"Yes," I confessed, "it's bullshit."

"I'm no Romeo," he said. "I don't pretend to any heroic stature. But think about my situation: I'm in a maximum security prison for love. I'm willing to put myself in this kind of jeopardy because I love Natalie. I'm a prisoner of love. How many people can say that?"

He sat back. It was breathtakingly grandiose, what he'd said. But it was also true. I decided to begin a different tack.

"The intensity of your passion," I began, as though trying to sketch out something with words. "Your persistence in the face of difficulty and discouragement—of danger. Your willingness to sacrifice. These are all qualities you and Romeo have in common. But it seems to me there's one essential difference."

He wasn't going to be drawn in. He'd chosen the terms of ref-

erence, and I'd agreed to fight on his ground. So he had antici-
pated what I would do and he was already there ahead of me,
waiting for me.

"The difference between you and Romeo," I said, treading very
carefully, tensing surreptitiously in my chair in case I had to move
quickly, "is that Juliet also loves Romeo."

I had thought he might explode in protest, in delusional rage.
When he reacted calmly, I expected some bland psychotic denial of
reality. But that wasn't quite what I got.

"So what is your point?" he asked, as carefully as I'd asked my
question. "That Juliet loves Romeo, and Natalie doesn't love me?"

"Correct."

"But you don't know that."

This young man, after countless rejections, letters and gifts
spurned, a restraining order, the threat of a prison term that
stemmed directly from actions initiated by his beloved in order to
make him go away, still held out hope that Natalie might love him.
I thought, If only his heart would break!

"Is that what she told you?" he persisted, looking at me as if I
were a poor fool. "That she didn't love me?"

I stared him straight in the face and told him, "Yes."

He held my gaze for a long time, but he wasn't looking for information about Natalie, or whether I might be a reliable reporter.
He was peering into my head to see how I could believe what I'd
just said.

"She may have told you that," he began.

"I would think it's consistent with what she's communicated to
you, on several occasions, in several different ways, including a restraining order. I don't see how it can be any clearer than that: She
doesn't want you in her life."

"Do you remember Sir Lancelot and Queen Guinevere?"

"Let's get real," I insisted.

"He loved her from a distance. They never—what was the phrase you used?—they never had a physical relationship."

"Lancelot was a monk on horseback. Is that what you are? Is that what your love is, a celibate charade?"

"Oh, Lancelot had balls all right. He was biding his time. He understood that first he had to prove himself worthy of the woman he loved."

"And how are you going to do that?"

"I have to pass the tests that she places in my way."

"You think Natalie took out a restraining order to see if you really loved her?"

"I don't think she figured it out explicitly. I don't think she said to herself, 'Now let's see how he handles this.' But I think, yes, that was her unconscious motivation. And I rose to the occasion. Here I am. Here with you. Doesn't that prove something?"

"It proves you're persistent."

"And that's the test. I'm sure Abby must have put some barriers in your way. And Natalie—"

"Wait a minute!"

It had taken me a full two seconds: to appreciate that Craig had used my wife's name; to hear it; to deny I'd heard her name from his lips; to replay the tape in my mind; to keep from lunging across the table to get my hands around his throat.

"What did you just say?"

"You didn't let me finish."

"You used a name."

He acted nonplussed, slightly flustered, as though he'd missed something. He was thoroughly enjoying this. "I was starting to say something about Natalie."

"No. The other one."

He looked aside, acting out the process of scanning memory. "You mean, Abby?"

"Where do you get off using that name?"

"I don't understand. What's wrong with saying 'Abby'?"

"You know damned well."

"It's your wife's name."

"It's not for you to know my wife's name. Or for you to use it here."

"Well, I don't talk about her with the other guys, if that's what you mean."

"You don't use her name here, period. Understand?"

He held up his open hands in surrender. "Sure. No problem."

I was trying to calm myself. The last thing I wanted was to reveal how furious I was. That would have given him power over me. When I spoke, my voice sounded strangled. "My life outside here is off limits."

"Hey, sorry. Okay? Look. I don't know the rules here."

"You know the rules."

He took a deep, exasperated breath, as if he were the one who needed to regain control. "All right. If I was out of bounds . . ." He nodded as if I already knew what he was going to say and so didn't really need to complete the sentence, but then did anyway as an extra measure of graciousness. "I apologize."

It was too easy. I felt violated. He'd invaded my home and a primitive part of me wanted to make him pay.

"So, can we go on?" he prompted me.

"Okay." But I couldn't remember where we'd left off.

He knew. This was his territory. "If you love someone, you have to believe in a certain inevitability." He held up his hand to fend me off. "No, not the crazy kind. You have to believe that love overcomes all things. That in time, if you persist, you will be together."

"What if the other person doesn't agree?" I was going through the motions. My mind was lagging, still snagged on the mention of Abby's name. While I struggled to keep up with him, I was simultaneously trying to figure out how he could have gotten hold of the information.

"If you're a romantic," Craig was saying, "you believe that love confers certain privileges."

I wanted to slow him down. It was impossible to figure out two things at once. I couldn't catch up, much less jump ahead of him. I wondered if some key piece of information had gone by me altogether. I said, "I guess I'm not that kind of romantic."

"We all suffer setbacks, but we persist. I know you've had your share of disappointment. But you didn't give up. You still have your marriage. Don't you?"

"We're not here to talk about me."

"You see, Paul, I have to disagree with you there. This desk between us doesn't change anything. You're on that side. I'm on the other side. For now. But we're more alike than different, you and I. You were tested and you came through. You persisted." He paused as if to let a telling point strike home. "That's all I'm trying to do."

"It's an interesting speculation. But the reality is that you don't know anything about my life."

"That's what I meant when I told you how helpful people are here. And they're very inexpensive. For a few Twinkies and a bag of Doritos, some helpful person will make a phone call to someone on the outside who goes on the Internet and plugs your name into a search engine or checks out back issues of your local paper. Anyone can do it. It's public knowledge. It's a First Amendment right."

I was breathing hard. I was angry, but also afraid, and I didn't know what of. Very carefully, I asked him, "What is it you want?"

"I don't want anything."

"You had this planned out."

"Of course I did. Didn't you have your agenda planned out?"

"This isn't going to get you what you want."

"We're all tested, Paul. You were set a test yourself. When your son was killed." He looked into my eyes to determine the degree of pain that he was inflicting. I had a patient from Iran who had been tortured, and described the same scrutiny on the part of his torturers, an almost medical objectivity. At the apposite moment, Craig uttered the name. "Adrian."

There are some pressure points so exquisite that the pain circuitry bypasses the brain. I was on my feet without thinking. When Craig leapt to his feet, too, my thumb reflexively pressed the button on the body alarm.

We stood facing one another across the desk and heard the distant sound of the alarm bell ringing in the officers' trap at the end of the corridor.

One, Mississippi: He asked, in disbelief, "Is that for me?"

Two, Mississippi: He looked around for the source of the bell, finally fixing on the alarm on my belt. I was almost as dumbfounded at what I'd done as he was. I'd pressed the button to save Craig from myself.

Three, Mississippi: I told him, "Take it easy."

Four, Mississippi: His puzzlement was clearing. In sudden realization, in rising anger, he said, "This is payback, isn't it?"

Five, Mississippi: "No," I said, "it's not like that." There wasn't time to discuss it. I had to stop the charge of the cavalry.

Six, Mississippi: I stepped out from behind the desk so that I could meet them at the door. But Craig came around his side of the desk. He was slowing me down.

Seven, Mississippi: "Look," I told him, "back off. We'll sort this out." But already we heard pounding boots, many, in the corridor, closing quickly.

Eight, Mississippi: He was angry but frightened. He took a step toward me as if safety lay in my vicinity.

Nine, Mississippi: The door burst open. "Hold on!" I yelled.

But I might as well have tried to persuade a Minuteman back into its silo.

Ten, Mississippi: They saw a patient with his hands raised, yelling at the doctor, "You asshole!"

The lead officer launched himself at Craig without breaking stride and took him down onto the concrete floor. The rest came a moment later and piled on. To my distress, Craig struggled hard, bucking and pulling, so that the officers bore down on him even more forcefully, and it was several seconds before the pile of bodies resolved itself into individuals who had each seized an arm or leg.

Craig was spread facedown on the ground with his arms pinned. Someone had a knee on the back of his chest. His face was red and congested. To my horror, I saw a trickle of blood slowly descend from his forehead.

He was pinioned like a farm animal, utterly helpless. With great difficulty, he turned his head to search for me, and when his eyes found me, I saw on his face such a snarl of hate that I knew I would be his enemy forever and that he would never forget me.

After the charge, Lieutenant Kovacs's arrival seemed almost leisurely. He surveyed what was now a motionless tableau, ordered a minor adjustment to be made, then nodded his head with professional satisfaction.

"Doc," he said, slightly more sharply than usual, as you do when arousing someone from a daydream. "You want us to lug him?"

I noticed the corridor outside had filled with clinicians. Maria was shooing them away, back to the staff room.

"Let him up," I said.

Sergeant Ramirez, who had hold of Craig's right leg, began to protest, but Kovacs cut him off with an upheld hand.

"Your call, Doc," Kovacs told me.

"I think it'll be enough to remove him from the interview room," I said.

Warily, loosening their holds but keeping hands in place at first, the men shifted their weight so that they crouched on either side of Craig's body. His eyes were closed. He made no move. Slowly, keeping hands outstretched to ward off any resurgence of violence, all but the two who had hold of his wrists rose to their feet. Then, with glances toward the lieutenant in case he should countermand the order, they backed away to the edges of the room.

Craig lay still. Blood ran from the wound on his forehead, down his cheek, then angled across his chin to stain the floor. I prayed it didn't indicate a serious head injury. I was anguished by what I had brought about.

Three long seconds passed while Craig lay motionless, face-down on the concrete floor. Finally, he stirred, and I gave a deep sigh of relief. He raised himself up, testing each limb as he got to his feet. Painfully, he held himself erect. The officer who had hold of his right wrist let him raise his hand to wipe his cheek; when he brought it down, Craig saw, to his surprise, bright blood on the back of his fingers. As he limped from the interview room between the officers, he allowed himself one glance at me, and in his eyes I saw the light of triumph.

eight

At the end of the week, I was still shaking my head in disbelief. Craig hadn't been injured seriously. The cut over his left eyebrow was healing, but I winced every time I caught sight of it. And it might have been my imagination, the sensitivity of a bad conscience, but it seemed to me he flaunted his wound. I'd been trigger-happy, and we both knew it.

Then Natalie called.

"I wanted to thank you for meeting with me," she said. Her voice was breathy, intimate.

I could have told her that it was my job, that she had been of more help to me than I to her, but I was in need of a little affirmation, and I enjoyed playing the knight-errant to her damsel in distress. It seemed harmless enough. "You're very welcome," I told her with, perhaps, a gracious flourish.

She told me about working through the trauma of the last months. She was happy, expansive, unreservedly grateful. I listened as she ticked off the phases of her recovery, making encouraging, therapeutic noises, until she started talking about a fresh start.

"I can't tell you how glad I am it's over," she said.

"Well, let's hope so."

She picked up the reservation in my voice, but she wasn't going to let it puncture her optimism. "What can go wrong?" she asked. "He's been arrested. He's locked up. I've had the best night's sleep I've had in years. I'd forgotten what freedom felt like. Now we just have to wait for the law to take its course."

"Right," I agreed, halfheartedly.

"But what can go wrong?" she repeated. There was a tremor of anxiety this time.

I didn't tell her that as far as the courts were concerned there was no such thing as a sure thing. "It's nothing specific," I said.

"Then, what?"

"Oh, I don't know." I was already backtracking. Why not hope for the best? Why spoil her happiness, when I didn't know what the future held? "Maybe it's just my cautious nature," I allowed.

"Well, if that's all . . ."

Her tone was teasing and lighthearted, a contrast with the studious young woman I'd interviewed at Widener Library, and all it had taken to effect this transformation was the removal of Craig Cavanaugh from her life. Craig had been imprisoned, and Natalie had been set free. She had blossomed. It wasn't hard to see how a man, a lonely young man like Craig, would be drawn to her.

"If there's anything I can do," she offered, and I had the feeling this didn't entirely relate to our efforts to keep her persecutor locked up. "Anything at all."

"I'll certainly keep it in mind."

"Will you?" she insisted.

"Of course I will."

"If you feel you have to interview me again, I'm more than willing."

"If you should think of anything that I haven't asked you about," I suggested, realizing that although I'd intended to gently extricate myself, I'd met her implicit offer halfway. "Then don't hesitate to call."

She was pleased. "I will," and, as she added, "I most surely will," I wondered what exactly I'd given her permission for.

If I felt guilty about pressing the button on Craig, it wasn't going to stop me from digging deeper into his history. That Friday, Brenda Gorn had called me as the prosecution expert in another case at the Exeter Superior Court, and we talked during a recess in the trial.

"A stalker doesn't go from zero to this all-consuming intensity," I told her. "You don't reach this level of expertise without practice. He's done this before."

"I don't have anything you can use," Brenda said.

"I don't believe he's never been in trouble before."

"No convictions. No charges. Not even juvenile stuff. But there was one complaint."

"There you go."

"It didn't go anywhere. He was young, for one thing. Sixteen. It occurred at a coed prep school in the western part of the state, out near Springfield. The girl was local, on scholarship. She and Cavanaugh had had some romantic contact, but she wanted to break it off when he got too intense. But he wouldn't let it go, of course. He started pestering her, following her. It didn't seem much more than a rich kid throwing his weight around when he didn't get what he wanted. Obnoxious, sure, but not criminal. Until the night one of the other girls got up to go to the bathroom at two A.M. and found him hovering over the victim's bed. This was on the third floor. What really freaked them was they couldn't figure how he'd gotten in. They checked the doors; they were locked. He had to have climbed up the side of the building. He was proud of it. He'd been doing it every night for three weeks, he said: a silent vigil by the bedside of his love. The girl's parents were incensed, especially since the school was getting a lot of pressure from the Cavanaughs and wouldn't throw him out without a review. The parents were red-hot to prosecute. I talked to the assistant DA who had the case. He had the witness who'd testify Craig was in the girls' dorm in the middle of the night. The victim could show a pattern of harassment that put her in fear. The Commonwealth had a strong case. They were ready to go. Then, all of a sudden, the parents pulled the plug."

"Someone got to them?"

"We think so. Nothing vulgar. An old money payoff. The DA I spoke to was very pissed. Even now, six years later. The case was pulled out from under him. So he kept an eye on the girl. She was the local star in a small town and the newspaper wrote her up from time to time. It seems the way was smoothed for her to go to Yale. She was given some summer intern job at a subsidiary of a subsidiary of Cavanaugh Wealth Management that paid her tuition."

"Old Man Cavanaugh pulled in a few markers to keep Craig viable."

"He had to keep the prince clean. You wouldn't want a felon managing your pension."

"And that's it? We don't have anything else on Craig after the age of sixteen?"

"Nothing in Massachusetts. After the school incident, the family sent him out of state. Old Man Cavanaugh didn't let him back until he was ready for his alma mater."

. . .

Every Sunday since we first moved in together, Abby and I have read the newspapers lounging on the sofa. We've been through a couple of sofas, but Sunday morning has remained an inviolable routine—although Adrian did put a dent in it. If we became too absorbed, if he felt he was being neglected, we'd be roused by a tiny hand smacking the edifice of paper that separated him from a parent. As he got older, a rooter of tousled blond hair would burrow through the wedge-shaped space formed by the paper's fold, followed by a beaming face that angled for a kiss. Then, more often than not, he'd be on his way again. He was an independent boy and would happily play for minutes on end surrounded by his animals. As long as we heard his voice, ordering bears about, urging on Donkey, admonishing a misbehaving Monkey in tones that were eerily familiar to my ears, we knew he was safely occupied. As were we, each occupied with our own section of the news, until, from time to time, when one of us came across something interesting, we'd read it aloud to the other.

When the house of a two-year-old falls silent, you run to see what he's gotten into. Silence—the absence of babbling, the absence of bricks collapsing—is a parental alert. I'm convinced that "Uh-oh" feeling is hardwired. This was what made moving on impossible: So much of love is hardwired. There was a moment, weeks after Adrian's death, when Abby and I simultaneously collapsed our newspapers in response to an imagined silence—a phantom silence much like a phantom limb—and turned to one another in implicit, parental speech: "You go." "My turn." The first time, we clung to each other as though we'd been visited by his ghost, half out of our minds with fear and pain. It felt like madness. After that, there were other occasions when I was brought to that same state of alert, but I kept them to myself. I suspect Abby experienced them, too.

Therefore, when we read the papers together that Sunday morning, I had taken the precaution of playing music—Rimsky-Korsakoff, Ravel, Rachmaninov—that refused to become background.

I wanted to talk over with Abby the way I'd reacted to Craig. She was good at this. In the old days, Abby and I would have analyzed the situation up, down, and sideways, until we'd whittled the issue down to a nub that could be emotionally stowed away. But when the time came, I couldn't bring myself to say to her, "I have this guy at Sanders who knows Adrian's name."

Instead I said, "I have this guy at Sanders who's love-crazy."

"That doesn't sound like such a bad problem to have."

"It is for the girl he's crazy about."

"Is he psychotic?"

"Not entirely. More like, crazy in love."

"But he can't get her attention?"

"He's handsome, charming, and rich."

"Where's the catch?"

"She doesn't love him."

"Ah." She thought this over. "Did she ever?"

"No. They've never even kissed."

"But there must have been something to get him started. Some encouragement. Maybe she flirted with him and didn't recognize what she was doing."

"He was her student. She showed interest in his work—that's all it was—and he misread the signs."

"But now he's hooked. He can't get free of his feelings for her. Is that the way it is?"

"More than that. He worships her. He'd die for her."

Abby, ever practical, considered this. "Shouldn't she at least go out on a date with this guy?"

"He's possessive. He follows her. He knows her every move."

"That would be spooky. I wouldn't want anyone knowing my every move."

She picked up the newspaper she'd laid aside and began to read again, holding it up like a curtain between us. Our conversations sometimes continued in this way, lapsing into silence, each in his or her own thoughts, like a river running underground, only to emerge in a few minutes in what appeared to be a different context, sometimes not recognizably the same conversation.

"There's an article here," Abby said, "that says that compulsive shopping's a mental illness."

"Does it say how you treat it?"

"Prozac, of course."

"Well, that's a problem we don't have."

"But shopping does relieve stress. It works for me. It's worth twenty milligrams of Prozac, any day."

"But you don't buy anything."

She was sitting with one leg hooked under her, the other straight out. The foot that was dangling off the end of the couch had been jiggling, and when I spoke it abruptly stopped moving, as if all the loose strings in her body had been pulled tight. She still held the newspaper as though she were reading. It hid her face, and all I could see were the fingers holding the edges of the paper and the one leg with the foot that was clamped stockstill.

"Sometimes I do," she said. "Sometimes I don't."

"When you took the day off from work, you didn't."

"I didn't buy anything?" she wondered aloud, scanning her memory. Then, more definitely, "No. As a matter of fact, I didn't." She paused, considering whether to let it go. "How do you know that?"

"I checked."

"You checked."

"I called the card company."

"Why did you do that?"

"I know." I started to explain, but I couldn't think of any extenuation.

She brought the paper down with a crash. "But why?"

"I couldn't figure out what you were doing."

"Why do you have to know what I'm doing?"

"You're my wife, for goodness sake!"

"But that doesn't give you the right to know everything I do."

"I don't want to know everything you do. But you said you were late for work. You told me, more or less, you were going to work."

"I was."

"Then I turn up at the agency, and you're not there. Never were there. Never had any intention of going to work."

"That's not true. You're wrong, Paul. I got halfway to Cambridge. I was stuck in traffic on Mass Ave, totally jammed up, totally frazzled, and I said, 'Screw it.' "

"You said, 'Screw it, I'm going shopping.' "

"I don't want to be interrogated."

"I'm not interrogating you. I'm talking to you."

"I don't like it when you quote what I say back at me. I don't want my words twisted around."

"I just want to get to the truth."

"What are you looking for?"

"I don't know." I sighed.

"What?"

"It sounds crazy," I conceded. "When you say it out loud, it sounds nuts."

"So put it into words," she urged me. I could have been one of her blocked, teenaged mothers. "Say it out loud."

"When I turned up at the agency and you weren't there, I thought . . ."

She was waiting for me to speak the words. She might have been ready to pounce. She was as tense as I was.

"I thought you were with someone else," I said.

Her lips were tight. She glanced at me and away, fleeing my eyes. I felt I'd betrayed her. I felt undeserving. I deserved no mercy.

"Now what do you think?"

"I think it was ridiculous."

She picked up the newspaper again, as if the conclusion of a logical proof needed no further comment. The newspaper was crumpled though, and when she tried to put it up, the pages wouldn't fall into place. But I didn't want the conversation to end there. Even though I'd made myself look like an idiot, at least we were talking openly for the first time in months. I could see only the top of her head and her eyes, which were fixed studiously on the text. She rattled the newspaper to free a kink and, in that adjustment, raised the curtain to cover herself completely.

"I'm not making excuses for myself," I said, speaking to the obituaries. "But I'm feeling disconnected from you. We don't talk to each other like we used to."

The paper didn't move. I looked at her fingers, the conch-pink nails. I felt I was talking to myself.

"I know you must discuss this in therapy," I said.

The fingers tightened infinitesimally.

"I don't want to get into that," I said. "Therapy's off-limits. I understand that. I think that's the way it ought to be."

One of the worst parts of our grief was my enforced helplessness in the face of Abby's misery. She had been in therapy when we first met. You didn't have to be Sigmund Freud to recognize that I was the latest in a series of older men with whom she played out the abandonment by her charming, unreliable father, a lawyer whose blarney got him into more scrapes than he could talk his way out of. In that time together, there was no secrecy about the issues she was dealing with. She spoke openly of the emotional impact of her father's absence, and I shared with her my own, oddly complementary problem, of a father who was always present. We speculated about whether her father had ever appeared before my father, and if so, whether as counsel or defendant. God knows what she told her therapist. But in those days, therapy wasn't such a desperate, Sturm und Drang struggle of the soul. Our neuroses mingled. Our hang-ups were bared. We shocked and delighted each other with raunchy incest jokes about our lovemaking. It wasn't that we were frivolous—far from it—but our coming together possessed a lightness of touch. For me, Abby possessed both the splendor and the emotional delicacy of a butterfly.

"What you say there is private," I told her. It was impossible to tell what kind of reaction I was getting on the other side of the paper. "I respect that. If that's what you want."

I couldn't be her therapist. She already had one. But that was the problem: the ponderous, aging, infinitely well-meaning, achingly empathic Ellen Hollenburg, who in her prime had been accorded the awe due a mythic figure. But Ellen's brand of therapy—digging deep, boring through the living flesh of experience until you hit bone—was liable to get people stuck in the past, bogged down in the pit that therapy had dug.

"But if it's not working," I said, "I think I have to say something. If therapy is making things worse."

The paper came down slowly, as though her arms were too weary to support it anymore. All this time, no more than two feet from me, Abby had been weeping in silence behind the curtain. Tears ran freely in glistening streaks down her cheeks, and she made no attempt to wipe them away before they gathered at her chin. Her hands collapsed, crushing the paper into a chaotic ball in her lap.

I made to come to her, but she raised her hands in something like a ninja stance.

"No!" she said.

She was anguished. She could scarcely keep her eyes open and blinked away tears as fast as they came.

I waited, and after a few moments she tried to talk, but the tears got in the way of speech. She gasped as though she were drowning while I waited at the shore.

"It's not a question," she managed eventually, "of whether therapy's working."

"Okay," I encouraged her.

"She says . . ." It took her a long time to bring this out. "She says maybe I'm not ready to recover."

My heart sank at this. "She says"? I wondered. Since when had Abby given her life over to another person to determine?

"But what do you think?" I asked her.

She shook her head, defiant and bewildered, both. "I don't think I am."

"You don't think you're ready to go on with life?"

"No." She had recovered herself and sat quietly with her hands resting still in her lap.

"Is it that you feel you have to punish yourself?"

"No. That's not it. I don't blame myself for what happened to Adrian." The mention of his name, after months of taboo, was so easy; the word was so simply enunciated. She turned to me with a sweet smile, reassuring, and gently grasped my wrist. "I don't blame you, either. Neither of us."

"What, then, Abby? Tell me what it is."

She stared off into the distance. "Oh, I don't know." She sighed, as people do at the moment they relax their vigilance and the fragments at the edges of consciousness start to come together and form an understanding.

"Tell me," I coaxed.

She shrugged, as if testing the weight of her burden. "I get up in the morning, and I tell myself, I'll go on. But I can't go on. Really, I don't want to. I don't want to get over Adrian. This is all I have of him now. I want to feel what I feel. It would feel wrong to get over it. I want to stay with it." She glanced at me to see my reaction. "I know it sounds masochistic. I know it's a familiar feeling—being left, being abandoned, feeling this way. I know I have a tendency to put it on myself, to feel I'm alone because I wasn't good enough. I know where it comes from—we both do. But knowing where it comes from doesn't make any difference. This feels true. To feel this way seems the most real way to be.

"Some things you get over. After my father died, I found a way to go on with life. I didn't think I would. The final abandonment. But I did. And you helped me. You were wonderful, Paul. But this is different. I've learned that a parent's death is something you get over. Losing a child is something you can't get over. Your heart breaks."

She drew breath to speak and then stopped. It was something new and more difficult to say, and she needed to give it further thought.

She touched my shoulder. "You keep your balance when everything goes topsy-turvy," she began. "You're so good at staying calm when everyone else loses their cool. You keep your perspective whatever other people say, because you have this inner certainty. It doesn't bother you what other people do. You have your own standards. You've been my rock. All the time we've been married, you've been my North Star, always true, never wavering."

She stopped short of the "But" that the cadence of her voice led up to.

"But now?" I supplied.

She held up her hands on either side of her head, fingers extended, shaking with the effort of opposing a force field that was pressing in upon her. I was afraid I might be part of that force.

"Now, understanding doesn't help. Understanding's going to take it away. I don't think this is about being rational. I know it sounds crazy. I just know I have to be here for a while. I have to find my own way. I don't know what I'm doing. I can't ask you . . ."

"I'll do anything," I told her. "I'll do anything to help you."

"I know," she said, nodding, head down. "I know."

"I'll fight," I said, "but I don't know what I'm fighting."

Suddenly, she gave herself up to her grief. She sobbed, crouched forward on the edge of the couch, precariously balanced with one foot under her, her hands covering her lower face like an oxygen mask.

I was wretched. Slowly, I reached out. I wasn't trying to do anything more than lay my hand upon her back; she let me put my arm around her shoulders and slowly draw her to me. She sobbed deeply and bitterly and I—lover, husband, doctor—enclosed her misery but was not permitted to enter it.

"I can't help it," she whispered. "I can't help it."

She leaned against me and I could feel that she was still shaking her head even as it rested on my shoulder.

nine

I met Brenda Gorn at the Exeter County Courthouse. Brenda takes many of the cases in which the victim is a child or a woman, and I knew that Craig Cavanaugh's case drew on this special passion for justice. She came late to the law, deferring law school until well after her children started grade school, and she seems to have no designs on her boss's job, though she is close to fifty, and her window of opportunity for moving up will soon close. She is still a good-looking woman, trim, with a somewhat muscular body, but there is in her face the hardness of someone who doesn't cut herself much slack, who has given herself over to her work. From our casual conversation, I have the impression that Brenda's private life after her divorce has pretty much shrunk down to her two daughters; they are through college now, and have left home.

I found Brenda pacing impatiently in the marble lobby. In spite of her elegant dark blue suit and impeccable professional appearance, she looked like she was preparing for a brawl.

"Sorry it's such short notice," she said. She was off already, stalking toward the courtroom.

"I don't have a report done on Cavanaugh," I told her. I had to walk quickly to keep up. "You know that?"

"It doesn't matter. We're going to have to wing it."

There had been a change of plan, she told me. The lawyers for Craig Cavanaugh weren't going the not-guilty-by-reason-of-insanity route anymore. They had some other strategy in mind, and they were in a rush. Ross Hamilton had managed to get his hearing moved up, an unheard-of feat in the face of an unresponsive and implacable court system.

"How did they do this?" I asked Brenda.

"Who knows." She waved it off. "Maybe someone Ross went to law school with fixed it with the clerk. Or someone whose divorce his firm handled spoke to a judge. Who cares? The main thing is, they think they can spring him."

I was uneasy about this; Brenda must have seen the uncertainty on my face.

"He's crazy, right?" she said. It was a demand more than a question.

"Kind of."

She stopped abruptly. "What does that mean, Paul?"

"He's obsessed. He can't think about anything except the victim. His whole life revolves around her and trying to get her to love him."

"That sounds crazy to me."

"He's only crazy if extreme love is crazy."

"Jesus, Paul—don't go all lawyerly on me now. We have to nail this son of a bitch. If we don't get him committed to Sanders, the court could let him go on bail. And if he walks, he'll make Natalie's life not worth living." She took hold of my jacket with thumb and finger and tugged at me until we stood face-to-face. She seemed to want to brace me. "Craig Cavanaugh is crazy-dangerous and he has to stay in the hospital. Right?"

"Look, I'm with you, Brenda. This kid is evil."

"But 'evil shit' won't do it, Paul. You know the court won't buy that."

"He's culpable. He knows what he's doing. He knows right from wrong."

"He has to be certifiably nuts, or he'll walk. This is it. You're all I've got. Next stop: bail hearing."

I deliberated a moment on how far I could stretch the sworn testimony I was about to give. I thought of the three-story building he'd climbed for his nightly vigil. I thought of Natalie and her dead cat and wondered how far Craig would go if he finally got the message that Natalie wasn't interested in him, would never, ever want him.

"He's dangerous. There's no doubt about that."

"He made threats?"

"Not to me."

"Give me something I can use in there." Brenda jerked her thumb in the direction of the heavy mahogany doors that led into the courtroom.

"He killed Natalie's cat."

I couldn't meet her eye. I knew it sounded lame, but it felt strong. To be convincing you need to have had certain experiences: you need to have seen a dozen Craigs plus a handful of serial murderers. Unless you've heard them describe the joy of stalking, the taking of trophies and mementoes and talismans, the torture of proxies, you won't get the creepy, uneasy chill that comes to an experienced clinician when he encounters a pet killing. Pets are embedded in an emotional context of a person's life; the stalker feels this connection as vividly as his victim.

"A cat?"

"I know. On the face of it—"

"Maybe if the judge is a cat person . . ." She made an ironic tipping motion. "Maybe that could swing it our way."

"It shows malice toward the victim. It's a strong indication that he's capable of resorting to violence. Violence is part of his repertoire."

"Okay, okay. Listen."

She now had a tight grip on the arm of my jacket, as though she needed physical means to hold me in place to stop me from dodging her question. She held my gaze as if by force of will she could draw from me the conclusion she needed to keep her victim safe.

"Answer me this: Is Craig Cavanaugh mentally ill?"

In my hesitation, I saw the dawning disappointment in her eyes. Soon it would turn to exasperation. We'd been friends for a long time, but this was business. For Brenda, the pursuit of justice is a blood sport.

"Yes," I said at the last minute. "There's a disorder of attachment. There's a narrowing of attentional focus. There's distortion of thinking, poor insight, grossly impaired judgment, aberrant behavior. But that's all soft stuff. There isn't something like a delusion that you can shake in front of the judge. He's not talking about a microchip implanted behind his ear that controls his thoughts. Nothing like that."

"What's he got, then?"

"There's falling in love here." I spread my arms with the palms of my hands separated by two feet to show the limits of normal feeling. Then I moved them wider, so that my hands were three feet apart. "This here is crazy. This is called de Clérambault's syndrome—the delusion that some movie star is head-over-heels in love with you. That's not where Craig Cavanaugh is. He's somewhere in between, in this gray area."

She started to say something, then glanced at my face and thought better of it. I knew what she wanted to ask of me: To nudge this one her way—not to lie or fake, only to tilt my testimony a little, "just this one time." But honesty is like virginity—once you give it away, you can't get it back—and perhaps Brenda thought it was worth preserving.

"Am I hearing you right?" she demanded. "He's not committable?"

"I'm saying it could go either way. We can take a shot at it. That's fine with me. But I'd think there'd be stronger grounds for arguing against bail."

"Not a chance. You think a judge is going to make an upperclass kid, with decent legal representation and no prior conviction for violent crime, await trial in jail?"

"He might."

"A white kid with real money?"

"There's something else," I confessed.

She waited, stony-eyed.

"He got banged up a bit in Sanders."

"Great." She shook her head in disbelief. "I suppose he was fending off some child rapist?"

"No. Actually, I pressed the alarm on him. The officers took him down a bit more zealously than was called for."

"Even better!" She threw her hands in the air in frustration.

"If we can't commit him to Sanders—if, I said if—we should focus on getting some restriction that will keep him away from Natalie."

"You're right," Brenda said, instantly practical. "This is about Natalie. We have to do what we can to keep her safe. She thinks you walk on water, by the way. I didn't have the heart to disabuse her."

Ross Hamilton came in with Judy O'Donnell, and Brenda and

Ross went away to a corner for a bargaining session. Though we've never hit it off, Judy and I have been colleagues at the Methodist for several years, and she came over to talk to me. Judy is a forensic psychiatrist who's taken a different career path from my own and stayed in town, at the center of things. She has a deft political touch, so that although she's one of many staff psychiatrists at the Methodist, she's close to Larry Shapiro and wields power informally.

Judy looks the way you might imagine someone's grandmother to appear as a younger woman: a folksy, thirty-six-year-old granny. Behind large glasses are candid eyes that sparkle with kindness and seem to peer into the better part of you. I've never been entirely certain whether Judy is sincere or an extraordinary actress. No one is. Judy has a knack for taking on thankless tasks, such as high-profile patients like Craig Cavanaugh, and emerging from the encounter covered in glory. She does sincerity extraordinarily well. She doesn't seem to be ambitious, but there she is at Larry's right hand. She doesn't seem to be mercenary, but she's in the witness box on all the most lucrative trials. She doesn't seem to be hungry for publicity, but she's forever turning up as a talk-show guest, willing to give her opinion on almost anything tangentially related to what she knows. I'm willing to acknowledge a twinge of jealousy at her success, but I still wonder how a saintly person like Judy can end up at the top of a dirty business like ours. Even when I'm pretty sure she's full of it, I feel a nagging sense of guilt for thinking badly of this good woman.

"Hey, Judy."

"Hey, Paul."

Mercifully, the lawyers conferred for no more than a couple of minutes—it soon became clear they wouldn't come to an agreement—and we passed through the great mahogany doors to take our seats at the front of the courtroom.

Halfway down, surrounded by an aide on either side and another in the row behind who was in the act of reaching to point to a detail in the document held before him, sat Old Man Cavanaugh. It was impossible not to notice him. He was eighty years old and an imposing presence—every bit as large in life as he appeared on television. He had been a football player at Harvard back when the college fielded a real team, and he was still a big man, with broad shoulders and a thick neck, so that when he turned to us as we came level with him, tilting his head to scrutinize us over his reading glasses, he had the look of a bull lowering his horns.

We sat down, and Craig was brought in just before the judge took the bench. He wore his own clothes, but even his Italian blue blazer couldn't offset the effect of handcuffs anchored by a chain to the manacles around his ankles that restricted him to an eighteen-inch stride. All the same, he managed to shuffle with a degree of panache. In fact, the hardware, which could have played against him, made him look young and vulnerable. The scrape above his eye, a dusky purple bruise fading at the edges to iodine brown which healing rendered even more conspicuous, definitely conferred victim status. He might have been a choirboy who'd been mugged for his collection money.

As Craig crossed in front of the judge's bench, he looked over our heads toward his grandfather sitting in the well of the court, and I wasn't sure whether he nodded in greeting to him or simply dipped his head in shame.

The judge entered, counsel identified themselves for the record, Judy and I were sworn in, and proceedings began. A commitment hearing is a battle of the psychiatric experts. There's no jury to impress so even the lawyers don't get much of a chance to spar. When a patient insists on testifying on his own behalf, it's almost always a disaster, and I knew Ross wouldn't permit that kind of self-indulgence. Besides, Craig didn't need to speak. Throughout my testimony, I was acutely aware of the apparent disconnect between the person I was describing and the person who sat before the judge, the clean-cut, preppy young man whom His Honor could—so it seemed—evaluate with his own eyes.

Ross Hamilton played Craig's injury with a light touch. There was no outrage, no mention of trampling by jack-booted paramilitaries. The wound itself carried all the rhetorical force that was necessary. Craig—at this point, Ross lapsed into the use of his first name, as one would a minor—had been held in the company of hardened criminals. The young man had been "brutalized." Ross spoke more in sadness than in anger. The judge frowned thoughtfully in my direction.

I had precious little hard evidence to show that Craig was dangerous, other than the pattern of following and harassment that had put Natalie in fear prior to his arrest. Brenda had scarcely begun to lead me through the circumstances of Craig's admission to Sanders when Ross was on his feet objecting that my testimony was hearsay. After all, I hadn't seen Craig creeping around outside Natalie's apartment; I hadn't seen him opening her mail, or following her when she went out. The judge allowed the objection, and there wasn't much else I could say on the subject.

When the time came for Ross to cross-examine me, he focused on Craig's hospitalization. A cross by a good attorney makes you feel like a ventriloquist's dummy. However smart a clinician you may be, however well prepared, you're powerless to shade or explain. You answer his questions and find that you have to agree to a series of three-quarter truths. You hate the words that are forced from your mouth. And if you try to twist free, to demonstrate that even though the cross-examination straightjacket holds you tight, you can waggle a finger to prove that you still have a mind of your own, you're smacked down.

"You have a unit at Sanders where patients who are too violent for the ordinary admissions unit are housed, is that correct, Doctor?"

"Yes."

"What is it called?"

"The intensive treatment unit."

"Did Mr. Cavanaugh's behavior make it necessary to be removed to the intensive treatment unit?"

"No."

"So he spent all his time on the regular admissions unit?"

"Yes."

"Was he violent toward any of the other patients?"

"Not to my knowledge."

"You're the attending psychiatrist in the admissions unit, right?"

"Yes."

"Well, wouldn't you know if Mr. Cavanaugh had been violent toward any of the other patients? Isn't it your job to know that kind of thing, Doctor?"

"If it's reported, I'll know about it."

"But you don't know for sure?"

"Not a hundred percent, no."

"Even though you're the doctor in charge? Even though it's your job to know what happens in the admissions unit, you can't give a straight answer to the question?"

"I think I've answered the question."

"Very well. Let's turn to something you do know about."

It was pretty standard witness baiting. The last thing you want to do is give someone like Ross the satisfaction of provoking you to retaliate. Sometimes you have to take your knocks and ride it out until your own team gets the ball back.

But Ross wasn't done. "Tell me, Doctor," he asked. "How did Craig receive that cut on the side of his head?"

He let me describe the situation while he looked over some papers in his hands and seemed not to be listening to a word I said.

"Did Mr. Cavanaugh threaten you?"

"Not verbally."

"Not verbally. You mean, he did something?"

"Yes."

"What did he do to threaten you?"

"He'd made some inappropriate remarks about my family and I'd gotten up to end the interview. He became very angry—"

He cut me off. "I'm not asking what you thought. Just tell the court what you observed Mr. Cavanaugh do that you interpreted as a threat."

"He stood up abruptly."

He waited a couple of beats, as though he thought there might be more to come. "That's it?"

"In my opinion, he—"

"So the injury my client sustained is the result of his standing up too quickly? Did we hear you correctly, Doctor?"

Brenda came in with the re-direct and got me to fill in the context of the encounter, but it was my sense that she was giving me an opportunity to correct the record for my own vindication rather than because it would have much effect on the judge.

Then Ross called Judy. He was now the courteous listener, and although Brenda did her best to interrupt the flow with objections, Judy had her own way in the direct. To hear her testimony, you might have thought she was a grade-school teacher talking about some behavior problem that time, patience, and a loving environment would surely enable Craig to outgrow.

"What is Mr. Cavanaugh's diagnosis?" Ross asked her.

"Adjustment disorder with mixed emotional features," Judy replied promptly.

"What kind of a diagnosis is that, Doctor? Adjustment disorder? Is that a serious mental illness?"

"Any psychiatric illness involves suffering and deserves appropriate treatment. I don't want to minimize that. But it's not a major mental illness like schizophrenia, or bipolar disorder."

"Not the kind of condition that in the normal scheme of things would require psychiatric hospitalization?"

"Heavens, no. Hardly ever. It's commonly treated on an outpatient basis."

"Would you tell the court how you arrived at that diagnosis?"

"Certainly." Judy beamed. "Mr. Cavanaugh is a young man who's gradually getting over a big disappointment. It's the kind of disappointment that everyone goes through, particularly during their teens and twenties: He fell in love, his love wasn't returned, and he's been having difficulty falling out of love. All this is perfectly normal. He just feels things more intensely than most people. Certainly, his thinking at one point was distorted. He accentuated the positive. Love by its very nature is optimistic. Love by its very nature is obsessive. To love implies a preoccupation with the person you're in love with and the hope that one's love is returned. There's nothing unreasonable here. If you're in love, then you do tend to think of the person you're in love with night and day."

She paused to spread the warmth of her smile over everyone in the courtroom, including the stenographer, as though inviting other members of the group to jump in and share their own experiences on the issue.

"Mr. Cavanaugh has been overly persistent. In fact, in talking things over with me, he's willing to admit that he's been a downright pest. I'm certain that he deeply regrets any distress he's caused Ms. Davis. And I think this in itself is a sign that he has insight into the way he's been behaving, and this indicates that he's not psychotic, or deluded, or in any way sick. I'm sure that, with the proper therapy, he's ready to move on."

Craig nodded on cue and hung his head thoughtfully. He didn't look plausibly mentally ill. He fit all too well the picture that Judy painted of him: a young man who loved too much.

Brenda gave her a tough cross-examination. She zeroed in on Judy's lack of experience with hardened criminals and then worked away at a line of questioning that implied Judy's judgment was Pollyannaish. But Brenda's difficulty lay in the fact that Craig had never fallen into the trap of saying that Natalie returned his feelings. He'd never crossed the line into psychosis.

After the lawyers' summations, we weren't much surprised when the judge turned down the petition to commit. All that lay between Craig and freedom was the bail hearing. I had promised to call Natalie with the outcome of the hearing, and was already thinking about what I'd tell her. I'd intended to leave, but Ross Hamilton had begun his argument. The judge interrupted Ross with a series of skeptical questions. It was one thing to safeguard Craig's civil rights against incarceration in a maximum security hospital; now the court had to address the other side of the coin.

The judge was paying close attention as Brenda mixed it up, playing off what would otherwise have appeared to be Craig's assets.

"The risk of default is substantial," she said. "This is a man of almost limitless financial means. With his family's resources, he can live anywhere in the world he chooses. He's not married. He has no children. He has no job that ties him to the area. He's well traveled and lived abroad for six months before starting college."

"What worries me is the safety of the young woman," the judge said. He turned to Ross. "What safeguards are there in the community to keep him out of trouble?"

"The restraining order is still in place, Your Honor."

"But Mr. Hamilton, hasn't he already shown that a court order alone isn't enough to keep him in line?"

Ross wavered and turned, in his first show of uncertainty that day, in Judy's direction. But she was conferring intensely with Craig. They were concocting some cover story, I thought, and she looked up long enough only to motion that she needed another couple of minutes to sell the deal to Craig.

"What's in place," the judge wanted to know, "that will ensure that your client doesn't relapse back into the kind of thinking that has brought him to this point?"

Ross turned again. Judy nodded as though she had the answer to the judge's question.

"If I may, Your Honor?" Ross asked.

Briskly, he crossed the few yards that brought him to where Judy sat and bent to hear what she had managed to put together. She whispered into his ear, and Ross nodded his head as she talked. He started to straighten up, as though uncertain; he glanced in my direction. Then, for a moment, I thought, his eyes sought out John Cavanaugh. Judy was still talking; she was emphatic. Ross turned to question Craig, who nodded agreement.

"Your Honor," Ross began, "my client recognizes his need for continuing psychiatric supervision during this period of recovery."

Judy was looking intently at me as Ross spoke. It was the kind of stare whose intensity, if you believed in telepathy, would have transmitted a message.

"Mr. Cavanaugh," Ross said, "is willing to undergo psychiatric supervision by Dr. Lucas."

He turned to indicate me with a generous wave of his hand. I had already thought of three plausible conflicts of interest when my eyes came into contact once more with Judy's unwavering, telepathic stare. The message, I knew, was not a personal one. She spoke for Larry Shapiro. The Methodist was calling in the markers.

"Dr. Lucas treated Mr. Cavanaugh during his stay at the Sanders Institute," Ross said. In one of those reversals of polarity that lawyers manage without even blinking, Ross now gave what sounded like a testimonial to my clinical acumen. "Dr. Lucas," he said, "knows the case intimately. Mr. Cavanaugh has confidence in Dr. Lucas. He trusts him. He agrees to meet with Dr. Lucas at a frequency determined by Dr. Lucas—weekly, if that's felt necessary— and for Dr. Lucas to file periodic reports with the court on his progress in therapy."

It was a setup, of course. The proposal was cynical enough that Craig might even have come up with it himself. Aside from that one hour a week, I'd have no control over my patient, but I'd be held accountable for what he did. Craig would have as much control over my future as I would have over his. I thought of the ancient Ottoman punishment in which the murderer is sewn up in a sack with a monkey and heaved into the Bosphorus.

The judge turned to me. "Dr. Lucas?"

Even as I rose, like an automaton, to my feet, I still hadn't made up my mind. Brenda was looking at me in a peculiar way. My mind was empty. Blank of all decision.

"Yes, Your Honor," I heard myself agree.

ten

I dreaded making the call to Natalie, but I'd promised. As soon as I got back to Sanders, I sat down at my desk to give her the bad news. There was a trip wire, I'd say. The instant Craig put a foot wrong—and she had to let the police know about the slightest thing—they'd yank his bail. I felt I'd failed her.

When she didn't answer, I was relieved. I left a noncommittal message on her voice mail with my number at Sanders. Natalie wasn't my patient. She was a witness, and, really, I had no obligation to her. But as an afterthought, I added my home number, which I'd never done before.

She called me quite late that night. Abby was watching a movie, and I picked up.

She said, simply and implicitly, "It's me."

There's an intimacy implied by someone announcing herself anonymously in this way. This intimacy deepens when the other person accepts the assumption—accepts it by omission, simply by not asking, "Who's this?"—that he must know who this person is by the sound of her voice, by the time of her call, because she has a place in his life.

"I know," I said. I found I was whispering. So I added, to undo any assumption, to dispel any hint that she'd been on my mind, "I recognized your voice."

"I know what you're going to say," she said. She was whispering, too, her voice slightly husky. "But I don't want you to tell me."

"Then I'm not sure how to help you."

"I don't know either."

I wondered, from the quality of her voice, whether she was lying down. Lolling on her back on a sofa, feet in the air. Or sprawled in bed.

"I wish we could meet," she suggested. "Are you allowed to do that? If you're going to tell me something, it would be better face-to-face."

I agreed, because I felt I owed it to her.

We arranged to get together the next day, a Saturday. It was on neutral ground, a Starbucks in a shopping mall. No alcohol. Good lighting. Lots of people around. Witnesses. Clean and simple.

It had been raining all day, and the Meeting House Mall was mobbed with people wandering around with nothing much to do. Starbucks was packed, and I was lucky to find a couple of stools at the counter that ran along the window. Our view was a corner where the two arms of the mall crossed. I was watching a group of teenage girls pretending not to notice a group of teenage boys and I didn't see Natalie come in. She walked up behind me and had to tap me on the shoulder to get my attention.

As a result, I turned quickly and caught her still leaning toward me, so that for an instant our faces were almost touching. The fine rain had gathered in her eyebrows and on her cheeks and the tiny droplets caught the light. She seemed to sparkle.

She stood upright. I gave her my hand. She was slightly out of breath, as though she'd been hurrying through the crowds.

"Thank you," she told me. She still had hold of my hand and gave it a squeeze before letting go.

She was wearing a tam-o'-shanter and she pulled it off and shook out her hair, and because she sat so close to me I smelled the fragrance of the shampoo or the conditioner she used, and I felt I was enveloped in the intimate miasma that surrounds a person.

I left her to get her coffee, something elaborate with skimmed milk and large amounts of caffeine. As I waited in line at the counter I turned to look at her and found her eyes already on me. When she saw me look at her she smiled, and I knew that she hoped for too much from the encounter. But I was the bearer of bad news, and couldn't cut her off without leaving her with some replacement for the faith she'd placed in me.

When I returned to our perch, she took the coffee from me with both her hands and looked anxiously into my face.

"I wasn't sure you'd come," she said.

"Of course I'd come." I was genuinely surprised. "I told you I would. Why wouldn't I?"

"On the phone, you sounded hesitant."

"That was because I wanted to tell you something that would cheer you up. And I didn't have any good news for you."

"That's all right," she said, as if forgiving me.

She stared abstractedly through the window at the passing crowds. The boys had sent an emissary, the class clown, to break the ice with the girls. Around the corner, a paunchy security guard took note of the loitering young people and spoke into his radio.

"I didn't expect anything good to come out of it," she said.

"It was just a hearing. It didn't decide anything except that he's fit to stand trial. Remember, he still has to stand trial."

"They let him go."

"There just weren't grounds enough to keep him locked up in a psychiatric hospital."

I sounded as though I was making excuses. At that moment, I felt very keenly that I'd let Natalie down.

"So he's out there, somewhere."

We stared at the people sauntering by with carrier bags from Banana Republic and Pier 1 and Filene's Basement, a flow that parted around the group of teenage boys still loitering at the corner.

"Or maybe he got the message," I said hopefully. "Maybe he got a taste of where this will lead if he doesn't let go."

"Do you think so?" She searched my eyes. "Do you really think that's possible? That he'll just give up and move on to something else?"

She had hold of my arm. "I think . . . ," I said.

She wasn't letting go of my arm. There were tears gathered in the corners of her eyes, and I couldn't hold her gaze.

"I know." She sighed.

"Sometimes they do switch to something else."

"To someone else."

"To someone else. We don't know what triggers it. They don't know. They wake up one morning and someone new strikes their fancy, and it's all over with the previous love of their lives. They fall out of love just as suddenly as they fell into it."

"That isn't what you said before."

"What did I say?"

"You told me to leave the state."

"That's something to think about."

I was angry at the injustice of the situation. That Craig, with the best lawyers that money could buy, as a prerogative of privilege, might force Natalie out. At this critical juncture in her career, she'd have to abandon all her network, the mentors and colleagues who could help her in the next leg up. I wanted her to stay and fight.

"You have to see what happens at the trial," I said. "They may lock him up."

"But the trial could be a year from now. And in the meantime, I have this creepy feeling that I'm never alone. I sense him watching me everywhere I go."

Natalie seemed to find in me powers I knew I didn't possess. I felt her tugging at me emotionally, trying to pull me in. Good sense told me to disengage. I should have walked away.

Outside the window, there were two security guards moving in on the group of teenage boys. But the boys were surly and inclined to argue. One of them stood face-to-face with the original security guard who had taken up a stance that he must have thought conveyed authority: feet apart, thumbs hooked into a wide belt from which hung keys, flashlight, radio, handcuffs, nightstick. Now the boys would have to make some gesture of defiance to save face in front of the girls. People who passed sensed the standoff and slowed to stare.

"If there's anything I can do . . . ," I began lamely.

She nodded in disappointment, staring down at the speckled froth of her untouched mocha.

"You have family around here—is that right? Friends?"

"Sure."

"You have to pull in your support network."

"I know. They try, but they don't really know what it is I'm going through. No one knows how alone I am with this." She looked at me to see if I really did understand.

"Yes," I said, staring into her eyes. "I know."

I felt myself at the brink. Either I'd fall into some crazy, quasi-professional liaison whose bottom I couldn't see, or I'd swerve out of the way at the last minute, now, and leave her sitting alone at the Starbucks counter.

She sensed this. She knew she had to hook me in at this moment, or I'd be gone.

She grasped my arm. "If I could call you once in a while . . . ," she said. "It would help a lot." She gazed appealingly into my eyes. She was afraid. Her lips were parted. Her hand touched my wrist. "If we could meet occasionally . . ."

I felt the erotic undertow in her plea. "Of course you can call me," I told her.

I took a deep breath. I moved the hand she was touching to take my cup of coffee and raise it to my lips. Momentarily, we were distracted by the scene on the other side of the window, where a crowd was collecting. People kept their distance, but they were curious to see how the security guard, nervously fingering the nightstick on his belt, would handle the teenage boys.

I stood up. "Anytime," I told her with a studied coolness. "You've got my number."

"Thank you," she said.

Then, before I could stop her, she was hugging me. I could have caught her by the wrists before she put her arms around my neck, but it would have been a rough move. I would have had to push her away, and I felt bad enough as it was. So I made the best of it and tried to subvert the gesture.

"Thank you for coming," she murmured in my ear.

I patted her on the back in a reassuring way. I was careful not to make any move that she could misinterpret as my clasping her. "You're very welcome," I said.

Over her shoulder my attention was caught by a shift in the crowd in response to a sudden movement. A shove, I suspected, delivered by the security guard who felt disrespected. I couldn't see into the center of the mass of people. There was something not right, and it took me an instant to notice what it was: One face in the far side of the crowd wasn't looking into the center, where the action was. Craig stared at me as I embraced Natalie in the coffee shop.

A moment later, the crowd moved again as one of the youths was escorted out between two security guards, and I lost sight of him. I broke away from Natalie abruptly enough so that she turned to see where I was looking. I was stunned.

"Did you see him?" I asked her. "Did you see Craig over there?"

She shook her head. She didn't seem put out by the possibility.

I searched the crowd for his face. I wanted to be sure. But I couldn't see him.

"I think it was Craig," I said.

Natalie was entirely calm. She shrugged fatalistically. Almost with indifference. "It probably was."

"But I only glimpsed him."

"Now you know what it's like," she said.

I had to be sure. I took off, out of the coffee shop, in the direction I'd seen him. If it was him. And if it was Craig, I had to tell him what it was that he'd seen. That the embrace meant nothing beyond an act of kindness. That I was trying to bring comfort to Natalie. Nothing more than that. I felt an urgent need to correct whatever impression he'd formed before his mind set.

That was why I ran. I was dodging people, pushing when someone with their back to me wouldn't move out of the way fast enough. People turned to look at me as though I were part of the earlier fracas. Some of them moved quickly aside in case I was violent. I must have looked wild and maybe a bit dangerous as I turned my head this way and that, oblivious to the stares of those around me.

I came out on the other side of the crowd, where he'd been, but I couldn't see anyone who resembled him. I spun around. Then I caught sight of someone hurrying in the opposite direction, toward the exit to the parking lot, and I sprinted after him. Before I'd gone a dozen paces he heard my footsteps coming up fast behind him and turned, and I saw at once it wasn't Craig.

I ran back, peering into the stores on either side, passing again through the people still gathered at the corner. They saw me coming and stepped hurriedly out of my way. I went around the corner to look down one arm of the main hall, then turned to see if I could glimpse him in the other direction, but Craig was gone.

eleven

"I don't have the whole story yet," Brenda told me over the phone. "But since you've volunteered to treat this character, I thought I'd give you what I had."

"I need all the help I can get," I agreed.

"I found out where Craig went after he left the prep school in Massachusetts. They packed him off to a military academy in Georgia. One of those places that's big on discipline. Drill before breakfast. Boys only."

"Sounds like the right move."

"The funny thing was, the school closed down right after Craig left. Even stranger, John Cavanaugh stepped in and bought the place up. It wasn't like the land was worth much—they'd closed the school, so it wasn't a going concern—but the principal and his wife were able to retire to a place in Bermuda. And they took their daughter with them."

"It sounds like his grandson's love life got pretty expensive."

"Get this: Old Man Cavanaugh turned around and bulldozed the place. He put in a golf course and turned the property into a retirement community. If you've got the cash, you can get a nice little place by the ninth green for a million bucks."

"Money loves money."

"That's all I could get at this end. I've got a call in to the county prosecutor in Georgia. I'll let you know if I get anything more."

I was prepared for a rough meeting when Craig walked through the door for our first session at the Methodist. He'd had a week to stew over what he'd witnessed at the mall. If it was Craig whom I'd seen.

He was formal and businesslike; his prime concern seemed to be making sure that I wasn't concealing any recording device in the office. I could have asked him what he had to hide. But in the session's first moments, I thought there was a possibility that we might eventually work our way to something close to candor. In that spirit, I invited him to look around.

"You could have a tape recorder in that drawer," he said, pointing to the bottom drawer of the desk.

It wasn't, in fact, my office. It's assigned to a child psychiatrist, and I have the use of it on the one day a week I'm at the Methodist. Hence the crayon drawings pinned to one wall, the blackboard and easel, and a toy box in a corner by a potted tree. As to the drawer Craig indicated, I hadn't the slightest idea what was in it.

"Go ahead," I told him.

He changed his mind and opened the one above it. Inside were a pair of teddy bears, dressed as male and female. Two blinks, and I was back in control. These emotional ambushes—memories of Adrian that were as sudden and painful as knife thrusts—could come at any time. I'd gotten quite adept at distracting any audience from the momentary leak of emotion.

"Go ahead," I urged Craig. "Pat them down. I think Daddy Bear might be wearing a wire."

"I know you have to report to the court," he said, almost in apology. "But if you're not taping the session, everything's deniable."

"I want to clear up any source of misunderstanding," I began, intending to meet at once, head-on, the issue of Natalie's hug in the shopping mall.

"Sure."

He gave a gracious wave of his hand. Perhaps it hadn't been him at the mall, after all. Or he had seen the woman he loved more than his own life throw her arms around me in a fervent embrace, and now concealed his feelings until he could arrange an opportunity for revenge.

"Whatever you may have seen . . . ," I began, groping forward.

I shouldn't have hoped that he'd help me out. He stared at me coolly. I was disturbed by how disciplined he was. For a man with an obsession this side of madness, to sit back in his chair, to feign mild incomprehension, polite interest, spoke to a self-control that was icy.

"How do you mean?" he inquired. "I'm not sure what it is I'm supposed to have seen."

Unless he hadn't seen anything, had been nowhere near the mall on Saturday, in which case I was about to hint that some incident had occurred that threatened his very emotional existence.

"Were you at the Meeting House Mall?" I asked.

"Could be."

I waited for the slightest flicker of those long lashes. I thought he observed me in the same way. We regarded one another stealthily, in a silent standoff. The suspicion in the room was almost palpable, like static electricity. Or, I was imagining all this.

"Have you been there since you left Sanders?" I asked.

He made a show of thinking about this, screwing up his eyes and peering into the distance over my left shoulder. "As a matter of fact, yes."

"Did I see you there?"

He started to speak, then stopped, staring at me for two full seconds with his mouth frozen around the first syllable. "Do you realize what a weird question that is, Doctor?" As if he suddenly recollected his manners, he sat up straight in the chair. "Oh, I'm sorry. I'm answering a question with a question. That's your department, isn't it? Let me see. Did you see me at the mall? Gosh, I don't know, Doc. Did you?"

"I'm not sure."

"You mean, like you might have hallucinated me?"

He was warming to his work. Psychotherapy can be an instrument of exquisite torture: fifty long minutes with no hope of escape, pitifully few means of self-defense, and no excuse for retaliation.

"I thought I saw you there," I said, "but I just caught a glimpse. That's why I asked if you saw me."

"Jog my memory. Were you with your wife?"

"No."

"Were you by yourself?"

"No."

We stared at each other across the desk, eye to eye, in what should have been one of those I-know-you-know-I-know moments, the poker faces giving way at the last moment with an arch of an eyebrow or a wry turn of the lip. But neither of us would let down his guard.

"What day was this?" he asked.

"Saturday. In the morning."

"Well, that explains it."

"How so?"

"Because I was there on Friday."

There was no glint of recognition or humor in his eyes. The absence of visible emotion made me very uneasy, because I still didn't know what I was dealing with. If he felt betrayed, why not rip into me? Or, more ominously, mere words were not enough.

"Well then, that explains it," I agreed.

"If you say so." He looked away. The matter was finished. "Are you going to cure me of Natalie?"

"I don't think that's what you want."

"You're right. It's not a disease."

"I don't think so, either."

"Apart from the occasional suicidal impulse, I don't think I have anything you could call a problem."

"But that is a problem," I suggested.

"I said you might call it a problem. Suicide's not a problem for me. Not that I have any plans to do away with myself right now."

"But there are times you might think life isn't worthwhile?"

"What's sick about that? If you can't have something that's essential to your life, then you might as well check out. That's what I think. I think the sickness is hanging onto a life that's meaningless." He was growing intense and inward and he caught himself. He smirked to discredit the person who'd just spoken. "But that's just a theory." He waved it away.

"Is there anything you feel you might want to work on in therapy?"

"Of course not."

"So we're just going through the motions?"

He shrugged to indicate indifference. "I guess you're stuck with me." He settled into the big, soft chair opposite me, stretching and shifting, as if he meant to stay a long time.

"I guess we're stuck with each other. So we might as well make the best of it."

"No, you're stuck with me. I can fire you any time I want."

"We could still do something useful."

He sneered. "Such as?"

For an instant, I glimpsed contempt in his eyes, and within it something more sinister, a sadistic desire to inflict pain.

"We might talk about your love life," I suggested hopelessly.

"Why don't we talk about you?"

"This isn't my therapy. This is about you."

"But you're here. You're part of the process. Aren't you?"

"Our positions aren't the same, though."

"Is that so?"

"That's the way therapy works."

"I still think we should talk about you."

"Do you have something you want to say about me? Is that it?"

"Yes, I do."

"Okay," I said, with a sense of dread. I knew enough about him now to know that he didn't bluff. He had something. "Go ahead."

"I really think you should do something about your house."

I didn't respond. I'd wait him out to see what he had. He searched my face for signs of discomfort.

He looked down to pick an invisible piece of fluff from his gray slacks, then looked up brightly, smiling as if he were trying to charm me.

"It's a nice house," he said appreciatively. "Really nice. In fact, I wouldn't have thought you could have afforded it on your salary. What have you got there, an acre? An acre and a half?"

He waited. When he didn't get a response, he said, "Anyway, at least one acre. On the ocean. Pretty."

No big deal, I thought. He'd gotten my name from one of the medical directories, then looked up my address in the Bristol phone book. It was a drive-by. Nothing more.

"So, you checked me out."

"Of course."

I took a deep breath. I didn't want anything to come through in my voice. "We've been here before, and I'm going to tell you again: My home, my family, my private life—they're out of the mix."

"I can understand your feeling that way, Paul. But the fact is—"

"I'd like you to call me Dr. Lucas."

"The fact is, Dr. Lucas, this is my therapy, and it's not really up to you to decide what we talk about."

"There are ground rules."

"If there are, this is the first time you're mentioning them."

"There are boundaries. Therapy only works if certain boundaries are respected."

"What if I don't want to play by your rules?"

"They're not my rules."

"I think you make them up as you go along. Whenever you don't feel in control of the situation, you make up a new rule."

"I'm sorry you don't like the rules. But they've evolved over decades, with countless therapists and patients. It's what works."

"That chair in your office?"

"Which office?"

"That is your office, isn't it, on the third floor? You have a beautiful view. What I was going to tell you is that that chair really needs to be replaced. The leather one. The one with the stain on the seat?"

My father's chair.

"It looks a bit shabby, that's all. It's really none of my business— but . . . Just a suggestion. Okay?"

Then, just as abruptly, he began to talk about an old girlfriend, Angie, and the breakup of that relationship. Even when he mentioned Georgia, I didn't pay attention.

"You went into my house?" I asked. I knew I sounded stupid. I was stupefied.

"I never said that."

"You said something about my chair."

He gave a shrug, exaggerated like a mime. "I guessed."

"But you said it had a stain on the seat. You had to have been there, to know that."

"Not really. I figured, from what I've learned about you in our sessions, that you're the kind of guy who'd let things like that slide. I didn't have to go anywhere. I certainly didn't have to break the law."

He was getting up to leave.

"We're not finished yet," I told him.

"Save it for next week," he said.

I remained in my seat for several minutes after the door closed behind him. Craig was out on bail thanks to my stepping up at the hearing. I'd made a good-faith effort. I'd paid my dues to the Methodist. Now I'd tell Larry Shapiro I was getting out—no ifs, ands, or buts.

"No, really, he's not here," Linda, Larry's secretary said. "He's got a Resource Committee meeting at the medical school. You just missed him."

I took off down the stairs, two at a time, across the bridge to the parking garage, crossed the road recklessly, took the diagonal through Children's Hospital, out the emergency room exit, skirted the power plant, and arrived at the far edge of the medical school campus in time to see Larry's tall, loping figure approaching from the other end of the path that skirted the lawn of the quadrangle. I stayed out of sight to take a minute to catch my breath and consider the best way to deliver my news.

It's rumored Larry put himself through medical school synthesizing acid for the San Francisco market. Larry still affects a leisurely, "California Dreamin'" manner. He likes to give the impression that his success is the absurd result of some cosmic wrinkle. But the truth is that he's busy becoming famous. For Larry is king of the NMDA receptor. It's still long odds, but incredible as it may seem to those who knew him in the early days, Larry has a shot at a Nobel. When the wind blows from a certain direction, even though Stockholm is more than four thousand miles away, Larry can smell the heady musk of the prize. In unguarded moments—there are few of them—I've caught the steely glint of ambition in Larry's eyes. It is not a pretty sight, and he does not like it seen, but beneath the easy affability of your friendly Haight Ashbury LSD dealer, Larry is utterly ruthless: a hippie shark.

Larry saw me coming at once. He waved as I started down the steps onto the path. Then, as I came within range, he injected some wiggle into his walk, with slow punching movements of his arms, that suggested a dance of tribal greeting. It was part of a softening process that I didn't usually rate, and I wondered if Linda had called him on his cell phone to warn him that I looked serious and unhappy.

"Hey," he said. He stopped early, ten feet from me, and made a friendly shooting gesture with his index finger like he had me in his sights. "Here's the man."

"That's what I want to talk to you about, Larry."

He hadn't asked how I'd managed to track him down. As far as he was concerned, this was simply one of those lucky encounters that shouldn't be scrutinized. He closed on me and swung his arm around so that it came to land across my shoulders, and although it rested lightly there, the influence was sufficient to sweep me onward in the direction that he was going. I was momentarily disarmed.

"You saved our ass, Paul. I won't forget it."

We strolled together on the gravel path at a leisurely pace, as though neither of us had much else to do except reminisce about the deal that had gone down.

"Man, that was sweet!" he said with a chuckle. "Old Man Cavanaugh wanted to do something for you, by the way. I acted embarrassed and said I couldn't discuss it. But he's a generous guy. As we know. That's between you and him. I'm looking the other way. I don't want to know, so don't tell me. But, heck, you sure deserve it."

"It's not really therapy, though, is it, Larry?"

"I'm no expert, but it's my impression psychotherapy covers a multitude of sins. If you don't want to frame it as psychotherapy, that's okay. I think you can call it anything you want."

"How about 'payoff'?"

I sensed the muscles of the arm across my shoulders tighten a notch. Somehow the load felt heavier. He stopped. I kept going a couple of paces until it was natural for me to come free of his embrace.

"I think that's kind of harsh, Paul." He appeared somber, almost troubled by the thought. "The family's helped us out in a number of tough situations. I look upon what you did as returning the favor. This is not just about you. You did this for all of us."

"Why sic him on me?"

"We needed someone. We didn't expect it, but the need arose. You were there."

"So I was co-opted to spring this guy. I helped keep a stalker on the loose."

"If I'd known you were going to have an attack of the vapors, I'd have given the job to someone else."

"I'm not about to wimp out. You know that, Larry."

"Of course I do. And I know it feels like we dumped him on you. But the fact of the matter is you got him for one simple reason: because you're the best man for the job." He pantomimed sparring, ducking and weaving in slow motion, then out of the blue let loose a right jab that stopped an inch from my shoulder. He was a lot faster than he looked. "Come on, Paul! You know that.

None of us comes close to your level of expertise when it gets down and dirty."

"He hasn't the slightest interest in doing therapy. All he uses the time for is to needle me."

Larry held up his hands, palms out, to plead no contest. "Hey, I know. The kid's an evil fuck. Bad seed. There are no illusions here. I'm not asking you to cure him."

"That's the point. I'm not a therapist, I'm a minder."

"It keeps him out of jail."

"Which is where he belongs."

"Listen, if you feel a crisis of conscience coming on, pop an Ativan, take deep breaths, repeat your mantra, wait for it to pass."

"I want out, Larry."

"I don't give a fuck what you want. This isn't about you."

"There's something I haven't told you."

He swiveled on his heel while he let his head flop back, openmouthed, so that he stared at the heavens in a gesture of impatience and skepticism. He sighed. "Yeah?"

"He's been by my house. He knows Abby's name. He's gone through back issues of the local papers and found out about the accident."

Larry's head was down. He kicked dirt reflectively. I thought he was finally starting to understand my predicament. I thought he was coming round to seeing Craig my way. He was ready for the clincher.

"I think he's been inside my house," I said. "He denied it, of course. But he described a chair in my home office. He had to have been there."

"But you're not sure?" Larry asked, without looking up from the dirt.

"Not one hundred percent. But close enough."

"And he denied it."

"Of course he did."

"Why, 'of course'?" He'd worried a patch through to the crushed stone beneath the gravel.

"It's a crime. He's not going to admit to that."

"Then why did he tell you in the first place?"

"Because he wants to mess with my head."

Larry looked up suddenly, eye to eye. I'd never seen such frank anger in his eyes.

"Look," he said. "I don't do therapy. I'm a receptor guy. Otherwise I'd have taken care of it myself. Yes, it's tough. But this is what you do. Whether the kid is sick, or whatever, it doesn't matter. What does matter is that you're a doctor and you can't pick and choose your patients. You can't not treat him because of what he is. You don't hear cardiologists say they can't treat someone because his coronary arteries are clogged and the guy won't exercise and he sits in front of the TV set all day guzzling cheeseburgers and smoking like a chimney. Don't like it? Tough shit!"

"Okay," I said. "I got it."

"Because that's what they do. We don't need them to do the easy cases. Anyone can do those."

He caught himself and stopped. He was out of breath. He glanced at me to see if I'd noticed the slippage in his persona.

"Look, Paul." He was back again, soft in tone, conciliatory. "I'm not saying this is a test of your manhood. God knows, we've all killed our lion. There's nothing you have to prove to me. If you want out . . ." He made a sign of peace, or benevolence—or, it may have been, cosmic indifference—that I associated with an Eastern religion. "If you want off this case, so be it."

I was about to thank him for being so understanding, but he beat me to it.

"All I'm asking—" he put in quickly, " 'ask,' mind you—is that you reconsider." He gave me a stare of man-to-man candor. When

Larry turned it on, his sincerity was of a very high quality. "All I want is that you give this kid one more shot."

"I don't know, Larry," I said, avoiding his eyes.

"He asked for you. You gave him the third degree at Sanders, and he came back for more. I think there's motivation there if you can tap into it. No one walks into their first session and says, 'I hate what I am and I want to change.' It doesn't happen. I don't have to tell you that."

I didn't know why, but against all reason, this shtick was working on me. You don't get into my line of business if you don't harbor the delusion that redemption might lie just around the next corner.

"This is a cry for help," Larry said. "You can't call it off unless he does."

"Okay," I said. "Give me your best offer."

"One session. Take a break. Give it a week. A couple if you think things need to cool off. Then see him one more time. If he's impossible, then he had his chance. We gave him a shot and he didn't take it."

"One session."

"That's it. If he shows any sign, any sign at all that he wants to do some work—and I'll leave it up to you; you be the sole judge of this—then we're in business. If not—screw him."

Larry's like a lot of manipulators who are good at the game: They can't quit while they're ahead. He'd started to walk on when he suddenly turned on his heel as if he'd forgotten something.

"That funding request," he said. "It's on my desk. In fact, it's working its way to the top of the pile. It's an interesting idea. Two groups, right? Sociopaths and controls. You're going to scan them in the functional MRI when they're paid to tell the truth and then when they're paid to lie. You won't have any trouble finding subjects, will you?"

"Oh, no," I said. "There's never any shortage of liars."

"My only reservation," he said, "is you make this thing work. If you hit on some way to tell who's telling the truth and who isn't, it could make life difficult for some of us."

As he turned again to go to his committee meeting, he flashed me the grin of the charming rogue who knows you know what he is and knows you know he knows, and so on, ad infinitum, to the vanishing point of a virtual truth.

twelve

My first instinct when I got home that night was to search for signs of forced entry. I found that it wasn't necessary to break into our house—the place was wide open to anyone who took the trouble to look around. The back door was loose enough to admit a credit card, and I pried it open in seconds. There was an unlatched window on the first floor. Even from the ground, I could see that another window, in the guest bedroom we rarely used, wasn't closed. Our house is set back from the road and screened from neighbors by trees, so that although the guest room is on the second floor, an intruder could climb unseen onto the garage roof and easily reach the window. We had very little crime in our town, and Abby and I tended to be relaxed about locking up. Once I started poking around with the mind-set of a criminal, it became clear that we'd been living in a state of denial.

When your home has been entered, you first look for signs of disturbance in the places where you've hidden your secret things. I'm not a person of many secrets. I don't have a thing for twelve-year-old girls or black leather masks with zippered orifices. No intimate photographs taped to the undersides of furniture. Not even a ribboned bundle of love letters from old flames lying at the bottom of a drawer. As for drugs, I hadn't used any since I was a resident—one last drag on a joint in somebody's kitchen at a party. There weren't any stashes of white powder in our house or pints of vodka concealed behind textbooks on the shelves of the library. Nor were the books themselves compromising; apart from a brief infatuation with anarchism during my junior year of college, I'd never been a political animal. I wasn't hoarding bullion or hiding bundles of cash from the tax man under the floorboards.

All I had was the gun.

Every marriage has its secrets. The gun was my secret from Abby. I knew as much as anyone—except Abby, a zealot on the subject—about the statistics of household deaths and accidental shootings and suicide. I knew it was dumb, but there it was. If you had to have an emblem for your midlife crisis, a handgun was a lot cheaper than a little red sports car. And the motivation was similar: something wild, something irrational, something dangerous. Or seeming to be dangerous. No one in his right mind wants to place himself in gun-related danger. Just the idea of it, the potential, is enough. That's what the gun was: an option on the wild side.

And it was one hell of a gun. Specifically, a .25 semiautomatic with an eight-shot magazine, a dangerous-looking blue steel finish, and a balance that made it feel so light that it fit in my hand like a lethal extension of my arm. It was a slick, marvelous machine, a paradigm of engineering whose only purpose lay in killing people. But only intruders. Most of the time it simply sat in a drawer in my father's oak desk. Every few weeks I'd slip it into a gym bag with a pair of sneakers and some sweats to pad the bag out so that it looked like I was going to work out, and I'd take off for a couple of hours of target practice. I blasted the heck out of some paper targets and returned home replenished.

You hide your secret where you believe an intruder is least likely to look for it. When you've been broken into, it's the first place you think he's going to look. I bounded up the stairs to my office on the third floor. I was afraid I'd find furniture tipped over, drawers ransacked, the computer screen kicked in, papers strewn everywhere: "Craig was here."

Nothing was out of place on my cursory survey of the room, except for one, small thing that might have been nothing at all. When I leave the office, I turn the old leather chair so that it faces the desk, a detail that evokes my father's orderliness. When I entered the room, I found the chair facing sideways. I could have left it that way myself. I didn't remember how I'd left it. I preferred to think that was the way I'd left it.

The gun. I went straightaway to the lower drawer of the desk. It was still locked, and I let out a long sigh of relief. Inside, the gun's carrying case lay as I had left it, and when I lifted it out, I was reassured to feel the weight of the weapon inside.

When I removed the gun from its case, though, I noticed at once that the safety catch was in the off position. I keep the gun unloaded, but I always leave the safety on as a fail-safe. Or, I thought I always left it on. It was a routine that I performed without thinking. Who remembers, as they drive away from a gas station, screwing up the gas-tank cap after a fill-up? When was the last time I'd put the gun away? Two weeks ago. Three, maybe.

I didn't want to consider the alternative, that Craig had left a message for me: From now on, the safety's off.

I was locking the drawer again when the phone rang. It was Brenda Gorn.

"I spoke to the DA about that military school in Georgia Craig attended. The school closed right after one of the students was killed."

She paused for effect. "Go on," I said.

"The death was ruled an accident. The case didn't go any further. The DA didn't know much about it, so I called the local police chief."

"Was there a girl involved?"

"Of course there was. The only girl in the place. The principal's daughter. The one who went to Bermuda. But she was never Craig's girlfriend. She was courted by all the upperclassmen, but it was a kid called Randall, the head cadet—Captain of the Guard, I guess he was called—who won her heart. It was all very proper and knightly. They danced together all night at the Christmas cotillion, and that seemed to advertise that they were an item. Craig was shut out and he took it badly."

"Do you know what she was called, the girl?"

"Her name was Angela. And by all accounts, she was an angel—with ethereal, strawberry-blond hair. The chief waxed poetic."

"Angie," I corrected her and heard, at the mention of her name, the doused cymbal from the Rolling Stones song.

"Angie. Right. That's what they called her. Do you already know this?"

"Just a hunch," I said.

"The accident—if you want to call it that—occurred on the firing range. 'A freak accident,' the chief said. Maybe that's what it was. Maybe it was just bad luck."

"Except Old Man Cavanaugh felt he had to come in and bulldoze the place."

"You be the judge. This was the setup on the firing range: Randall and Craig were both on the shooting team, and they'd practice most days after classes. It was an outdoor range, the firing positions two hundred yards from the targets. The targets were run up and down on a pulley. They'd take turns, shooting, changing targets, manning the telephone. The cadet changing the targets would take off the old target, put on a new one, then stand up in the trench to pull up the new target; then he'd go to the dugout and crank up an old World War I telephone and report to the telephone operator at the firing position the score of the last shooter. At the same time, the fact that he was making the call from the dugout signaled the all clear. The only time the routine changed was when the telephone operator told him the fresh target wasn't right; when the cadet climbed out of the dugout and went back to fix it, he'd be standing right behind the target, invisible to the shooter. That's what the chief figured must have happened."

"And there was a communication mix-up—the freak accident—and Randall, who happened to be behind a target at the time, got shot."

"No, that's not it. It wasn't Randall. The cadet who was killed was just some poor kid who happened to be in the wrong place at the wrong time."

"Then that's what the mix-up was. The freak accident was that Randall was meant to be behind the target and Craig shot the wrong guy."

"Craig didn't shoot the cadet. Craig is too devious for that. That's why you have to be very careful with him. It was Randall who shot the cadet. He blew the kid's head off. When he saw there was something wrong, he sprinted across those two hundred yards and he was the first one into the target trench. You've seen crime-scene photographs. You know what a high-velocity rifle round does to a head. Randall wasn't prepared for what he'd find in the trench. For what he'd done. He had a place at West Point, but he couldn't pick up a gun again. He didn't even go on to college. He's working as an auto mechanic, the chief said."

"Then what does this have to do with Craig?"

"Craig was the telephone operator. Craig gave the all clear."

I searched the house, but I didn't really want to find anything that would force me to accept that Craig had been in my home.

The patient files were all in order. I looked at the alignment of checkbooks in the desk drawer and tried to remember how I might have tossed them there after paying the bills the week before.

I went to the mailbox. Intruders snatch mail on their way into your house. If you know what you're doing, there's plenty of useful information in the mail. But the box contained an average stack of junk mail, a couple of bills, and the answer from the insurance company about the increase in our auto premiums: the citation for Abby's speeding ticket. I scanned it absentmindedly and put it aside on the counter in the kitchen. The name of the officer who stopped Abby seemed familiar, and I thought he must have been on one of my cases.

I went back to my tour of the house. Maybe John Cavanaugh hadn't been cleaning up Craig's mess when he bought up the school. Maybe he saw a business opportunity and gave the principal what turned out to be a fair price for the property. Our housekeeper had turned the chair around when she'd cleaned my office. As for the safety, I resolved to be more meticulous in ensuring the gun was secure when I put it away.

I didn't know what I was looking for. I wasn't used to considering my home a crime scene. It was perhaps fifteen minutes before I realized that I wasn't thinking like Craig. I was standing in my own house thinking like me. I had to look for an opportunity to punish Paul Lucas, to hurt him for embracing Natalie, brazenly, before my very eyes, in a way that I had never been privileged to do.

Then the target became clear. Craig would come at me through those I loved, as he had in our interviews. I went back to the second floor and for a moment stood still in the middle of our bedroom. How could I tell whether he'd been through Abby's drawers? How could anyone tell, in the disarray of her dressing room, that something was missing?

Abby is an intensely private person. I respect her desire not to be completely known, even though I find it difficult. Some of her self-possession is not abstract at all but frankly territorial. The idea of my violating her space by searching the drawers of her bureau or turning over her dressing room was anathema. Her dressing room was emotionally electrified. You could turn off the current, and I still wouldn't risk it.

That's why I went down to the basement instead. It's a large space covering the entire footprint of the house. The furnace and the water heater sit off to one side. In a corner near the bulkhead is an old toilet that I suspect was for the use of the gardener in grander days. The rest of the space is taken up with haphazard groups of discarded furniture, an upright piano, bikes that I never got around to fixing, obsolete skis and superseded exercise machines. This was where I found our worst omission: Somehow, I'd left the bulkhead to the cellar unbolted. I paused in the dim light and looked around, imagining myself a stranger to the place. Perhaps he had entered here.

I circled back through the house, checking the photographs that we had on display. Photos are magnets for people who want to break into your life. They take them as trophies. They leave them for you ripped up, mutilated, defiled. I was afraid of what I'd find, because I knew I'd have to hurt Craig if he'd trashed Adrian's picture. But there it was intact, in its place on the mantelpiece, and I breathed a sigh of relief. I lingered over a wedding picture in which Abby looked impossibly young, and I knew that I couldn't evade the fact any longer that if Craig had targeted Abby, he'd go through her dressing room.

When I edged open the door, I found rows of skirts and jackets and dresses and slacks, somewhat askew on their hangers, as if tossed there in haste. I sat at her dressing table and cast a guilty glance at myself in the mirror. I did look a little shifty. But I reminded myself that the principle—her safety—justified what I was about to do.

I pulled out the top drawer on the left. It contained letters, old concert tickets, and other papers, and I figured I had no business there. Even without rummaging, I felt I was trespassing. The drawer on the other side held a jumble of lipsticks and cosmetics. When I tried one of the bottom drawers, I came upon her underwear.

Most of the garments were functional, workday panties: white cotton, a few skimpier ones in bright colors. There were others I hadn't seen for a while: a couple of slight satin things I'd bought for her at Victoria's Secret. "Friday night specials," we'd called them. At the back of the drawer were two more sexy items, still in their boxes.

I hadn't bought them for her. Of course, there wasn't any reason why my wife shouldn't buy her own sexy panties, except that she never had in the past. Early in our relationship, that had become my job. But change was good, I thought. Our lovemaking had become routine. Maybe Abby had plans.

I hadn't heard the SUV, the back door open and close. The sound of Abby climbing the stairs made me start, and I knew that I might just have time to close the drawer, get out of her dressing room, and step into the bathroom. Flight was my first impulse. But I felt justified and wanted her to know what I'd done, so I stayed, and as the seconds ticked by, I made discovery inevitable. I even left her underwear drawer open.

She came quickly up the stairs, and I heard the click of her heels on the oak floor of the hall, then softer footfalls as she came along the carpeted corridor. Then I heard her stop when she saw the open door to the dressing room.

"It's me," I called out so that she wouldn't be frightened.

"Paul?" She was incredulous. A burglar would have made sense. But not her husband.

I pulled the door open so that she could see me sitting in her seat in front of the dressing table.

"I had to check on something," I told her.

This sounded crazy, even to me. She was frowning, but more from her inability to understand the oddity of this event than from anger that I had violated her space.

"Oh," she said, as though I was making sense, as though things now were starting to click into place. Her eyes went from my face to the profusion of panties in the drawer. She saw I'd found the new ones.

"It's okay," I said with a desperate smile. "I haven't turned into a cross-dresser."

"What are you looking for?"

"I'm not sure."

"You were checking on me?"

"No. It doesn't have anything to do with you."

"But . . ." She gestured to indicate where I was. "If it doesn't have anything to do with me, why are you going through my things?"

How much to tell her? I wasn't sure whether Craig had been in our home, and had no business alarming her. I'd warn her, I thought, but also reassure her that whatever threat he posed could be contained.

I said, "I have this patient." My hesitancy made it sound as though I was improvising. "He said—or anyway, he implied—that he'd been here. In this house."

"Then why don't you call the police?"

Hard to argue with that conclusion. "It's complicated," I began, but Abby was gone.

She was back in a moment, thrusting her open cell phone at me. "Here," she demanded, "call them."

"I'm not sure. That's why I'm checking."

"Why are you checking in my room? What are you looking for in that drawer?"

I sighed. "He's a stalker. I was afraid he might be transferring to us."

She didn't believe a word I'd said; she'd already made up her mind on that score. She was staring at my face trying to assess some other thing.

"It's okay," she said. She gave a small, tired smile. "We're grown-ups. You can say what you think."

"That's it." I closed the drawer. "I was looking for something, and I didn't really know what it was."

"It's okay," she said, not resigned, not tired, but with an angry edge. "Say what you think. Say it, for God's sake!"

I spread my hands in surrender. "I'm sorry," I told her. "I had no right to be here. I've let this whole case get out of proportion."

She was furious. "You had your hand in my underwear and it was a mistake? Is that it? A technical error?" She threw her hands in the air in ironic incomprehension. "So . . . what?" she asked the ceiling. She turned to me. "What is it—you think I'm having an affair?"

We stared at each other across the divide. I saw she wasn't really angry at all. There were tears in the corners of her eyes.

"No," I said quietly.

I got up and came through the gap in the door that separated us. She stood tensely with her face turned away and her hands clenched rigidly at her sides. I reached out my hand and touched her shoulder, and although she didn't move away, she didn't relax, either.

"No," I told her, "that wasn't what I was thinking at all."

Later that evening, though we talked over dinner, the silence seemed to continue between us. After dinner, Abby went to listen to music through headphones. I wanted to get out of the house.

"I'm going to work out," I told her. "It's been a brutal day."

I had the gym bag in my hand and, even with my sneakers and a T-shirt and shorts, I imagined I could feel the weight of the .25.

When I pulled up outside the industrial building that housed the shooting range, I saw Lieutenant Kovacs sitting on the bench outside. A number of the officers who live nearby use the range for target practice, and from time to time I'd run into Kovacs, though usually this elicited only a nod and a gruff "How're you doing?" as we passed. This evening he seemed to be in an unusual state of repose, enjoying the evening sun, and he looked up as I approached as though he might not be averse to a few minutes of casual conversation.

For someone who, for my money, embodies lethality, he is not a physically imposing man. Kovacs is in his early fifties, with salt-and-pepper hair trimmed short and the tanned and wrinkled face of an outdoorsman, a hunter. He is mostly in motion, stretching, hunching his shoulders, shaking loose a tightness, as though he might in the natural order of his body become too tightly wound. I sense he's uncomfortable with proximity. The human element disturbs him. When he talks, he avoids eye contact. Instead, as he addresses you, he often seems to be considering the middle distance over your shoulder.

He squinted as I closed in on him and looked up at me curiously.

"Hey, Doc," he said. There was something close to a smile of greeting on his face, or, at least, an expression of tolerance. "What brings you here on this fine summer evening?"

I shrugged. "Thought I'd bang off a few rounds."

"Catharsis, right?"

He enjoys ambushing me with my own technical jargon. Once

he asked me if I knew where the medulla oblongata was. He knew. It was the ultimate target. The sniper's Holy Grail. "See, you hit him in the medulla oblongata," he told me, "you get what's called a flaccid paralysis. You hit him anywhere else in the brain and what you get is a spastic paralysis—that means all the muscles go into spasm, which is bad news if the target has his finger on the trigger and he's holding a weapon to a hostage's head. You hit him in the medulla oblongata—see what I mean?—everything turns to jelly—plop—and he falls on the ground. It's over. Clean."

He takes a wry enjoyment in these games with me, but I've learned that there is more to them than mere entertainment, that Kovacs often has some other agenda that he's obliquely introducing. He is a shrewd judge of a man's inner state. He had done little more than glance at me as I'd walked toward the bench, but it was enough for him to pick up that I had some tension in need of release.

"You could call it catharsis," I said. I took a seat beside him. "It's a good way of letting off steam."

He would never ask me where the steam came from, no more than I would ask him a question about his family. If Kovacs has one.

We sat silently on the bench for a time, enjoying the last rays of the sun on our faces.

"You ever have someone come into your home?" I said.

He was silent for a while, as if I hadn't spoken. I'd overstepped the boundaries of our acquaintance, and assumed that he was passing over my faux pas in discreet silence, when he spoke.

"You mean, when you're not there?"

"Right."

He considered this for a while. "I knew a guy once. There was this other guy that had a thing for his wife."

"It's not quite like that."

"No, that's not what I'm saying. The wife didn't know anything about it. It turned out the guy who was sneaking into the house was someone she worked with. A nut."

"He was breaking into the house when no one was around? Taking stuff?"

He pursed his lips in a gesture that indicated the conjecture might or might not have merit. "I guess."

Now that he'd told his story, now that he'd defined why I was at the shooting range, he appeared to have lost interest. He was punctilious in his own way. He avoided prying, and he adopted an air of studied boredom in order to protect my privacy. In certain ways Kovacs possessed the sensibility of an Edwardian gentleman. Lethal, but courteous.

"What happened to him?" I asked.

Now that I'd taken it to the next step, he turned to look at me. "My friend? Or the nut?"

"The nut."

He shrugged. "He might of moved out of state."

"But it stopped? The thing with sneaking into the house didn't happen again?"

"Oh, yeah. That was the end of it, sure enough."

The fate of the nut was conveyed by the certainty in Kovacs's voice. If Kovacs had wanted me to know the details, he'd have told me; therefore, I couldn't ask. A gap opened between us, difficult to close. I wanted to find out what his friend had done. I'd come as far as I could as a forensic psychiatrist: Craig had crossed the boundary where my experience ended. I couldn't see any further down that road. Kovacs had been there. He'd been to the end of it.

"These people who come into peoples' houses," he said. "Stalkers. Perverts after underwear. They're not normal. The law won't stop them. They don't give a fuck about cops. And the judges are useless. The courts give them a slap on the wrist and tell them not to do it again. But they do. Once they've got the idea in their head, they'll keep at it forever. You have to take care of it yourself."

"In my house—"

It was the wrong move. Kovacs cut me off by holding up his hand. "Don't tell me," he said. "I don't want to know."

"Look, it's not something I'd ever do."

"Right. We're just talking."

"Absolutely. I'd never do anything."

"You never know."

"I'm just letting off steam."

Kovacs nodded reflectively. He wanted the moment to pass, so that what he was about to say had no connection with what had gone before.

"Doc," he asked delicately, "did anyone ever tell you the three rules of murder?"

He wasn't much older than I, but in the fastidiousness of his manner he might have been a favorite uncle communicating advanced sex education: foreplay tricks, the timing and placement of the condom, holding back.

"No," I said, feeling the inadequacy of a virgin. "I don't think I've ever heard of them."

"They're nothing much," he said. "Obvious, really. Except people can't stick to them. That's how they get caught. Think about it: The only murderers you see at Sanders are the fuckups. All they've got between them and natural life is some no-hope insanity plea. All because they didn't obey three simple rules."

"Okay," I said. "I'll go along with that."

"Rule one: Do it yourself. If you can't do it yourself, don't try to hire someone else to do it. They'll take your money and turn you in. These contract killers you see in the movies, the hit men—they don't exist. You go into a bar, ask around, the next guy you talk to is a state cop. The same goes for anyone else you take along to keep you company: If you can't do it alone, don't do it. All an accomplice does is turn you in to get a deal for himself. It's only natural."

He spoke with the assurance of a man who has argued these propositions back and forth with himself for years. So this is what went on in Kovacs's head during those long, slow days in the front trap. I might have fine-tuned my research proposal or planned the vegetable garden for next year; Kovacs pondered the deeper reaches of homicide.

"Murder's hard." His brow was furrowed in concern. He sounded eerily empathic. "Specially the first time. People are scared. It's all so new. After, they get lonely. That's why there's rule two: Tell no one. You've no idea how hard it is to keep it to yourself. Even for hardened criminals. It's not that they feel guilty about what they've done. They can't keep it to themselves because murder's too big for one person. It's in the papers. It's on TV. There's the manhunt. The suspects. The interrogation. The attention's overwhelming. When the perpetrator talks to the police it's not like going to confession. He's boasting. It's the biggest thing he's ever done. The only big thing, for most of those losers. He wants the credit for it.

"You're different, though, Doc. You've got professional training. People tell you things—really hot stuff, some of it, I'll bet—but you're duty bound not to say a word."

"I'm used to keeping secrets."

"Right. They all think that. Until it hits them. Then you're in a place you've never been before."

"I don't intend to go there, believe me."

"It's rule three that's the important one. Without rule three, there might not be any murder. Without rule three, you're liable to screw it up so that the alleged victim survives—worst of all possible worlds, because you've done the crime and you've left a witness. Rule three: Don't rush it."

"I'd want to get it over with as quickly as possible."

"No you wouldn't. You'd want to be sure you finished the job."

"A bullet through the medulla oblongata should just about do it. That's quick."

"I'm different. I'm a professional. When I pull the trigger on a target, there's nothing personal about it. Plus, most times, I'm under a time constraint. Hostage taking, for example, where you don't get to choose your moment. But murder in the first degree is a whole different type of situation. You pick the spot, and the time. You're in control. Or you should be, because you planned it.

"You don't rush it," he said, turning to me to bring home the crucial nature of the third rule with dual chopping motions of his hands, "because you want to be sure you get it right. So your first shot isn't the head shot. Right?"

He scrutinized my face for a moment to see if I appreciated the counterintuitive elegance of this point. He was a passionate teacher. A master craftsman imparting his skill to a callow apprentice. A Zen master interrogating his pupil to discern if he had truly plumbed the zero of death.

"Right," I agreed. His plain practicality was making me nervous. Once I envisioned it, the scene began to take on substance. It began, against my will, to seem possible.

"The purpose of your first shot is to acquire a stationary target," Kovacs said, as if he were quoting from a manual. "Take the man down. If you're using a handgun, hit him in the gut. Take his legs off, if you've got a shotgun." He held up his hand to forestall objections. "I know that sounds callous. It's messy. It's gory. There's no two ways about it. But if talking about it makes you queasy . . . You know the rest: Consult rule one. If you're not up for it, don't do it."

He got up and, with a nod of the head, indicated the door to the range. "Let's do it."

"Sure," I said, picking up the .25 in its carrying case. The package didn't look deadly at all.

Kovacs started toward the range, then turned with a second thought.

"You know, Doc, if you do anything—"

I laughed. "I'm not doing anything."

He wasn't laughing. "If you do. You can confess to anyone you want. Just don't tell me."

There was no shame in naïveté now, so I asked him, "Why not?"

He gave a make-believe punch to my arm; it landed with the gentlest of pressures, hardly contact at all. It was the friendliest gesture I'd ever received from him. But he still wasn't smiling. "Because I'd turn you in," he said.

thirteen

Against my better judgment, I'd let Larry talk me into one more
session with Craig. But the funny thing was, over the next couple
of meetings, I thought I was making headway with him. It wasn't
that we'd turned a corner; sudden progress would have been suspect. But I had a sense that Craig was starting to realize how one-
sided his love for Natalie had been. All the same, I stayed on my
toes, ready to discover that this understanding was another feint.
But if it was, I didn't see where it would get him. The court had
mandated therapy, but he could fire me and hire another therapist—someone naive, incompetent, indulgent; some rube from the
rent-a-friend agency; Ma Coffeeklatch; Dr. Ponytail—any time he
wanted. He didn't have to prove anything to me. If there was a
payoff to acting the good patient, I couldn't see it.

And Craig was a good patient. When you ignored the fact that
he was a tenacious stalker with violent tendencies, Craig was the
ultimate YAVI that all psychotherapists crave: young, attractive,
vocal, intelligent. He was all of those things and more. He applied
himself. He listened. He gave me information about his life and

his emotional reactions. Plus, he didn't bait me anymore. In moments of giddy relief, I wondered if we'd entered a new era of collaboration. I didn't feel his eyes on me, scrutinizing my every expression and gesture for possible advantage. In fact, I seemed to fade into the background, which is exactly where an effective therapist belongs.

As for the break-in at my home, I was inclined to believe that it was nothing more than a coincidence of minor details. At the end of a particularly productive session, I felt we'd come far enough to ask him about it.

"Just for my information," I began.

He turned at the door of the office, relaxed, attentive, willing to please. "I know," he said. He sucked in his lower lip in a grimace of regret. "It's what I said about the office in your home."

He was phenomenally quick and intuitive. I nodded, somewhat taken aback that he could anticipate me so well.

He took a couple of steps back from the door, closer to where I sat behind the desk. He held one hand braced against the other, a point of tension, as though struggling with something. Then his hands spread themselves, as some internal resolution broke, and they were freed.

"I was gaming you," he said.

He gave me the direct, eye-to-eye candid stare that sociopaths can't resist, as if sheer force of will could create belief in the recipient.

I felt cheated by this stare of sincerity. I was disturbed, not so much that he lied to me, but because I really wanted to believe that he hadn't been in my home.

"I looked up your address," he said, in confessional mode. "I drove by once, before we started therapy."

He looked vaguely uncomfortable, one hand messing with the

other. He was reflective, eyes downcast. The eyes came up suddenly. The expression was manly, big.

"I guess I owe you an apology," he said. "I've never been inside your home. I never would."

The sociopath is like a fussy painter who can't resist adding one more brush stroke that wrecks the canvas. He piles on layer upon layer of deceit because he doesn't have a feel for what candor is. I saw in Craig's stance a forward tipping, mixed with hesitation, that I knew portended movement. Most likely, I thought, he was preparing an impulsive rush toward me, hand outstretched for an expiating handshake whose spontaneity would take me by surprise, whose good feeling would disarm me.

"Okay," I said. "I'm glad we clarified that." And I quickly added, eyes down, breaking off contact, "See you next week, then."

Abby didn't buy it.

"If someone had been in this house they would have taken something," she insisted.

"It's not about money," I told her. I'd kept Craig anonymous and indistinct in my discussions with her. "He has more money than we do. It's about control. It's about possessing some aspect of our lives."

She looked at me, suspicious, wary, as if trying to understand what motive I'd have for telling her this detail of my case. She still hadn't forgiven me for going through her underwear drawer.

She shrugged. "But there's no proof—is there? That he's been here?"

Without that irrefutable detail, without the pebble in the sneaker that keeps you wondering and doubting, the possibility of the break-in faded. Occasionally, with Craig sitting in the chair beside my desk, in a moment of silence, I'd find myself wondering if . . . But most of the time, I was busy. I'd promised Larry I'd go the extra mile. If there was a shred of Craig's complex persona that inclined toward change, I stood ready. Larry was right about one thing: You never know when someone might just decide to turn his life around. Craig was in a crash dive from the pinnacle of privilege to the squalor of jail. If he was going to pull out of this dive, he'd have to do it now.

The next week, he began to tell me, in fits and starts, that he was getting interested in someone else.

"She reminds me of Natalie," he said. Promptly, he held up his hand to forestall my objection. "I know you don't want me to talk about her. But this is different."

"How's that?"

"I kind of like her."

"Kind of?"

"That's what I mean. That's what's different. I may end up liking her . . . a lot. Or I may end up not liking her at all."

"You're not plunging in headfirst, anyway."

"Exactly."

"Do you want to tell me about her?"

He seemed bashful. It wasn't overdone. It could have been genuine. Clinically, some shyness at this juncture would have made sense. His feelings for Natalie had been fierce, undeviating, and public; now, his emotions were more nuanced, budding. If this was real, he wouldn't be sure what he felt. And Craig certainly didn't want a therapist there ahead of him. Hence the vulnerability, the wariness of disclosure.

"If you want," I suggested with an expansive gesture, as if the subject could wait until a better time.

He took a deep breath, as though preparing to swim beneath the surface. "Okay."

His head was down. I glimpsed a secret smile. Not for me. A memory pleased him, perhaps.

"It's up to you," I said.

"Sometimes when I bring up Natalie you cut me off."

"Sometimes," I agreed. "If I decide it's not therapeutic."

"If I'm going to talk about this other person, I have to feel I can say what I want."

I don't like bargains. Experts like Craig know exactly what they want. In those situations I've never had a clear idea of what I'm giving away until it's too late. I'm bound to keep my end, and the patient isn't.

When I didn't offer anything, Craig said, "Look, you have to trust me on this."

I searched his face, but found no hint of irony there.

"Okay," I agreed. "What have I got to lose?"

"All right, then," he said, to himself it seemed, as though he needed prompting, as though he had to urge himself over a hurdle. He was restless and couldn't meet my eye. The secret smile recurred and was immediately smoothed away. "Okay," he muttered. He seemed like a man preparing to dive, to plunge into a new medium and swim a distance beneath the surface through a strange substance.

"The thing is, she does look a bit like Natalie."

He glanced up to see if I'd stop him, and when I didn't interrupt, he took that for a green light, and then it all came out, coltish, full of youthful enthusiasm and optimism about the possibilities.

"She has the same hair coloring. And the same height. She's slim, too, like Natalie." He looked to see how I was receiving this.

"And different, in some ways?" I suggested hopefully.

He nodded agreement, but didn't reply at once. He was thoughtful, considering, perhaps, where to begin.

"She's a bit older than I am."

He waited to see if I would disapprove. I shrugged like a man of the world, a Gallic gesture of infinite indulgence. It seemed to satisfy him.

"So she's more poised than Natalie," he was saying. "Natalie was quite insecure. A lot of things bothered her that shouldn't have. But this person is solid. She's not in process. She's not becoming. When we talk . . ."

I was intrigued by his use of the past tense in referring to Natalie, but I thought better than to point this out to him. I was full of questions about this new woman.

"When we talk, I don't feel like there's another agenda, like there was with Natalie. She's there, with me. Not looking over my shoulder, glancing at the clock."

"You think she's interested in you?"

"I think maybe she is. Maybe."

I was impressed that he would tolerate the uncertainty.

"It's too soon to tell," he said seriously. "She's certainly friendly. And I think it's more than politeness."

"What does she do?"

He blinked. It wasn't a conclusive sign of trouble. But a blink is like a flinch. It's the mind changing gears, and as far as I knew the topic hadn't changed. Other than noting the hesitation, though, I paid it no mind.

"What does she do?" he repeated. "You mean, like what kind of work does she do?"

"Exactly."

I wondered why he was having difficulty with this small item. Even if, for reasons of his own, he chose to lie to me, it lay easily within Craig's capability to proffer a seamless answer. I speculated that if he were really undergoing these psychological changes, they might well undermine his deceptive abilities.

"My grandfather has this idea I should get to know the business from the bottom up. So he has me working for the summer in the proverbial mail room. Literally. I trundle a cart around the building delivering the mail. No one knows who I am. I'm just the mail guy. Even the summer interns have better jobs than me. But I like it."

I nodded. The job sounded like stalker heaven: He had the run of the building, a plausible reason to stop by whomever's cubicle he took a fancy to. Plus, all the mail went through his hands, to be perused, delivered, or diverted on a whim. For Craig, it must have been like drinking from a fire hose. But I was being cynical. I told myself I had to listen and hold back judgment. Craig was expansive; all I had to do was let him talk.

"I get to meet all the bigwigs who I'll be dealing with one day, and they haven't the slightest idea who I really am. I could be invisible. Anyway, she works in my grandfather's company as an analyst."

I was trying to figure out how old she was. If she had an MBA, with a few years work experience before that, she'd be in her late twenties.

"She analyzes health-care stocks, as a matter of fact."

"Go on," I said.

"How we met?"

"Sure. I'd like to know."

I thought he would have been taken with her, love at first sight, as he prowled the building with his mail cart. Then he would have researched her, scrolling through her personnel file, reading her mail, checking her e-mail, figuring out from the patterns of communication who she was connected with. Then, at an opportune moment, the chance meeting. Perhaps it would have been a crisis he himself engineered, with Craig on hand at the critical moment to save the day.

"It wasn't anything special," he said. "I delivered her mail, and we just got talking."

It was hard to visualize this. The MBA stock analyst and the kid from the mail room: the frog who, with the magic of a kiss bestowed—and Cavanaugh DNA—turns into a prince.

I said, "I suppose it doesn't hurt that you're the boss's grandson?"

"I know. It's not the kind of thing you can keep hidden indefinitely. And then, you're right, you've got to use what you've got."

I smiled at this. "Why not?"

This sounded real. He was using what he had to win her, and the outcome was in doubt. This was a far cry from the automatic assumption that whomever he loved would love him back. Must love him back. I went back and forth, oscillating between hope and cynicism.

He said, "I just have this feeling of emotional connection with her. I sense that she's lonely. And I think, from small hints she's let out, that there's been some tragedy in her life. There's an aura of melancholy about her."

"Some people find that attractive."

"I do. Very. She has a way of looking down and away when she's thinking, and I sense this tremendous sadness. When we were having lunch on Thursday—"

"You had lunch together?"

He nodded modestly, his mouth hanging slightly open. "Yeah, actually." He was very pleased with himself. The older woman: a big score.

"Like, a date?"

He pretended embarrassment. "Well." He almost squirmed. "Not exactly a date."

"But a beginning."

"Maybe. I'm not sure. I think she likes me. I know there's this difference in our ages, but she went after me. She tipped her hand first."

"How so?"

"She took an interest in me. She started with the idea, 'What's a bright young guy like you doing in the mail room?' after I made a comment on one of the annual reports I delivered to her, and she kind of took me under her wing. I became her project. Then I had to tell her that, actually, this was a summer job and I was about to finish up at Harvard, and she checked out the name on my ID, which usually I keep turned around."

We took the lunch encounter and decomposed the words she'd said and her responses to what he said, and the gestures that accompanied the words, and her facial expressions, and the stance of her body in relation to his. As he answered my questions I sensed that he was looking at this person as someone who existed independently of his fantasies. He was describing a living, breathing woman, rather than some goddess.

Against all expectations, Craig's therapy seemed set on the right track. I might be able to fix him so that, even if he wasn't entirely turned around, he would be better enough for me to declare victory and depart the case. I'd have done my duty by the Methodist, and I'd be off the hook. I was starting to believe in this therapy—not in Craig himself so much as in the inexorable leak of truth.

"She sounds delightful," I said, sincerely.

I envied him. In a moment of inattention, I found myself thinking, with a sadness that surprised me, of Abby and me coming together, of the sense of endless possibility, of the intoxicating pull of falling in love.

"You never told me her name," I said as he was leaving.

He stopped. For a moment he was flummoxed. He could come up with an excuse, an alibi, in the blink of an eye. But names are hard to invent on the spur of the moment. Why Craig would have to lie to me about the name of this woman, I didn't know. But there was no need for me to go after this. A name is a powerful thing. I remembered the first time I interviewed him, when he'd jumped in to prevent me from saying "Natalie." Let him keep his secret until he was ready.

"Next week," he promised.

The next week we talked about nothing else. Her name was Susan. He was full of excitement, but he didn't see his next step in the courtship. Whatever social abilities he'd possessed were overwritten by the heavy investment he'd made in the more specialized skills of a stalker. He had to relearn, now, how a man woos a woman.

"Are you going to ask her out?" I asked him.

He balked at this step. He'd scaled a three-story building and taken risks in his pursuit of Natalie, any one of which could have landed him in jail. Now he was shying away from asking a woman out on a date.

"Sure," he said. "It's just that, I'm not sure we've reached a stage where this is going to work."

"You have to be the judge," I said. "But on the other hand, you don't want things to go cold."

We rehearsed some simple invitations, then discussed the logistics of the date itself. I suggested he take her to lunch at one of the restaurants at Faneuil Hall Marketplace.

"Sure it's touristy," I said, "but it's close to the financial district, and there's a whole different ambience when you sit outside under an umbrella."

From time to time he'd shake his head in disbelief at his luck, as though he had to wake himself up to what was really happening.

"If this works . . . ," he said. "Man!"

Again, the secret smile, followed by a glance at my face and the smile's fast fade. I let it go. There's no need for a therapist to know everything. He'd report back on his progress the next week.

The next day, Tuesday, I got an invitation to lunch myself. It was an e-mail from Abby, and I almost missed it. I was surprised. Abby likes the personal touch of voice mail if she can't reach me directly. She rarely uses e-mail, and when she does, her messages are about practical, numerical matters like details of refinancing the mortgage. She wrote:

Impromptu lunch at the Patagonia Café. 1 pm. Be there or be square.
Love you, Abby.

I was mesmerized by the words. They were so playful, so uncomplicatedly affectionate. In another context, at another time in our marriage, the message would have been prosaic. But now my spirits soared. Wherever Abby had been, she was coming back.

By the time I opened Abby's message, it was after noon. I dropped everything, called around to the other doctors and found someone who'd tie up my loose ends. Within ten minutes I was accelerating out of the parking lot, intent on making the fifty-minute journey to Cambridge in forty.

I felt like a kid again. I was going to win my wife back. I started to think about what had to be said, then reconsidered. Best not to stir up the past. Not today, this beautiful summer day. Better to stay with the present. The present was perfect.

I was full of life, driving like a typical Boston maniac, cutting people off with abandon. I changed lanes without signaling, swooping into the breakdown lane, ignoring fingers and blasts of the horn. I couldn't have cared less. I was a man on a mission. Be there or be square.

By the time I reached the parking garage under the university health building I was only five minutes late. I jogged a couple of blocks, dodging pedestrians, skipping off the curb into the path of relentless bicyclists. On an impulse, I ducked into a flower shop and picked up a bunch of roses. When I came out, I paused to straighten my tie and peer in the store window to make sure my hair wasn't out of place. I realized I was breathing hard and that it had nothing to do with running.

The Patagonia Café is in the heart of Harvard Square, down a quiet side street slightly removed from the press of traffic and the crowds of pedestrians. It has half a dozen tables outside, clustered on a tiny triangle of real estate so that it more or less spills onto the street. The food isn't anything special, but it's a great place for a leisurely lunch, where you can loll beneath an umbrella, pick at a salad, and watch the world go by. When I'd talked with Craig about the setting for his date with the mystery woman, I now realized, I'd been drawing on memories of the Patagonia Café. It had been our regular lunch spot before Abby and I were married, and the fact that Abby had chosen it for this occasion suggested an appeal to a time when we had a simple, uncomplicated love for each other, a return to our roots.

I came around the corner. The café was fifty yards down on the other side of the street. I was hoping she'd managed to snag an outside table. Maybe Abby had worked on the owner, with whom we'd been on a first-name basis during our courtship, to save us a table outside for old times' sake. I was looking for her among the cluster of people sitting under the umbrellas, but in the bright midday sun, it was difficult to make out who was sitting in deep shade.

Abby had her back to me. She sat at one of the inner tables, with a noisy foursome between her and the street. They wouldn't bother us. Her shoulder and a lock of golden hair shone in the sun. A couple were taking their time getting up to go; a waiter was picking up the charge receipt and checking the tip; another couple were hovering, the man ostentatiously consulting his watch, waiting for the table to be vacated.

I checked my own watch: ten minutes late. But Abby was no

stickler for punctuality. I thought that she'd turn around to look up the street to see what had happened to me, but she didn't. I'd come up behind her and give her a surprise.

I slowed my pace, hoping she'd glance round at this moment and catch sight of me as I crossed the road. I'd wave, filled with anticipation. It would be like old times.

It wasn't until I was about to step off the curb that I noticed the other person sitting at her table. He had been expecting me, evidently. I couldn't make him out. My mind couldn't see him. My brain was momentarily at a loss to compute his presence here, this intrusion into our intimate table à deux.

As I balanced on the curbstone, about to cross but holding back in horror, Craig rose into the sunlight. I could see him clearly now. Craig was smiling. The perfect gentleman, he pulled out a chair for me to join them. Abby, a glass of iced tea halfway to her lips, looked up at him. She must have asked him a question. Perhaps she asked him why he'd stood up. She wasn't expecting me, evidently. Nor was she curious enough to look round to see who, for three whole seconds, Craig grinned at.

fourteen

I turned away before Abby could catch sight of me. Dazed, I walked along Massachusetts Avenue. It was several minutes before I realized I was still clinging to a dozen pink roses, and I ditched them in a Dumpster full of construction waste.

It was my routine to work in my office at home on Tuesday afternoons, but I was in no mood to consider my research project. Instead, I paced the path beside the Charles, mulling over the encounter.

I'd been burned, but that didn't matter. What hurt most was that my hopes for Abby and me had come crashing down. Rationally, I knew there never had been a date. But I had come forward, expectant and vulnerable, eyes closed, lips ready for a kiss, and been smacked silly.

As I tramped the path beside the river, blind to the beauty of my surroundings, I thought about the scene at the café: Abby was not under any obvious duress. She looked relaxed. She gave every indication that Craig was familiar to her. I thought of their heads bent together over the table: She had no misgivings about him.

And why should she? Craig was plausible. He had a sense for what you wanted to believe. He'd played me. Somehow, he'd gained access to Abby's computer to send the e-mail. He'd charmed her, won her confidence. It wouldn't work if I bluntly warned her off.

I called Abby as soon as I thought she'd be back in her office, but Nan told me she hadn't returned from lunch. I tried an hour later when I picked up my car, but according to Nan she still wasn't available. I finally spoke to her at the end of the afternoon, by which time I'd returned home. She had a board meeting and would be late, she said. I wasn't to wait for her for dinner, but I said I would. The conversation meandered briefly—what she was up to, what I was up to—until her opportunity, if there was something unusual to tell me, had passed.

"Oh, you know what I wanted to ask you?" I said. "My e-mail got garbled. Did you send me something today?"

"No," she replied blankly. "Why would I do that?"

"I don't know. I had this fragment and it looked like your name on it. It must have been old."

"I guess."

"Everything okay with you?"

There was a pause. Her hesitation worried me. I pictured Craig holding a knife to her throat. "We have to talk, Paul."

"I know," I said. "I know we do. That's what I want. I almost called you today so we could have lunch together."

"I couldn't have, anyway."

"Why not?"

"I had a work lunch."

I wanted to ask her, "A work lunch, at the Patagonia Café?" but instead I said, "But you're okay?"

"Yes," she said. "Why wouldn't I be?"

It was very late—after ten—when Abby got home. She looked

wan and exhausted, but her makeup was fresh, and I wondered why she'd bothered, with the day almost at its end. She had brought a rice dish from a Brazilian restaurant in Central Square, and we shared it at the kitchen table. I hadn't eaten, but I wasn't hungry.

We ate, acutely conscious of one another and the silence that was like a vacuum sucking speech into it. Then we both started talking at once. I'd forgotten that she had something she wanted to talk about.

"No, you first," Abby said.

In the past, when we'd been happy together, it would have been an act of generosity; now her offer to hear me out seemed like the lesser of two evils.

"Something very strange happened to me today," I said.

Abby scarcely glanced up from her plate. She seemed preoccupied, and a couple of times during the conversation she didn't seem to register things I said, or even hear a question I asked.

"Oh?" she asked, matter-of-fact, without curiosity. "How so?"

"I thought I had a lunch date with you."

"I told you, though. I had a working lunch."

"We didn't have a date. I was fooled into thinking we had one."

"Like, a practical joke? I don't get it."

All this time she continued eating, her eyes down on her plate. She cut a piece of meat and stuck her fork into it, then chewed mechanically, going through the motions of dinner while her mind was elsewhere.

"Not a joke," I said. "More like a setup."

She glanced sideways at me, as someone does who knows the other person well and wants a quick reading on their present state. She spoke very carefully. "Why would someone want to set me up?"

"Not you. Me."

"Oh." For an instant the furrowing of her brow that I'd taken for concentration of thought smoothed in relief.

"I turned up anyway."

"That's too bad." She was more attentive now. She smiled into my eyes and her fingertips brushed my arm in sympathy. "You poor thing! All for nothing."

"I turned up where you were having lunch. Someone sent me an e-mail in your name saying to meet you at the Patagonia Café at one."

"You were there? I didn't see you. Why didn't you join us?"

"You know, the person you had lunch with at the Patagonia Café is the stalker I treated at Sanders. He's the one I thought had been through the house."

"Why would Craig stalk me?" she asked. "He sees me every day."

We each looked at one another as though the other had gone mad. I was acutely aware of how tenuous belief is, how finely balanced, how the word of a husband does not necessarily outweigh the convincing evidence of a wife's own experience. I moved very slowly, very carefully. I sensed that if I made any premature attempt to close the argument, I'd invalidate my own position.

"How does he see you every day?" I asked her.

"Because he works at the agency. He's a summer intern."

"He works there every day? Every day of the week?"

"Of course. We don't take people who won't commit."

So the entire story Craig had told me about working in Patriarch Cavanaugh's mail room, the meeting with the older woman, the shy courtship, the big brother tips on how to find out if Susan was interested—all this was bogus. Over weeks of psychotherapy, I had given my best effort in coaching Craig on how to get a date with my wife.

"Does he deliver the mail?" I asked. I couldn't hold back the bitter laugh that rose, sharp and corrosive in my throat like gastric reflux.

"No." She was puzzled by the question and looked at me with a worried frown, as though she thought she should understand the significance of what I'd asked. "We wouldn't use someone like that. Besides, Craig has pretty good clinical skills."

"Whatever clinical skills he's got, he owes to Sanders. That's not true, though. He's a natural. He has an uncanny ability to figure people out, except the women he's in love with."

"He did mention he was at Sanders. We discussed it. Not in great depth. Frankly, I didn't want to go too much into it. I think it's a strength that he never made a secret of. He's been pretty up front with us. And he's been entirely appropriate with the clients."

"Oh, for God's sake!" I exclaimed in exasperation. "You let him loose on clients?"

"That's what he's there for. He's interested in a career in psychology and he wants the clinical experience. You know, I've mentioned him several times to you. Maybe you weren't listening."

Once more, I was overcome with a sensation of madness that was akin to nausea. Craig had been part of our dinner conversation? We had talked about him over tandoori chicken and swordfish kebabs and meals that stretched back weeks—and yet I had been totally oblivious to his presence among us? I thought back: Abby had mentioned a summer intern. Maybe she was right; maybe I hadn't been paying attention. He'd come in beneath the radar.

"It doesn't worry you that he's been charged with stalking?"

"Are you meant to be telling me this, Paul? If it's confidential, I think it should stay with you."

"This guy doesn't play by the rules. He uses the rules. I had a session with him this week—"

"He's in therapy with you?"

"As of now, he's not. As of the moment I saw him having lunch with you."

"But if he's your patient, do you think you should really be telling me this about him? I mean, it's like he's my colleague."

"Which is nuts."

"I think we have to respect his confidentiality."

"It's a setup. Don't you see it?"

"No, I don't."

"Well, ask yourself this: How come my patient happens to land a summer job at the agency where my wife works?"

"We accept Harvard students for the summer. We're down the street. I happen to work there. It's not that complicated. I think he had an experience at Sanders that changed him. Sure he's made mistakes. God knows, we've all loved too much at some time in our lives. But that doesn't make him dangerous. He's a vulnerable soul, Paul. If he's in therapy with you, I think you should be able to recognize that. Now he wants to give back. If he gets a little mothering in the process, that's a bonus."

"He chose the agency because that's where you work. He'd already learned your name before he'd even been discharged from Sanders. He knew Adrian's name."

She was silent for several seconds at the evocation of our son. Then she sighed.

"This is not about you," she said. "Everything isn't about you. I know you have to be careful of your patients. But everything's becoming so . . . self-referential."

"Paranoid, you mean."

"I just think you're blowing this out of proportion."

"I know this guy. He's smooth. He's slick. He's dangerous as hell."

"I know him, too."

"But not in the way I do."

"That's right: I've spent a lot more time with him than you have. Plus, I've spent time with him in a normal environment."

"You don't know his history. You have no idea, Abby."

"You mean, his dark side?" She regretted the sarcasm immediately. "Sorry."

She closed her eyes and lowered her head to her hands. She released a long, slow breath through pursed lips, as though she had come to the end of a piece of emotional work and was clearing her mind. But the hands on which her brow rested were clenched into fists, the knuckles blanched, the tendons in her forearms sprung tight.

"Are you done?" she asked from behind her hands. "Because there's something I have to tell you."

She lowered her hands deliberately and took a deep breath, as a person does who must summon inner strength in order to begin the next, more difficult thing.

"I just have this," I insisted. "He's a stalker. He terrified one of his teachers and made her life a living hell. I'm warning you: Once he fastens on to you, he'll never let go."

"Can't you listen when I'm trying to tell you something!"

"Okay!" I almost shouted. "I'm listening!"

"I had some bad news today, Paul."

She looked at me as though she'd already determined I wasn't in a fit state of mind to receive anything more than a summary. She was right: I wasn't listening. I was seething. I was filled with the helpless panic of someone in a dream who sees the catastrophe but can't move, can't make his larynx work to sound the alarm. She had some bad news. A potentially lethal stalker hooks up with my wife, dupes me into conducting a pseudo-therapy, and she had bad news to tell.

"Abby," I began, in a tone that conveyed a thin veneer of calm and rationality. I was at the very edge of control. "Do you have any conception of what you're dealing with?"

She looked at me uncertainly. "You mean . . . ?" she began. Then started over. "Which one are you talking about?"

"I'm talking about the homicidal maniac you've hired for the summer. What do you think?"

"I'm trying to tell you something important!" she yelled.

"You don't think that's important?"

"This isn't easy, what I'm trying to tell you, Paul. Why won't you listen to me? Why in God's name can't you just listen?"

"Because I'm trying to get across to you that this case is exceptional. The last thing in the world I want is to bring work home. I respect that you want Sanders to stay . . . where it is, out there, behind the wire. But this is different. Craig is different. He's meticulous. He's infinitely patient. He's diabolical!"

I saw I'd gone too far. Abby slowly shook her head, pityingly.

There is a still point in the center of the vortex. That is where I found myself. I felt stilled. The buzzing in my ears was gone. I was poised, emotionally silent. If it came to it, I'd handle Craig without her. I considered the three rules of murder. I thought, "Okay. This is what rule one feels like. This is what it's like when you act alone." It wasn't real. I wasn't about to run up the stairs to the third floor and grab the gun out of the desk drawer. But I did need to imagine it. I needed the pretended action of killing him, of seriously envisioning his murder.

"All right," I told her softly, "let me hear your news."

She looked hard at me as though I'd become unfamiliar to her. As though I might be someone who closely resembled her husband Paul but in fact was someone else.

"You're losing it," she said quietly. "Don't you realize, Paul, that you sound clinically paranoid?"

fifteen

What scared me about myself was that in my most sober clinical assessment, I accepted there wasn't any other way. For stalkers like Craig, stalking is forever. If you know the psychology of stalkers, if you know the law on stalking, if you know the capacities and proclivities of law enforcement agencies, then you know that if you're the victim of a certain kind of stalker, the only rational solution to the problem is to kill him.

I was starting to think about how I'd do it. And Craig had to know that. When it came to human beings, he had tunnel vision, but within that laser-narrow focus he was extraordinarily gifted in assessing other peoples' vulnerabilities and motivations. I realized that he'd learned as much about me in our sessions as I'd learned about him. Now I was as obsessed with him and Abby as he was with me and Natalie. I was as blindly protective, as unreasoningly dangerous as he was. This had to stop.

I called Natalie. Stalkers aren't promiscuous; because of the very nature of their obsessive focus, it's rare for them to be interested in more than one person at a time. So I reasoned that if Craig was still stalking Natalie, Abby was in the clear. If he was still interested in Natalie, then the lunch with Abby was a feint, a maneuver intended to warn me off.

She was as hard to get hold of on the telephone as before. I left several voice mails at her office, but it wasn't until the next day that she finally picked up.

She treated me with a certain coolness at first. I realized several weeks had gone by since we'd met for coffee in the shopping mall, and if she felt I'd neglected her, it was with some justification.

"I'm in a difficult situation," I told her. "There's not much I can tell you, since I've been treating Craig. As you know."

"Yes," she said. She sounded disappointed in me, as if I were fraternizing with the enemy. "Yes, of course."

"But I've been meaning to give you a call to find out how you are."

"I go from day to day, pretty much."

"How's your thesis going?"

"I'm going to defend it next month, actually." She became more animated as she talked about the future. "I took your advice. I'm going to finish up and move out of state. It's the only way to stop this."

She didn't use his name, or even designate him with a personal pronoun. It was as if Natalie wanted to depersonalize the presence that had insinuated itself into her life. Craig was "this." He'd become a process, something to escape from like the harsh New England winter.

"It's still going on?" I asked her.

"I don't know. I think so."

"Do you want to tell me about it?"

"I don't know." She sighed. She might have said, "What's the point? What can you do about it? What can anyone do?"

"But you think he's still . . . active?"

"My mail's been tampered with, if that's what you mean. And I've been getting weird e-mail."

"What's it about?"

"It's supposedly not from him, but it's about him. It's a woman writing to tell me—shit, I hate to use the word—to tell me how loved I am. 'Love' will never be the same for me now. It'll always mean this insane obsession. I'm not sure I can trust anyone to love me. Is that crazy, too?"

"No," I told her. "It means you have to move on and start over. You have to begin to live again."

"The e-mails purportedly give me advice on how to get along with him. How to get to know him. As though she's trying to help me heal this troubled relationship. They're nauseating."

"You mean, like something a therapist would say?"

"He signs off as if it's an advice column in a newspaper. Do you know the one I mean—Dear Abby?"

Craig's message had been routed through Natalie and had sat on her hard drive waiting until, at a time of my own choosing, I was ready to pick it up. I felt as though I'd had the breath kicked out of me. I marveled at his patience. All the skills that he'd amassed as a persevering lover he had now turned on me, the interloper, the rival.

"Yes," I managed, "I know that column."

I had put off calling Brenda Gorn until two days after seeing Craig at the Patagonia Café. I felt like an idiot, and I didn't want to tell her I was off the case until I'd had time to mull it over. Brenda was hard to reach, too. Each time I called, I got her paralegal: "Assistant District Attorney Gorn's office?"

She was brisk and official. The DA was in conference. No, she didn't know when she'd be available. Did I want to leave a message?

How was I to phrase my plea for help? I needed to walk around my predicament with someone on the outside looking in. I needed someone with a police perspective. I needed to know what kind of big, law enforcement stick I could swing at Craig. Mainly, I needed to talk.

"No. Thank you. No message. Just tell her it's important that I speak with her directly. Tell her I'll call back later."

Brenda must have sensed my distress. When she called me I was with a patient and couldn't get to the phone, but she left a cell phone number.

"Sorry," she said, when we finally made contact. I felt better hearing her voice. "I've been tied up on this cop homicide."

"I must have missed it," I said.

"It made the news last night, but we didn't want to let the media get hold of much until we knew more about what was going on. It'll make the news tonight, big time. He was a lieutenant in the state police."

"Anyone I worked with?"

There was a pause at the other end, and I thought Brenda was running through the cases I might have been on that had involved the dead cop.

"It was Lou Francone," she said, as though she were breaking bad news to me.

Her tone implied both that I'd recognize the name and feel sadness at his passing. It was familiar to me. I'd read his name on the report from the insurance company when they'd jacked up the premium. Beyond that was a vague feeling of a human presence at the very farthest point of memory, like a footfall so soft you're not quite sure you heard it.

"I know that name." I was about to tell her that the lieutenant had given Abby a speeding ticket, but through habit that inhibited needless disclosure, I stopped myself in time. "Help me out, Brenda," I prompted her. This trick of memory, of an indistinct whisper from the past, made me feel like I was standing at a high point, above a drop. I was filled with the premonition that some slope of destiny had suddenly steepened for me, that a gravitational force was pulling me in a direction I dimly recognized. "Give me a clue," I asked.

"Paul, he's the cop who pulled Abby out of the car wreck," she said softly, apologetically.

"That's right," I said, as though remembering him. He had been a shadowy figure. In the background.

Lieutenant Francone was certainly important in the practical sense. He had arrived at the intersection soon after the drunk in the pickup truck plowed into us. Then others came. The helpers, Francone among them, were generic. I stood outside the car clutching Adrian's body. The only person I remembered was Abby. She was in the tiny, compacted world of crushed steel. She was very pale. The hand I held was cold. I saw an ominous sheen of sweat on her brow, and when I felt for her pulse I could hardly count the beats as her heart sprinted to make up in speed what it lacked in substance, as her blood drained away.

I asked her where she was hurt. She shook her head. I yelled to get a response from her. She shook her head at my useless question. Her door was jammed. She wanted me to go in the ambulance with Adrian. I couldn't tell her he was dead. I turned to hide his body from her. Then I stepped back when someone came with a huge pry bar. Maybe that was Francone. There were two of them on it. They were madmen, frenzied with a violence not unlike murderous rage.

Brenda waited a moment for me to regain the present. "You remember him now?"

"Yes. It's coming back." I wondered if Abby had remembered Lieutenant Francone when he gave her the speeding ticket. "Sorry. A blast from the past. I'm a little dazed."

"Look, the wake's at five at McCarthy's in Somerville—why don't you go, pay your last respects? Maybe it would be helpful."

"It's not a bad idea."

"And we can talk about the other thing."

She was about to hang up, but I realized I hadn't asked her what had happened to Francone.

"Shot in the head, in bed, in his own apartment. Lived alone. No immediate family. Divorced. Son killed in the Gulf War. No drugs. No booze problem. No gambling. No debts. He was clean, as far as we know—no unsavory connections."

"Who killed him?"

"Persons unknown."

"For now."

"Oh, yes," she said with a grim confidence. "Lou was one of our own."

McCarthy's Funeral Home was a large white clapboard house on a residential street of single family homes. A dark blue awning stretched from its front door to the street, where two beefy men in dark suits directed cars to the parking lot and helped the infirm disembark. It was something of an institution. There were more political deals concocted at McCarthy's than at any of the taverns within a ten-mile radius. For the wake of a slain police officer, the functionaries of the body politic would be out in force, not to mention Lou's many colleagues who spanned a long and honorable career. When I arrived, I was glad that Brenda had suggested we meet at the end of the afternoon session, before the heavy hitters came in the evening.

Even so, the parking lot was full and a group of police officers, uniformed and in plainclothes, stood smoking in groups on the street around the awning. As is the way of lifelong cops, their eyes frisked me for weapons without the brain even engaging in conscious thought. It was a quick, utilitarian glance that in an instant appraised social class, sobriety, and level of psychosis. I felt their eyes ping on me like a radar contact, establish my irrelevance, and, at once, without curiosity, redirect.

There was a line as soon as I got in the door. I took my turn to sign the book of condolences. I nodded to a couple of people I knew: a medical examiner I'd sat through a trial with, a detective who had bitterly resented the successful insanity plea of a man he'd arrested. As we shuffled forward toward the casket, I looked around for Brenda but didn't see her.

Even in death and overlaid with the grotesque art of the mortician, Lou Francone was a handsome man with rugged good looks. He had been in his mid-fifties and appeared to have dyed his hair a dark brown. The head above the brow was covered by the high-peaked uniform cap, pulled well down, but it couldn't entirely hide the entry wound just anterior to the left ear. I had forgotten the trim mustache.

As I knelt on the stool and stared at the remains, trying to penetrate the inscrutability of the corpse, the man started to come back to me. He hadn't opened the door of the car. Some other helper had done that. He was the one who had reached in—there had only been room for one person to do this—and lifted Abby out of her seat to the waiting gurney as she clutched at my hand as though Death himself were grasping her, enclosing her in his powerful arms to take her from me.

In a sense, that was what had happened: Abby had never entirely come back to me. That part of her that had been Adrian, that part of our mingling, had died in the wrecked car.

Memories flooded back. There were images that I hadn't recalled before and I would have lingered at the casket, but I was aware of the press of people who waited behind me. Reluctantly, breaking the spell, I tipped back onto my heels and rose to move on. I was grateful to Brenda for suggesting I come. She had been right; this was a healing process, the silent parting of one more of a hundred ties that bound me to the trauma. I'd thought of calling Abby but rejected the idea. Abby was at a different, more precarious stage.

I wondered again at the encounter between her and the lieutenant. He'd stopped her on Route 128. He wasn't looking for speeders. Lou didn't have a quota to make. But, as I imagined it, Abby had been daydreaming and hadn't noticed the police cruiser come up behind her, and when she still hadn't slowed down, he'd had no choice but to pull her over. He'd asked her if she knew what speed she was doing. She would have replied, truthfully, that she had no idea. Abby cruised on mental autopilot while she thought of some problem of one of her clients: It could have been eighty; it could just as easily have been fifty. And then—what? He recognized her face, though no longer pale and diaphoretic from impending shock, from a year before? Or was it the name on the license she handed over? Or did Abby, with that turbo-charged consciousness that hemorrhaging people possess as they teeter on the brink of death, remember Lou's face?

And then? The man in the coffin had played it by the book. Maybe he had made some gruff acknowledgment before writing out the citation. As I imagined him, Lou was that kind of guy. A straight shooter. A cop who played no favorites. Strange, though, I thought: You help save a woman's life, then you give her a ticket.

Or did they go their separate ways oblivious, with the crossing of paths nothing more than a pun of fate?

Brenda caught sight of me and waved. She was trading war stories with a group of prosecutors and plainclothes cops. They had pulled their chairs into a circle, each with an elbow on his knee leaning inward to the center, and she had happened to look up as I passed the door of the parlor. I wasn't in the mood for introductions, small talk, graceful exits, so I was grateful when she broke away and motioned for me to join her in a deserted corner of the room.

"This has really shaken people," she said. She touched my arm solicitously. "And you, too, huh? You remember him now, don't you? It's so weird seeing him lying in a coffin wearing lipstick. I never get over these corpses."

"He was a good guy," I said, somewhat lamely. "He pretty much saved Abby's life." He was becoming vague again as memory closed in like dusk.

"A neighbor found him. Naked in bed. Single shot to the head from close range. No signs of forced entry. He'd just had sex. God, you hate to intrude in a colleague's private life like this! I can't stand the intimate details."

"You're looking for the lover."

"We've got a description. The state police are on it. You can imagine the kind of intensity that goes into an investigation like this."

"I'm sorry to bother you with my stuff."

"No. No, it's okay."

She drew me to a chair, then pulled her own out of the line against the wall so that we sat almost in the confessional position.

"You wanted to talk about this rich-kid stalker. Cavanaugh. He's misbehaving. What do you know? You cut the kid a break, and he can't resist the urge to fuck up." She took a deep breath. "I'm sorry, Paul. I'm cynical and I'm mad. My head's still with Lou."

I was going to tell her that my problem could wait and I'd catch her at a better time, but she put a hand on my arm.

"Tell me," she said. "I'm back in the here and now."

"I just found out he's working as a summer intern at Abby's clinic."

She glanced at my face to read my expression. I could tell that she didn't want to say anything that would put the fear of God into me. She said, "I don't like the sound of that at all."

"Abby thinks it's coincidence."

"You've told her who he is, though?"

"She says he's a perfect gentleman."

"But she must be spooked. One day she discovers that the kid who fetches the coffee, whatever, is actually a patient of her husband's, that he's just got out of Sanders?" She gave a shiver and hunched her shoulders. She had been playing out her own imagined emotional reaction, but there must have been something in my face, or a lack of something there, that gave her pause. "Abby is spooked, right?"

"Not entirely. That's part of the problem. She's not as spooked as she should be."

She sensed some delicacy in my manner and held back, waiting for me to choose the level at which I'd feel comfortable explaining the situation.

"It's complicated," I said. "Abby tends to take him at face value."

"And what's that?"

"That he's a smart young Harvard undergrad getting some real-life experience."

"Maybe I could haul him back in front of a judge, but it's not clear this is a violation of his parole. It isn't entirely a question of law and order, is it? A bit of this is between you and Abby. You know what I'm saying."

I started to tell her that the situation was spinning out of control. That whatever Abby thought, we had to take some action. But it was obvious Brenda wasn't paying attention. As I spoke, her eyes followed someone, beyond my left shoulder, who was passing in the hallway.

When her gaze came back to me she was puzzled. "Was that

Abby that just went by?" she asked. "I didn't know she was here."

She stared at me critically, as though I'd been keeping something from her. She must have seen the momentary confusion on my face, because she was decent enough not to ask any questions.

"There are crosscurrents." I sighed. "As you can imagine. Look, I'll go and see how she is." I got up. "I'm sure she'll want to come and say hello."

I found Abby at the end of the hall by the coats. She'd found a corner that shielded her from the sight of the other mourners and was half turned to the wall. I called her name, though I think she was aware that it was me, and I touched her shoulder. When she turned her nose was red with weeping and her eyelids were raw.

"I'm okay," she insisted, holding up a fist that contained a damp, compacted tissue. "Please." She meant I was to leave her.

"I can drive you home, if you like."

"No. I drove here. My truck's in the lot." She made an inchoate, helpless gesture. "It's too complicated to explain right now."

And then the sobs broke from her, and I realized she'd been holding them back all the while I'd walked down the hall to her. The sobs were abrupt and convulsive. They bent her over until she moaned with pain, lost in a world of weeping, centered inward, unaware of her surroundings.

sixteen

I stayed at the wake another half hour after Abby left because I knew she wanted space, but when I got back to the house, she hadn't returned home. I was worried about her. It was clear to me the cop's death had reactivated the original trauma of the accident, and while I hoped that this freshening of memory would give new impetus to her stalled therapy, it was her suffering in the present that I felt.

It was two hours before I heard her SUV in the driveway. She came into the kitchen and sat slumped in a chair, staring blankly ahead. She looked wretched.

"Do you want something to eat?" I asked. I felt like a mother who had waited up for her daughter to return home: anxious, happy she had returned safely, angry with her for causing so much worry. "I'll make you an omelet, if you want."

She didn't look up. She didn't seem to have heard. It was as though she was continuing an imaginary debate she'd been having with herself for the last two hours.

"How did you know?" she asked.

"About Lou Francone?"

"What else is there?"

"It was a coincidence. Brenda Gorn, the DA, told me."

She looked up sharply at this: her head snapped around with a speed quite at variance with the morose apathy she had shown until then.

"I happened to call her about something else—Craig Cavanaugh, as a matter of fact," I explained. "And she mentioned that Lou had died."

"Killed."

"That Lou had been killed."

"Why is it you call him Lou?"

She looked at me intently, all her attention focused on how I might answer this innocuous, irrelevant question. Her gaze was fierce, as though she wasn't so much asking me for information as challenging my claim to familiarity with the man.

"I don't know," I said. "Brenda called him Lou."

"I don't know why you keep using that name, like you know him."

"I did. He helped us."

"Did you work with him on a case?"

"No, I don't think I ever did."

Abby had disappeared back into herself. Her jaw was working with the stress of inner dialogue, and I watched her eyes dart back and forth as the brain shifted gears from one perspective to another. Without any change in her expression, big tears gathered in her eyes and ran down her cheeks unheeded. A constant stream flowed along the side of her nose, then laterally through the hollow of her cheek beneath the bone, around the mouth, then curved along her jaw to drip off her chin.

She didn't pay the slightest attention to her tears, only blinking occasionally to clear her sight so that a new packet of fluid was ejected from her eyes. I took a seat beside her and very slowly dabbed her chin with a tissue.

"Please!" she whispered. She held her hands, stiff and spiky, trembling with the effort of self-control, in front of her.

I felt she was surrounded by invisible razor wire, but I said, "I know, in a way, you want to be alone. But that's not a good way to do it. Not for you, or for the two of us. We need to deal with this together."

She turned on me. "Why are you torturing me?" she screamed. "Isn't it enough he's dead?"

I hadn't realized she was so close to the edge. She was agonized. Her eyes were screwed tight and she shook her head as though trying to clear it of a great pain. I wanted to put my arm around her, but I knew she'd fight that—physically fight loose from me.

She bit on the knuckle of her left hand and sobbed, but the pain she inflicted on herself wasn't even close to the intensity that was needed to distract her. Her head came back and she opened her mouth in a spasmodic grimace that stretched her lips and contorted the skin around her mouth.

"Let me help you with this," I urged her.

She nodded her head in agreement, but when I moved toward her to comfort her, she warned me away. She fought to control her emotions. She wanted to tell me something, and she started to speak, but her grief got in the way. She paused, struggling with herself again. She waited for a gap in the emotion that would let her get the words out.

"I want you to know I love you," she said.

"I know that."

"I want you to be sure that I love you more than anything in the world."

"I do know that."

"No, you don't."

She stated this with such certainty that I stared, wondering, into her eyes. She flinched from my gaze.

"You have to take it on faith," she insisted. "You just have to believe I care for you."

She saw I didn't understand and that I wanted to ask questions.

"I can't," she said. She got up. "I can't take any more right now. I have to be by myself."

I sat in the leather chair in my office in front of my desk and spun slowly like an autistic boy. I kept going. It really was comforting to feel the gentle pull of the centrifugal force, to come slowly to rest as the chair lost momentum.

The strangeness of Abby's behavior worried me. I wondered if the cop's death had precipitated a psychotic reaction. You don't want to think of the person you sleep next to every night crossing that line. But the more I considered how she'd reacted downstairs, the more it seemed to me that Abby—with the crazy accusation that I was torturing her, then the avowal of love as if she were taking leave of me—was losing it in a serious way.

I would keep a careful watch on her, but I had to let her be for now. I was restless without answers. I spun in the chair one way, then the other. I tapped on the desk with a paper knife, thinking, trying out different perspectives on what might be happening with Abby. I leaned back in the chair and opened and closed the drawers of the desk with the tip of my shoe. I'd hooked open the drawer which held the gun and I'd tapped it closed again before registering that it should have been locked.

With deepening unease, I sat up. I reached down to open the drawer. The case for the handgun was there, sure enough. But as soon as I lifted it out of the drawer I knew it was empty.

The eight rounds that should have been lined up in a row were gone. The indentation that held the .25 was an empty footprint.

I tried to make it right. I wanted this manageable. Abby, I told myself, had been looking for the checkbook for our brokerage account and had mistaken which drawer I kept it in. She'd opened the drawer, seen the case, and taken the gun. She'd taken it and hidden it to give me a shock.

When it came to considering the alternative, my mind balked. If Craig had stolen the gun, my life would take a turn down a street I'd never been down before. I had been there vicariously. This was the street most of my patients lived on: where people got shot. The danger of this scenario was almost unthinkable. It was Abby. It had to be.

When I went downstairs, I found Abby watching TV in the den. She was cried out. She seemed tired and emptied and didn't look up when I came in or change her posture when I sat down beside her on the couch.

She had the news on. It was a report about Lou Francone's death. They were showing a photo taken shortly before he was murdered. He was in uniform, standing with a couple of other officers. They went to a close-up of his face. I glanced sideways to see Abby's reaction. She was mesmerized.

"Don't you want to give it a rest?" I asked.

She didn't reply. She might have been a zombie. I thought she was worn out, beyond decision making.

I tried to think of a good way to ask her if she had the gun. There didn't seem to be any segue into the topic, so I decided just to come clean and deal with the consequences later. I had to know.

On the TV, a reporter was describing the discovery of Lou Francone's body in his apartment. She was making a lot of the fact that he'd been shot at close range; that Officer Francone, an experienced police officer, had allowed the assailant to get right up to him; that there'd been no signs of forced entry. She speculated, but attributed the speculation to unnamed sources, that the killer was a lover. He was naked, in bed. Gently, I removed the clicker from Abby's limp fingers and switched the TV off.

We sat for a long time with only the ticking of the clock to break the silence. I'd never noticed it before. We stared at our looming reflections in the glass of the TV set.

Finally, I said, "Abby?"

You know there's something unpleasant coming when your spouse starts a new sentence with your name. I sensed, in a slight relaxation of her posture, Abby's attention turn from the TV set toward me.

"I wanted to ask you if you had my gun."

She hesitated a moment. Maybe she had to consider what her ultimatum would be, now that I'd come out in the open. On the other hand, maybe my gun was news to her.

"Don't play games with me, Paul," she said, fast and tight. She had her arms wrapped around her. She glanced at me quickly, accusingly, then away.

"This isn't a game. I wish it was. I know this isn't a good time, but if you have my gun, I need to know where it is. I need to get it back."

She turned on the sofa so that she faced me. "You're playing head games with me," she said. She was close. Her eyes were level with mine, aligned front on, scanning back and forth as people do when they're actually consciously looking at someone's eyes instead of allowing their brain to do the work for them. She was desperate.

"I'm not playing games with you," I said levelly, quietly.

"Look, Paul, I know you're really good at this. I know you're the world's expert on lying. I know you can get anything you want over on people. You're the master manipulator, and I'm just me. I'm no match for you. I'll do what you want. You don't have to maneuver me. Just, please don't do it. Please."

She was genuinely afraid of me. I was shocked. I was starting to think that, given the instability of her emotions and the emerging paranoia, the grief process was taking on a life of its own. Psychotherapy was stoking the fires instead of helping them burn out. Abby was losing touch with reality.

"All right," I told her. "No head games."

She let me take her hands so that we sat almost knee to knee, facing one another. Her hands between mine were trembling.

"Let's play it straight," I said. "Straight down the middle. No games."

"Okay," she said. She smiled bravely.

"I just have to ask you one thing. And then, that's it."

"Go ahead," she said, nodding her head, as if she could will us to work this out.

"Do you have my gun?"

She let out a gasp of terror and jumped up and away from me as if I'd stung her. "Oh, God!"

She stood with her hands up before her in a pushing gesture to stop me from coming after her.

"I'm sorry, I'm sorry, I'm sorry!" She was begging. "I'm sorry. But don't drive me mad!"

"Okay," I told her. "I'm not getting up. I'm just sitting here. I'm staying here."

We were both terrified.

"I'm going to tell you something." She had difficulty talking. She was swallowing hard, but I could hear the smack of her dry tongue against the roof of her mouth.

"Good." I sat back on the sofa to give an appearance of comfort, of respectful attentiveness. "I'll listen to whatever you want to tell me." I was pretty sure now that she was psychotic.

"I'm going to tell you something, and then we'll never mention it to each other again. All right?"

"Sure."

"You swear?"

"I swear."

She seemed out of breath. "Tuesday afternoon . . ." The rest of the words wouldn't come.

"Okay," I encouraged her.

"Tuesday afternoon . . ." She was nodding her head as if reminding me of an agreement that was already implicit between us. "We were together."

I started to protest. "But that was after the phony lunch date."

"It doesn't matter. We were together. You were here, at home, your usual Tuesday afternoon—"

"No, I didn't come home."

"Don't tell me!" She held up her hand as if she might jam the words back in my mouth.

"I was upset. I went for a walk along the Charles."

"Okay." She relaxed. "That's fine. In fact, that's good. We went for a walk along the Charles."

"If you like," I said. I wondered if this fit with some delusional notion of hers.

"Together," she said through clenched teeth.

Was she hinting at telepathy? Was she suggesting a mingling of consciousness? "Okay," I assented reluctantly.

"We were walking along by the Charles. Together. All afternoon."

"Sure," I said.

She insisted, emphatically and terminally, "You were with me."

I still didn't get it.

seventeen

I was pleased when Larry suggested we sit down together over lunch and hash out the Cavanaugh case. I thought it was a way to resolve what had become an impossible situation in a win/win way. Peace with honor. Discussion over lunch was a familiar format and one I felt comfortable with. We'd stroll down to the cafeteria and make small talk about family and friends as we wended our way through the lines, balancing plastic trays of salads and sandwiches, then find a quiet corner away from patients' relatives. In the midst of white-coated professionals equally engaged in their own business, we could talk frankly, without concern of being overheard.

But when I met Larry in his office, I saw that he'd had food sent up. Larry had inherited the office and the chair of the department from Boris Kudzov, a legendary and inscrutable psychoanalyst. It's a beautiful room with a view of one of the last green spaces that the medical school hasn't gobbled up. The walls are lined with shelves of bound journals and obscure tomes on defenses of the ego, holdovers from Boris. Larry has little time for books; in his line of research, anything that has been around long enough to make its way into a book is already out of date.

"I hope you like salads?" he asked.

"Fine with me," I said.

I don't care about food at these meetings; it's a distraction from the business at hand. But I did notice that there was more of it than the two of us could reasonably consume.

"It was that or meatballs," he said apologetically.

Larry seemed awkward. He had turned away from me and was fussing with plastic forks laid out on the credenza next to the clear plastic containers of salad, as if he felt he had to play the role of host but wasn't sure quite how far he had to go in serving me. An academic department is an egalitarian gathering at lunch, and we wouldn't think twice about fending for ourselves. I hadn't before seen Larry so socially ill at ease, so concerned with niceties.

"Larry," I said, "you tell me how you want to do this. Lunch first, then talk? Or shall we get right into it, so it's out of the way?"

He didn't respond immediately and he didn't turn around. I had the feeling he was hiding from me. "We should wait for Judy." He turned now and walked to his elemental chair, a chrome skeleton upholstered in black leather. He said, as if an afterthought, "I told you she was joining us, didn't I?"

"No, I don't think you mentioned it."

"You're okay with it, though, right?"

"Actually, maybe you and I should discuss the situation first, before Judy arrives."

"By 'situation,' you mean Craig Cavanaugh?"

"Yes. There have been some new developments. I think the situation's very different from the way it was when you and I last discussed my being his therapist."

"I agree."

"All right, then."

When people reach agreement, particularly on an issue that might lead to conflict, they acknowledge this with a nod, a handshake, or simply by making eye contact, but Larry was staring with a troubled frown at the end of his shoe. I became increasingly uneasy as I sensed some other order of business, some issue of which I had no inkling that was circling, waiting to drop out of the sky.

"Judy always has a valuable perspective on things," I suggested, "but in this case, given that she was a defense witness for Craig, there may be a conflict of interest."

"I'd like her to be part of this discussion."

"Some of what we have to talk about is private stuff," I said. "I was hoping we could discuss this in confidence."

Larry made a gesture of reluctance, helplessness, a shoving gesture to indicate that it was out of his hands. "I think, Paul, it's already gone beyond that stage. I mean—" He shook his head, then turned to me with a smile that was one notch short of goofy. "I think it's out there."

It took me a moment to recognize what the smile was: Larry was humoring me. I was emotionally out of tune, he implied; I wasn't in a position to make demands about how this discussion should proceed. Larry wasn't ill at ease at all. He was carefully keeping his distance from me.

It was an uncomfortable few minutes. At one point Larry glanced at an open journal on his desk, and I sensed he would have preferred to immerse himself in receptor biochemistry until Judy arrived. I struggled to come up with small talk, casting around for a neutral topic, not knowing which one might turn out to be radioactive.

It was clear Larry meant to fend me off until Judy arrived. Why he needed her, I didn't understand. It worried me. I wondered if he was going to say something to me that required a witness. Perhaps he had questions whose answers needed to be recorded.

But I didn't want to wait for whatever the two of them had in store for me. "Larry," I said, "I want off this case."

There was a knock on the door that came before Larry had a chance to respond to what I'd said. Judy had knocked softly and at once entered without waiting for his call to come in. She hadn't even felt it was necessary to pause a moment between her knock and entering. The arrangement implied a certain intimacy. The door to Larry's office was not a boundary that stood between them. Nor, for Judy, would there be any surprises inside.

"You got it," Larry told me.

There it was, right there: what I'd wanted. I'd done my business, but they hadn't even started theirs.

Judy had come into the room at the moment Larry had spoken; though she hadn't heard my question, she didn't feel the need to ask him what he meant. They were rehearsed. She was confident Larry would stick to their script.

She greeted me with a smile of inverted lips—the sucked-in smile you use to commiserate with someone going through a tough time—as she went at once to help herself to one of the salads laid out on the credenza. She caught herself, looking from Larry to me, and gave a good imitation of someone realizing no one else in the room has food.

"Are we going to eat first, or talk?" she asked.

"Talk," Larry said.

Judy was brimming with good humor. "Let's eat," she said play-fully. "What do you say, Paul? I vote we eat first."

It was a nice touch: a semblance of conflict with the boss, an in-vitation for me to gang up on Larry, possibly to defeat him, or to side with authority against her. Either way, I would seem to be a winner and Judy would not seem to have already worked out what was to happen in the next twenty minutes.

"I'm with Larry," I said. "Business before pleasure."

"Spoilsport!"

She took a seat on the couch and sat primly with her hands in her lap, back straight, beaming through her round glasses first at Larry, then myself. There was a moment of silence while each of us figured out the trajectory at which we wanted to get into the topic.

"This therapy with Craig Cavanaugh," I said, "is totally out of control."

A look passed between Larry and Judy.

Larry began to say something, something intemperate, then stopped himself. He let out the breath he'd held back in a deep sigh, like steam escaping under pressure, and started over. "You can say that again."

Judy gave Larry a sharp look: His tone was wrong; this wasn't the way they'd scripted the interaction.

She turned slightly toward me, kindly and desirous of understanding. " 'Out of control'?" she echoed. "How so, Paul?"

She was leaning in toward me in full listening mode, attentive, concerned, oozing empathy. She might have been my therapist. It was hard to retaliate against her without making it seem you were willing to hurt the feelings of your favorite auntie.

"I can't do therapy with someone who's harassing me."

"You know," Judy began reasonably, "you have to accept a certain amount of harassment. Especially if you're treating someone for a personality disorder. I think it's just part of the job."

"I already know that, Judy."

"I know you do, Paul. Of course you do. But in the heat of the moment, we tend to forget these obvious things."

"I'm talking about harassment outside of therapy."

They were watching me very carefully, marking my words. I felt I'd reached some objective that allowed them to skip a few pages of the script they'd prepared.

"This guy is getting into my private life. He keeps tabs on me. He follows me."

"You have proof of this?" Judy asked.

"Of course I don't. How could I get proof of someone following me? Are you saying I should hire my own security?"

"I'm not saying anything."

"That's a pretty safe position to be in."

The sarcasm was a mistake. Judy looked puzzled, and Larry came to her defense.

"Judy's not part of the problem," he said. "So let's focus on the solution, shall we?"

"Okay," I said. "How about this? Craig took a summer job at Abby's agency. That's a problem, to my way of thinking."

Larry shrugged. "Hey, it's a free country, Paul."

Again, Judy stopped him with a glance. "That is a problem, Larry. That's a boundary violation."

This seemed promising. I looked from one to the other, but they didn't appear to have any further comment to offer on the matter of a stalker taking a job with my wife. They waited for me to go on.

"Screw this!" Larry burst out.

"Larry," Judy warned.

"No, damn it!" Larry stormed on. "He's been harassing you? Craig Cavanaugh's been harassing you?"

"Yes, he has."

"He's been harassing you—or you've been harassing him?"

"How would I be harassing him?"

"You're supposed to be his therapist, for Chrissake!"

"Not anymore."

"Damn right!"

"I'm out. I quit."

"No, you don't. I'm taking you off the case."

"Okay. We agree. I'm not working with him anymore. That's all I want. I don't care how you do it."

"Paul," Judy said evenly, "I think you ought to care. We've worked together a long time. We go back a ways. That's why I'm going to tell you this straight up: You're in deep doo-doo."

"I'm in what?"

"You're fucked," Larry said. "You're fucked up in the head, Paul. You are seriously out of control. You'll be lucky to keep your license."

"My license?" I was dumbfounded. "What does my license have to do with it? You asked me to take the case. I didn't want it. I had serious reservations from the start. But I took it anyway. I've been a good soldier."

"But that doesn't allow you to act out your frustrations, Paul." Judy was firm, understanding, above all, nonjudgmental. "You still have to maintain your professional stance. You have to hold back your own emotional reactions. You can't be . . ." Judy seemed to have difficulty pronouncing an epithet so extreme: "Retaliatory."

The word hung in the air. Retaliation is the greatest sin. It strikes right at the heart of what a therapist is supposed to be: He must provide the holding environment in which the patient can resolve his fiercest conflicts. That environment must be safe. The patient must feel certain that whatever he says will not be acted upon by the therapist. This is the essential, the virtual quality of therapy. If, in this process, the therapist comes under attack as a stand-in for an earlier figure in the patient's life, he must withstand the most accurate abuse, the grossest provocation. Even though it may require the forbearance of a saint, he cannot, ever, retaliate.

"When you say 'retaliatory,'" I began carefully, stealthily, searching both their faces for advance warning of the direction from which the blow might come, "what exactly are you referring to?"

Judy gave no indication that she was going to answer my question, even though she'd introduced the topic. This was Larry's part: Everything had been leading to this.

"I had a call from John Cavanaugh yesterday," he said. I saw the anger in his eyes. This was personal. The patriarch must have driven over him, then backed up. "I had a lot of explaining to do. And frankly I couldn't come up with much of a defense. The guy is eighty years old, but he's as sharp as a tack. It was not a pleasant experience."

"I'm sorry he gave you a hard time."

"Do you want to tell me what he said?"

"I've no idea."

"Really?"

There was a trap here. It was too late to avoid it, because I'd fallen into it days before. Maybe weeks ago. With a growing feeling of liquefying dread in the pit of my stomach, I acknowledged that it hadn't been set by Judy or by Larry. For all their savvy, they weren't even playing in the same league as Craig.

"No," I said. "How could I possibly know what John Cavanaugh said to you?"

"I was hoping you'd come clean."

"I don't have any idea what you're talking about."

"Paul," Judy said. "I'm no lawyer—God forbid—but it's always better if the person tells what happened for themselves, rather than have other people accuse him. That way the story comes out from his perspective. I'm not talking about spin. I'm talking about the multiple facets of truth. The *Rashomon* thing."

"Old Man Cavanaugh told me that you've been harassing Craig.

That you're the one who's out of bounds." He twisted his arms in an openhanded gesture to indicate it was my turn.

They waited.

"This is a waste of time," Larry said, swiveling in his chair in exasperation.

"I can't confess to something I haven't done," I said. There was an *Alice in Wonderland* feel to the whole proceeding. "Think who we're dealing with here. Think how he operates. This is nuts! You can't believe a word he says."

"Come on, Paul!" Larry said in rising anger. "We've got the tape!"

I hadn't paid any attention to the TV set on the steel trolley strategically placed against the bookshelves. We tape interviews all the time, and you'll find a dozen VCRs in any academic psychiatry department. Now that Larry had mentioned it, I saw a tape protruding from the slot, ready to go. From where I sat, I couldn't read the handwriting on the label, but I could see a company logo that was familiar to me.

"This is a surveillance tape," Larry said. He raised his hands in a gesture of futility and resignation, disgust. "I know. It's basically a fascist tool." He shook his head in disbelief. "I never thought I'd side with Big Brother. But there it is."

"You said there was no way of getting evidence that someone was being followed," Judy said. "Well, this is it."

"Good," I said. "This should be interesting."

This time Judy and Larry didn't exchange looks. They didn't need to. They both stared at me incredulously, beyond comment.

"The tape was made with a surveillance camera at the Meeting House Mall. Which John Cavanaugh happens to own. The camera is situated where two halls cross. Just outside a Starbucks. Ring any bells, Paul?"

I tried to convey a sense that none of this was stressing me, but the truth was, I was having difficulty simply drawing breath. "Could be," I managed.

I hoped I wasn't sweating. I fought the impulse to run a fingertip across my forehead. There's a natural protective reflex of putting your hand up to your face—to rest your chin, to tap your lips, to scratch lightly at the corner of your eye—all these gestures serve to shield your face, and they're a dead giveaway that you're feeling vulnerable.

I thought back to the meeting with Natalie and ran through all the horrible things the camera could have caught. Not that I'd done anything wrong. There were no base motives there. But robbed of their true context, innocent gestures can be made sinister.

"There was some kind of disturbance," Larry was saying, "so the security guys in mission control happened to zoom in on this small piece of real estate. We'll skip the previews."

And there it was. From an elevation of about twelve feet, the camera closed in on the group of teenage boys who were already engaged with the security guard. From that angle, in shades of gray, slightly blurred, they appeared more menacing than they had at ground level from the Starbucks.

"There's our guy," Larry said.

I thought he was talking about me. I thought I was "our guy," but he couldn't be pointing to me, I realized, because at that point I was still inside the coffee shop.

Larry took out his laser pointer and drew our attention to the right upper corner of the screen, as though he were picking out some of the finer points of the NMDA receptor. The red dot of Larry's pointer indicated a figure in the crowd, somewhat in the background, out of focus, and often hidden by other figures closer to the camera.

I drew my chair closer. Larry and Judy had viewed the tape several times before, evidently. No doubt they'd fast-forwarded and freeze-framed and endlessly discussed the significance of each and every motion of the principal players. I watched the screen while Larry and Judy watched me.

Craig stayed mostly at the back of the gathering crowd of spectators. He didn't glance at the security camera or show any awareness of it. The ambush hadn't been contrived. He'd improvised. All his attention was focused on one spot. While in front of him the confrontation between the teenagers and the security guard escalated step by step, his attention never wavered. Because of the camera angle, you couldn't tell whether he was watching them or something further away, off camera. But I knew what he stared at so avidly, with such crushing intensity: me, with my arms around Natalie.

None of this was visible on the tape. You couldn't make out what his expression might be. There was no soundtrack. No music to set the emotional tone. There wasn't even color that could have revealed the flush of anger on his cheeks. You could only infer the mental state of the participants from their movements.

The camera came back to a wider view as Craig turned and walked away. I think the security people wanted to see how many people were liable to be involved if trouble developed. Craig moved quickly but without hurry. He glided between shoppers, like a trout swimming in a stream of people, gliding upstream against their movement toward the commotion.

Then I came on the scene. I didn't move smoothly. I was ruffled. I rushed into view and stopped suddenly. My movement was abrupt enough to cause people close by to turn to me. One woman with shopping bags in both hands glanced at me and moved away. I was oblivious to everyone around me. I turned my head this way and that. I went off in one direction, then, after only a couple of steps, I seemed to change my mind and rushed off in another. I was stopping and starting like a lunatic. A tall man in a tank top started to walk away at the same time I changed direction and we collided. I had no recollection of the contact. It must have been minor, glancing at worst, but in the tape it looked like I shouldered him out of the way.

It was easy enough to discern my motivation. I was looking for the vanished Craig. I was more than looking, though. The frantic intensity of my search, its desperate urgency, was evident even in the diminished images from the security camera. I watched myself: a man to watch carefully, a man with clear potential for violence. Suddenly—all my movements seemed abrupt and strangely random, the decisions of a man with a mind like a pin-ball machine—I fixed on a direction. There I was, exiting bottom right, head, eyes, limbs fixed straight ahead as I ran like a berserker in the direction Craig had gone.

Larry clicked the remote and the TV shut off. The tape clattered halfway out of the slot.

I said, "I know how this looks."

You can explain anything. I know, I've listened to these explanations. How the CIA implanted a microscopic amplifier behind this person's ear that allows other people to know what he's thinking, so that . . . It's not the delusion, per se, it's the explanation that's offered in support of it that really brings home to you how crazy the other person is. And so . . . And because . . .

I heard myself telling Larry and Judy what was really going on in that tape. Clear, cogent reasons. And so . . . And because . . . I looked at their clinical, professionally blank faces, and I knew what it was like to be paranoid—not to think paranoid thoughts—but to experience the profound invalidation of the paranoid life. To live among people who don't give any credence to these goings-on that you believe are utterly crucial. To talk to people who can't see the evidence staring them in the face. And the more you try to convince them . . .

Say no more.

eighteen

The next day, at Sanders, I had a call from a Detective Carol Dempsey.

"I'm with the state police," she said.

I knew her name, but I couldn't think which of my cases she might have been connected with.

"I think we've talked before," I said.

"I'm sure we have, Doctor."

Her tone was clipped and professionally neutral. Usually, I'm calling the arresting officer to get information from them on the crime scene or the way my patient had behaved on arrest, and I accept that they will try to use the opportunity to extract information from me that they might use in the prosecution. They don't get anywhere, but the exchange is good-natured, and we banter back and forth. Detective Dempsey, though, seemed to actively discourage any sense of camaraderie.

"Jog my memory," I asked her. "I don't recall offhand which case you're calling about."

"That would be the Lieutenant Louis Francone case, Doctor."

I was taken aback. "I don't know if there's much I can do to help you there."

"We sure would appreciate it if you'd come in and talk to us."

"All right. Of course."

"Anything you can tell us would be helpful, Doctor."

"Let me get this straight. You're not asking me for my professional opinion? I mean, you're not going to ask me about profiling, and that kind of thing?"

"No, Doctor. We're not going to ask you about profiling."

I was mystified as to how I might be of use to them in their investigation, but I was soon busy with the new admissions and didn't give any more thought to the detective's call. I agreed to drop by the state police barracks on my way home and give them any advice I had—not much, I thought. Perhaps one of my ex-patients was on their list of suspects. I was a loose end that had to be tied off.

I'd never been inside the barracks before. I'd read many statements obtained here and had to call them for one reason or another several times a year. I felt I knew the place, but I really didn't. It is a new concrete building off the highway, functional without being forbidding. It could have been offices for any of the many high-tech companies in the area except for the communications gear that sprouted from the top of the building and the line of gray and blue patrol cars that lined the parking spaces out front.

Although I hadn't been able to give her an exact time when I'd be there, Detective Dempsey was waiting for me in the foyer. She was a woman in her mid-forties, short and a little overweight, and she carried herself with a rigidity of posture that suggested she'd come to the police via the military. She measured me as I came through the doors and walked toward the reception desk; though we both suspected who the other was, she made no move to introduce herself, instead waiting for me to say my name to the officer.

"Dr. Lucas," she said gruffly, "thank you for coming." Her tone of voice was uninflected and empty of emotion, empty even of the gratitude her words indicated.

She wore her hair long and dyed blond and pulled back from her face. She had a very experienced face; a face, I thought, that had seen a lot of bad crime scenes that had left her pessimistic and depleted of compassion. There was a weariness about her, but she seemed more than tired. It was a condition I'd seen in other professionals who come into contact, day after day, with the terrible things people do to each other. It was a condition I monitored in myself: to be worn smooth by the constant abrasion of human nature to the point that you achieve a state of independence from lies, blandishments, flattery, promises, and bluff; a skepticism that approaches numbness to the spoken word; a point of cynical enlightenment that brings no satisfaction. She held me for a moment in her cool gaze, and I felt a kinship with Detective Dempsey and a certain fascination, as though we suffered from the same disease, and in Dempsey I could observe an advanced stage of what I had.

With a brusque wave of the folder in her hand, she indicated I was to walk in front of her toward the back of the building. I proceeded along a corridor past offices from which people looked up curiously as I passed. As I walked on, I heard the sounds of a man and a woman in conversation in an office ahead of me; I couldn't make out the words, but I caught the tone of friendly joshing, a chuckle. And then, when I came level with the door, they stopped abruptly and stared at me. It could have been the sight of a stranger in their midst, the security-consciousness of a cop that is always present. But when Detective Dempsey came after me, they didn't start up their conversation again. It was the case, I concluded. The dead cop. Lou Francone, one of their own. Anything connected with it, even someone connected as tenuously as myself, cast a pall.

I wasn't accustomed to being the subject. I was used to having the run of the place, for the institution to be my institution, and the staff to be my colleagues and allies. When I'd walked in the front door, I had implicitly assumed I'd continue in this role. I was in law enforcement, too, and in my mind there was a kind of continuity between Sanders and the state police barracks: We were all part of the same process, with my job downstream from the work conducted here. So I wasn't expecting to feel vulnerable as an object of scrutiny. I was suddenly keenly aware that I wasn't the one to decide what would happen next—that I didn't even know what would happen next.

At the end of the corridor, past a row of vending machines, we headed down a ramp toward another section that was below ground level. Detective Dempsey, I noted, was following closer behind me. There was a change in décor that signaled that we were entering a zone with an altogether different function: Carpeting gave way to a nonslip rubberized material on concrete and the walls were covered by a durable blue-gray paint that looked like it could be hosed down if the need arose. Surveillance cameras were in evidence at each corner. A yellow line ran down the center of the corridor.

We passed one door and then, when we came to a second, Detective Dempsey said, more as a command than a request, "Stop here, please."

She leaned past me and unlocked the door, then gave it a push so that it swung open before me. Inside was a room without decoration or windows except for a large one-way mirror which took up much of one wall. A table was bolted to the floor. She indicated the chair by itself on the side of the table facing the viewing room.

"Take a seat," she said. "I'll be back in a minute." She started to leave the room, but turned abruptly with an afterthought. "Coffee?"

"Thanks, no."

She closed the door behind her. I took a seat and wondered what she would have done if I'd asked for a double mocha espresso. Or any kind of coffee. Because I was listening for the sound, I heard the door of the viewing room next door close. Would Detective Dempsey really have fetched coffee from the vending machine for me?

I was a little giddy at the novelty of the situation. I was having an adventure, intrigued to be at one of the places where my work at Sanders began. I was curious and slightly anxious, the kind of anxiety anyone feels when a cop car comes up behind you on the highway, even when you're not speeding. I was not afraid.

Detective Dempsey was gone about ten minutes, during which I sat in the interviewee's seat and appraised the room with a professional interest. They'd gone with a different strategy in regard to the chairs; instead of the concrete-upholstered monsters at Sanders, the one I sat in was made out of an aluminum alloy and light as a feather. You could block it with one hand. On the whole, I thought the room was well arranged. Obviously the state police were more generously funded than we were.

There wasn't much of me to observe through the one-way mirror, and soon Dempsey came back with her partner.

"This is Detective Wolpert," she said.

Wolpert was younger, maybe in his early thirties, and though he was heavily muscled from working out, his face was rounded, almost pudgy. He wore round, rimless glasses and showed a readiness to smile, so that his face puckered around twinkling eyes in an appealing, friendly way. Detective Wolpert showed none of his partner's jaded attitude. He readily shook hands and beamed at me as if he were meeting me at a family gathering. He seemed very pleased to be in his present job, and I wanted to ask him how long he'd been a detective, because I wondered if there was an emotional progression in their line of work in which a Detective Wolpert became a Detective Dempsey. I was still curious, easily distracted by nonthematic details. This wasn't about me.

Wolpert gave me the standard police greeting for physicians. "It was good of you to make time, Doctor, in your busy schedule."

"I only wish I could be more helpful. I don't think I have a lot to contribute."

"Well, look . . ." He spread his hands in supplication, as a priest does at the end of the service to invite good fortune. "Why don't you let us be the judge of that?"

He wanted to put me in my place. The gesture could have been confrontational, but he carried it off well, and the message—that I was the amateur in their more knowledgeable hands—came across almost as if he were the one making a concession. He appeared young and eager, but if I'd had anything to hide, he was the one I'd have had to watch. Not Dempsey, with her borderline rude manner. If I'd had anything to hide.

"Why don't you tell us how you came to know Lieutenant Francone?" Dempsey asked.

"Well, I didn't, really."

"I see," she said. "You didn't know him, but you knew him well enough to go to his wake." She tossed a piece of paper at me. "Isn't that your signature there, from the book of condolences?"

I glanced at it, wondering if they'd copied the whole book. Had they asked the family for permission? I was annoyed at this intrusion into the private realm of grief. Anything that approached the Adrian zone made me aggressive.

"The mayor was there, too," I said. "Did you interview him?"

"No, we didn't," Wolpert admitted.

"But we might," Dempsey said.

She intended this without the slightest shred of humor, to let me know that status, a doctor's, a mayor's, would make not the slightest bit of difference to her. I was annoyed that she was treating me with such a heavy hand. I was trying to help them. There wasn't any need for the third degree. That was why I got a little snippy. A mistake.

"My wife signed the book, too," I said. "Why don't you interview her?"

There was a pause during which neither looked at the other. Though they might have been thinking the same thought. Dempsey stared fixedly at me. Wolpert pushed his pen across the surface of a notepad with a forefinger. I lived in that interval when, creeping through the jungle, the soldier realizes he's tripped a wire, but the mine hasn't yet exploded. By some unspoken agreement between them, Wolpert was the one to speak.

"As a matter of fact, we already did. We interviewed your wife yesterday," he said.

They allowed several beats to pass in order to allow my brain to fully absorb this. It didn't.

"You didn't know that?" Dempsey asked.

For the first time in the interview, I had the feeling that it might be dangerous to admit that I didn't know something. Or that I did. Or to say pretty much anything at all.

"No. I didn't know that."

"She didn't mention it at dinner last night?" Wolpert asked, with the delicacy of an outsider looking in, with the politeness of a stranger inquiring about a long-sick family member. He might have been the fire chief asking, ever so kindly, taking into consideration that my home had burned to the ground, if there was any chance I might have forgotten to turn the stove off.

"Strange, though. Don't you think, Doctor?" he asked in a conversational way.

I started to see how they worked. They were pretty good, the two of them. I hadn't been paying attention before; I hadn't thought to notice that they were working. They were working me. I suddenly realized that I had a lot of catching up to do. They knew a lot about something, and I didn't know what was at stake.

"Your wife's interrogated by the police," he suggested quite gently, "and she doesn't mention it to you?"

"You interrogated her?"

"It's just a word."

"Why? Why would you interrogate Abby?"

"Because she knew him." He waited: one beat. Then he asked, "You both did, right?"

"We were in a car accident. This was a while ago—a year ago. A drunk went through a red light and broadsided us. My wife was trapped in the passenger seat. Our little boy was killed. She must have told you this already."

They didn't respond. They didn't look down or away to afford the teller a modicum of privacy in the telling of his tragedy. They were experienced interrogators and they weren't going to let kindness slow them down. They stared at me unblinking, not skeptical, not sympathetic, not cynical. Merely and only listening.

"Anyway, Lou—"

" 'Lou'?" Dempsey interrupted. There was an edge to her tone she hadn't used before.

"Yes. Lou came along at that moment."

"You called him 'Lou'? That's what you called him?"

"Yes. That's his name."

"Only," Detective Wolpert put in, almost apologetically, "you said you didn't know him."

"I felt like I did."

Wolpert's expression indicated he understood that the reality of feelings could transcend facts. He nodded to invite further disclosure. I didn't see any harm in it.

"He pulled my wife out of the car wreck. She probably told you. We lost our son. That . . ." It was impossible to explain in a couple of sentences and I didn't want to go on more than that. To keep it simple, I said, "It creates a bond."

"A bond?"

"Yes."

"What was it?" Dempsey asked sarcastically. "A guy thing? He pulls your wife out of a car wreck and you're blood brothers for life?"

I let a couple of seconds pass so that they could be sure that what I said wasn't some impulsive emotional reaction.

"Look," I told Dempsey. "I'm willing to help you. More than willing. But I'm not here to take abuse."

"You can't take a bit of tough talk?" she said.

"I can take it. I don't want to."

She pursed her lips and shrugged, as if the question she'd asked was of no great importance one way or the other.

"We appreciate your help, Doctor. We're not here to abuse you or to keep you from going about your business. You're free to leave any time you want."

I should have got up and left right there, at that instant. But I was curious. There was more to it. Abby hadn't told me last night that she'd been interviewed. They'd hooked me. There had been several baited hooks that they'd dangled before me, but that was the one I'd gone for. And when I'd bitten, they'd leaned back and pulled on the line. And they'd made sure the hook had sunk deep.

I didn't get up. I missed a beat.

Wolpert didn't. "So he was more than just an officer doing his duty?" he asked. "He was more than that to you?"

"When your child dies . . . ," I began.

His question distracted me from deciding whether to leave. And the fact that I didn't get up, tell them, "Screw you," and walk out, made them all the more hungry to hear what I had to say. A guilty person has an almost irresistible urge to confess. He's drawn to police interrogation like a moth to the flame. Cops know this. Who better than a cop can appreciate the guilty person's crime? It stands to reason. That's what the second rule of murder is all about.

"When your child dies," I was saying, speaking in a way that I sensed was totally irrelevant to the real matter at hand, "anyone connected with that event takes on a particular importance."

"And Lieutenant Francone was important to you?" Wolpert asked.

"Lou was the person who saved my wife's life."

"His name was Louis Francone," Dempsey said, correcting me harshly. "To you, he was Lieutenant Francone."

"Look," I told her. "I came of my own free will to help you out. I didn't think I had anything to say that would be particularly useful in your investigation, but I came anyway. So I don't see why you're treating me with this hostile attitude. Unless there's something I'm missing?"

Their breathing changed. They both shifted positions in their seats as though we'd come to a critical point.

This felt ominous, but I didn't see what the danger was. I'd been honest. I'd said what I was thinking. I didn't think I was bluffing. You don't bluff if you have nothing to hide. I couldn't think what had alerted them.

They looked from one to the other and concurred on some

point that was hidden from me, and I sensed that they also agreed that Detective Dempsey would take the lead from here.

She was going to take her time. She was waiting for the moment to come to her, as though preparing to seize the opportunity from some imaginary conveyor belt. In the interval, she made a play at being relaxed, shrugging and stretching her neck. She glanced up at me in the middle of one of these exercises with a look of amusement. She chuckled softly, shaking her head, in disbelief, it might have been.

"You know what, Doc?"

"No, I don't."

"You're something."

"I don't know what you're talking about," I told her, and she turned to Wolpert as if my answer were a demonstration of exactly what she'd just said.

"You are really something!"

I was annoyed by their behavior. To my way of thinking, as a professional interviewer, there was a lack of seriousness in the way they were going about their business. I thought they were abusing my goodwill. I thought they were amusing themselves at my expense. It was time to wrap it up, I thought.

Perhaps they sensed that I'd had enough. Wolpert said, "Do you mind telling us where you were last Tuesday?"

"Well, I think . . ."

I paused as though to call the day to mind. I was calculating furiously—work I ought to have done before I even walked into their interrogation room. Tuesday had to have been the day when Lou Francone was killed. They were tying me into the murder. At least, they suspected I was a witness of some kind. Or a potential alibi.

A second passed without an answer. They stared at me implacably, without expression, though I knew that they must have been feeling some sense of triumph as each second passed. If their subject had to compose an answer, he had something to hide.

"It's hard to say, right off the bat."

They waited stealthily. They said nothing.

They knew I was stalling. But what I had to consider was whether I ought to take Abby's advice. Somehow, for reasons I dimly perceived as no more than dark, looming shapes, her alibi seemed like a good idea. She had been here, perhaps in this same room. They would have asked her the same question. I felt I should back her up—for her sake. Then again, I wasn't sure whether the alibi was for her sake, or for mine.

"Yes," I said with more certainty, as though the actual memory gave conviction. "As a matter of fact, I was at the hospital during the morning; then my wife and I went for a walk. We had some things we had to discuss. We walked along by the Charles."

"You're sticking with that?"

"Of course. Why wouldn't I?"

"I don't know. Why wouldn't you?"

"It's the truth. I'm sure my wife already told you."

"How would you know that, if you didn't know that she'd talked to us?"

"I don't know what she told you. All I know is where I was the afternoon Lou—Lieutenant Francone—was killed."

"I don't think anyone said anything about Tuesday being the day he was murdered."

"You didn't have to."

"That's your connection, though. That's the connection you made."

"But that's why you asked me where I was, wasn't it? To establish where I was the afternoon he was killed?"

"Is that what you and your wife agreed you'd say?" Dempsey cut in.

She wasn't expecting me to break down and deliver a confession. It was the kind of question you fire off to see how someone reacts in the quarter-second before they bring consciousness to bear on it: a flinch, evasive eye movements, inspiration with lip movements preparatory to speech which is censored.

"No," I replied. I kept it simple. No explanation. No outrage. No reasoned response as to why it would have been foolish for us to concoct an alibi. No dueling eye contact, each daring the other to cede victory by looking away, a test of truth.

"Did she tell you the rest of it?" Dempsey asked. She put a nasty twist into the question. She was trying to provoke me, but she was overplaying it.

"I don't know what you're talking about."

"You really don't know?"

"No."

"You don't know much, do you, Doctor?"

Wolpert, the softer touch, took up the theme. "Did she mention Lieutenant Francone stopped her for a speeding ticket?" he asked.

"Yes, she did, as a matter of fact."

He nodded, as if this was the point. "Okay," he said. "Good."

"So what?" I looked from one to the other. "What is it you want me to say?"

"I don't know, Doc," Dempsey said. There was sadness in her voice. A sense of resignation that all things, eventually, end up at this point. It was out of character with the toughness she'd shown up to that moment. Maybe it was an illusion fostered by the room's acoustics. "What do you want to tell us?"

"I don't have anything to tell you. What's going on? What's happening here?"

"Tell me," Dempsey asked, almost whispering. There was a tone of intimacy, almost of sensuousness. She leaned forward and looked down and away so that her ear was closest to me.

"I don't get it," I said. I sat back in my chair, breaking the mood she was trying to impose on our exchange, pushing physically further away from her. "Fill in the blanks for me."

Dempsey sat back with a snort. She let her head hang back so that she addressed the ceiling. "Shit—you are good!" She tilted back so that she was eye to eye with me again, staring along her nose, shaking her head in disbelief. "Doc, I've got to hand it to you: You are a piece of work!"

"Your wife didn't tell you what happened after Lieutenant Francone gave her the speeding ticket?" Wolpert inquired.

"The premium on the car insurance went up."

They looked at me pityingly.

"You didn't know," Wolpert began apologetically, "that after that encounter they started seeing one another?"

"Seeing each other, as in having an affair," Dempsey clarified. She was watching very carefully for my reaction.

I didn't have one. I couldn't get up to leave. I couldn't rise out of the featherlight aluminum chair. I was paralyzed. I was burning. I felt I'd been sitting through the entire interrogation doused in gasoline without knowing it. The stink of it had been in my nostrils the whole time, but I hadn't noticed. Then Dempsey had tossed the match. The flame enveloped me. I couldn't see beyond the blinding light of emotion that consumed me. They were shadows beyond the dancing flames.

One of them had asked me a question. I didn't know what was asked. The words were mumbo jumbo. But other things were falling into place. The jigsaw puzzle of the last two months had been tossed, like confetti, into the air, and now it landed with every piece in place. I thought of the day I'd turned up at the agency to take her out to lunch.

I let out a deep long sigh.

"So, what do you say, Doctor?" Wolpert asked.

"We're talking about Lou Francone," Dempsey prompted. "Lou. Remember? The guy you had the special bond with? The cop who was murdered? The man who was fucking your wife?"

nineteen

It wasn't until I was standing on the steps of the police barracks, looking around in a dazed way for my car, that things started to make sense. The process began slowly, one connection at a time, until the implications cascaded through my mind. Once it started, a veritable rock slide swept away everything in its path, everything I had taken for granted.

But it was a rock slide that ran in reverse, uphill and backward through time. When I had turned up at the agency on the spur of the moment to take Abby out to lunch, she'd been with the cop. I didn't know what to call him anymore. Dempsey was right: It was ridiculous for me to use his first name. Her sarcasm about the bond between us had been on the mark, too. What crap I'd talked! And I had said that only twenty minutes ago. Twenty minutes ago I had been blind.

Now I saw that all sorts of small incidents in my life with Abby, which before had seemed nothing more than details scattered at random, formed a pattern. Her little white lies, apparently casually tossed off for the sake of expediency, now revealed a deeper deception. Her secretiveness about the speeding ticket, for example. Surely that was something she would, in the normal course of our lives, have mentioned at supper. Why not? It wasn't that we had all that much news to discuss, apart from our work. But she hadn't said anything about it. Because? Because she'd already agreed to a date with Francone. He could have let her go with a warning, but he'd been the picture of rectitude: He'd handed her a hundred-dollar ticket and asked for a date.

All this time, Abby had maintained a subterranean life. Others had known, while I had continued on my way, oblivious. My ignorance on that score, my being the dupe, was a minor humiliation that somehow added torque to the sense of betrayal out of all proportion to its real capacity to wound. I wondered if Nan, the receptionist at her agency, had been in on it when I'd turned up to take Abby out to lunch. Maybe Nan covered for her all the time. The retroscope is an exquisite instrument of torture, and I was its prisoner.

These conjectures ricocheted around my head as I walked like a zombie across the parking lot in the humid summer evening. It was getting dark. The interrogation had gone on longer than I'd realized. I should have walked out. I should have had a lawyer. If I'd been involved in any way with Lou Francone, I would have refused to talk to them without a lawyer. It was too late for that, too.

I drove home on autopilot, one moment replaying the interview with the detectives, the next immersed in the implications that flowed from the revelation of Abby's affair. I flipped back and forth between thinking and feeling. One moment I gamed the moves in the interview or calculated the time line of where Abby was when, the next I was overwhelmed with rage and sadness. At one point the urge to vomit rose in me so suddenly that I had to pull the car over onto the road's sandy edge. I threw open the door and leaned out into the gathering dusk with only the chest strap of the seat belt supporting me as I gave way to spasms of dry retching. Then came inchoate tears and sobs like gasps that took possession of me and stopped all thought.

Afterward I felt relieved and drove on. It was good to drive. I chose back roads and stayed within the speed limit. Beneath all my thoughts ran the bitterness of betrayal like a toxic slime that broached the surface as soon as I began the slightest digging.

Affairs happen, of course. You don't own someone. A relationship can't satisfy all a person's needs. And a sexual fling doesn't destroy a marriage, unless the relationship's already in trouble. This way of thinking didn't help me. Abby's affair hurt deeply because I didn't think it was about sex, or even romance. In hooking up with Francone, the older man, the rescuer, Abby was searching for restitution. It was an impossible quest—the urge to make things right, to undo an event that has occurred, to fill the hole that had been Adrian. No one could really have given her what she sought. But in turning to another man for consolation, in turning away from me, I felt far more deeply betrayed than if she had chosen him for sex, however consuming, however passionate.

I steered through the curves of the darkening back roads. I drove more carelessly now, as I realized I was approaching home and Abby herself. I circled the house twice, taking the road that ran along the back shore, driving with the windows down so that I could inhale the smell of the sea. It was low tide, and the air came in with the slightly fetid scent of decomposing seaweed. Even after all the loops and detours, I was afraid of my anger. As I got closer to our house, I veered away down a side street. The nausea returned, and on my second pass, I stopped the car by the ocean and stepped out. The moon was hidden behind high clouds, and in the darkness I made out the waves breaking on the rocks by sound as much as the phosphorescence of their foam. I breathed deeply the aroma of decay and tried to be rational about the coming encounter.

For the last hour, I'd done nothing but think about Abby. Or rather, different Abbys. Abbys with alternative motivations and degrees of deception. But now I was going to come face-to-face with the real one, whomever she might be. Francone had been killed, and the detectives who'd just leveled me were looking for someone with a compelling motive.

Abby was making supper. "I stopped by the store on my way home," she explained.

"I entirely forgot," I said.

"It's okay," she said brightly. "It was on the way."

She chattered nervously about things that didn't matter. I didn't ask her how she knew I'd be late. How she knew, on her way home, that I'd forget it was my night to cook. I didn't know where to start. Each entry point to the real conversation seemed dismal.

"They had this great halibut on special," she said. "So I scooped some up for us."

It was a relief to fall into the comfortable routine of small talk. The irony was that we hadn't been able to have a lighthearted conversation in months.

"What did you do with it?" I asked.

"Oh, nothing much. I chopped up a little basil, a shake of parmesan, and then I sprinkled some bread crumbs over it. Oh, and lots of fresh ground pepper."

All the time she'd been talking she'd been busying herself, head down, with checking on the fish in the oven and slicing tomatoes for a salad. Now she looked up. She was smiling nervously and she had the big kitchen knife in her hand, point up. She noticed this and self-consciously lowered it to the cutting board.

We made eye contact for a long second. Neither of us could hold the gaze. We both looked away at the same time. But silence held its own dangers. Though we'd spent months with long stretches of the evening unbroken by speech, silence between us now was intolerable. If eye contact was blinding, silence was darkness. It held an intensity of its own.

"In the fish store, they were talking about the fishing restrictions," she said.

Abby is a rapid-fire prep-chef who can slice and dice so fast the knife on the cutting board sounds like a machine gun, but tonight she deliberately cut the spring onions one at a time. I looked around for the newspaper to give me cover, but it wasn't to be seen. I could hardly bear the reality of her physical presence.

"If they catch too much of cod, say, they have to put it back in the ocean. And of course, after it's been up on the deck of the boat, waiting to be sorted . . ."

It doesn't matter what you talk about. All topics lead to The Topic. All thoughts fall inward toward the central hole in your mind that drops you down into the abyss of your darkest emotions. Words are like pinballs; however energized they may appear by their collisions, they are wending their way down, and they will eventually, inevitably, drop through that hole at the bottom.

I thought of the majestic cod, almost as big as a man, flopping about on the deck of a dragger. I wondered how long Francone had taken to die, whether he'd seized and flopped around on the bed before expiring. Abby, I realized for the first time, was bereaved. Hence the widow's tears at his wake. How many people recognized those tears for what they were? All those state cops standing around, shooting the breeze, not missing a trick. And it was hard to explain my presence, too.

"So they throw them back and they die," I said.

"Yes," she said, relieved I had completed the thought.

"Do you want some wine?"

I wanted to keep a clear head, but it was part of our evening ritual, a glass of wine while one of us cooked, and I felt the need to keep to the routine. I got glasses from the cabinet and the bottle of white wine from the refrigerator. When I had the bottle in my hand, an Alsacer that I'd opened for dinner the night before, I felt a sense of bewilderment at this continuity, that something so trivial as a bottle of wine should remain the same while the entire world about it had been transformed. I tasted it, half expecting it to have soured, and was momentarily soothed by the fragrance of grapes.

Abby was still chopping the spring onions. The process was deliberate, precise, interminable. As I looked at her, I had a feeling of unreality, of the familiar made alien. I didn't know who she was. For several horrifying moments she was—literally—a stranger I didn't recognize. I felt myself disappearing, too. I sipped the wine and made myself concentrate on the faint, musky perfume that lay upon its acidity.

Abby was talking, talking, Scheherazade-style. If she stopped talking, we'd have to confront the truth. I felt the need for truth growing inside me, pressing for release like a baby whose time has come to be born. Abby was telling me about Ellen, whom she'd seen in the fish store, someone she played tennis with whom I'd never met. It was a complicated story about Ellen's car breaking down on the highway and someone coming to fetch her, and a misunderstanding, so that she was stranded for several hours. I soon lost track and didn't notice that it had come to a conclusion.

I felt I should say something. I had to make it up. "I don't understand why her husband didn't simply come and get her," I suggested.

"Well, she's . . ." Again the difficulty with putting a name to reality. "Alone."

"Alone, like divorced?"

"Yes. Divorced."

"What's wrong with that?"

"I don't think there's anything wrong with it. It's just that . . ."

Instead of lifting the board and whisking the chopped onions with the edge of the knife into the salad bowl all in one go, Abby stretched out the operation by using cupped hands to scoop them up, missing some, going back for the remainder, and finally picking up those fragments left behind one by one off the board. In the meantime, all conversation was suspended.

"What?" I asked impatiently.

"I mean, it's just the way it is." And then she added, as a hurried afterthought. "For some people."

"Just one of those things?"

The tone of my voice made her look up. "For Ellen," she said.

"Not for us?"

I wouldn't let her look away. She wouldn't answer my question.

"We have to talk, Abby."

"No, we don't."

"We've both been talking to the police, but we don't have anything to say to each other?"

"I don't think we should."

"How are we going to live together if we don't talk about what's been going on?"

"It's over."

"Apparently."

"I certainly don't think we should talk about that."

"About—what are we going to call him? There should be an acronym for what he is. Sorry—was. Detective Dempsey had a choice phrase."

"My lawyer said we shouldn't discuss it."

"Your lawyer?"

"Yes."

"How did we get to here so fast? Or maybe we didn't. Maybe

I'm just catching up with the rest of you—you, Francone, the cops. I'm the last to know. The husband. This is what it feels like to be a cliché."

"I'm sorry, Paul, I really am."

She really was. To the extent that I could see through my own tears, her eyes glistened. The forward lean of her posture told me she wanted to come to me. I wanted to take her in my arms and in the tight clasp of an embrace and the intoxication of the moment reverse time, undo betrayal, affirm love. But tears are fungible. I recalled the tears—the heartfelt, contrite tears—of a hundred just-indicted murderers. Everyone's sorry once they get caught.

"I'm sorry, too," I said, meaning it.

The idea that she'd been with another man was still too raw for me to go any further. The wound would have to be probed, but that could wait till tomorrow. Next week.

"I had to protect myself," Abby was explaining.

"But, a lawyer. It really wasn't necessary to get a lawyer." I gestured to include the kitchen, the entirety of the structure around us. "The house is yours," I told her. "I'd never dispute that."

"He's not a divorce lawyer, Paul." She waited a moment to let this sink in, looking at me with a puzzled frown. "He came with me yesterday, when the police wanted to talk to me."

"But why did you need a lawyer?" I asked her.

"I told you."

"To protect yourself."

"Yes."

"From what?"

She sighed, exasperated. "From anything that could have come out that would be . . ." She made a waving gesture of word-finding, the empty-handed gesture of the frustration of coming up empty. "They twist things. They have a way of asking questions—you know. They can make things seem the way they weren't."

"What were they trying to do?"

She was a long time in responding. She'd given up on chopping a piece of celery some time ago and had put the knife down. She now stood with both hands on the counter, arms straight, bracing her shoulders in a tight, hunched position, neck flaccid, head down. I had the impression of her sinking into something, of her tense, braced body holding the place but her spirit sagging and her mind falling into a dark region.

I'd assumed that the detectives had interviewed Abby because they thought she might have information as a witness. It never occurred to me that she could be a suspect. I considered her as she stood hunched over the cutting board. The anger came over me in waves, and I think that's why I was so open to imagining her as a possible killer. So much of her life recently had been hidden from me that I couldn't be sure that I knew what Abby was capable of.

Could Abby have killed a man? Was murder within her range? I didn't know. You never know, in advance. In any movie-theater audience, only a handful of people are capable of murder, but the killers who passed through Sanders came from all walks of life, all classes of people. There weren't any features that distinguished the murderers from the rest of the patients. No mark of Cain on the forehead. They were ordinary, mostly, except for that one thing: They'd taken life.

"It was over, you know," she said with her head still hanging down. "That's what I was trying to tell you."

"When?"

"The other night. Before . . . Before he was killed." She looked up and I saw for the first time that her face was contorted with the effort of holding back her anguish. "I was trying to tell you that this thing was over now. It was over!"

She said this last sentence with great emphasis, and I didn't understand why. I was still caught up on the idea that I hadn't noticed, in the wasteland of our silences, that she had been trying to communicate something vitally important to me, something marriage-saving. I was amazed I could have missed even a partial, garbled, stifled confession.

"What did you say, to tell me?" I asked.

"It was hard to begin. Oh, God, I tried so hard to tell you!" She looked up at me and there was a fervent look in her eyes as if it was crucial that I believe her when she said how hard she'd tried. "I talked it over with my therapist. We rehearsed it. But when the moment came, I couldn't hurt you."

"So you never got started?"

"No." She hung her head in something I suspected was shame. She whispered, "I'm so sorry!"

The familiar, customary urge to comfort her was overcome by a cold anger at her betrayal. With the scanty goodwill I could summon, the best I could manage was a halfhearted, "Well, it probably wouldn't have made any difference."

She gave a bitter little laugh. "You know that isn't true."

"If I'd known before Francone died? It wouldn't have changed anything."

She nodded, evasive, as if agreeing with the party line. "Sure," she said. "Look, I'm just going to say this once, so you know, then we won't talk about it anymore: I'll do everything I can to help you."

This seemed important to her, but I couldn't see how it would matter to me. We seemed to be conducting two separate conversations, almost touching at some points, but each running parallel to the other. I didn't understand what she was offering me.

"Like what?" I asked.

"Anything."

There was something wrong here. I didn't understand the change in tone. All of a sudden, Abby was collected, self-possessed. She looked me full in the eye with a steely expression, communicating—not guilt, contrition, a desire to make amends—but her resolve.

"Anything," she said with unexpected fierceness. "Because, whatever's happened, I do love you, Paul." One look told her this avowal wasn't having the intended impact on me. "You don't have to believe that now. Right now, all you have to know is that I'll do anything to help you. Anything."

With a shock, I understood. Abby believed I'd killed Francone. She thought that if I'd known the affair was over I wouldn't have done it. She was convinced that if she'd spoken up, Francone would still be alive and I wouldn't now be the prime suspect in his murder. She owed me. She would lie for me. She would hold to the alibi.

"I didn't do it," I said. "If that's what you're thinking."

She held up her hands, like a cop blocking traffic, to stop me from saying more. "Of course not," she said.

I started to say more. The longer the denial, the more suspect it is. But now I understood the desire to exonerate; it's compulsive, like the urge to confess.

"Of course you didn't. But we're both suspects. You know that, don't you? They're treating us gently now. But that'll change as soon as some hard evidence turns up."

"But it won't. Will it?"

She sighed in exasperation. "It won't work, Paul."

"What won't?"

"Acting dumb won't cut it with these guys."

"The reason I don't get it, the reason I'm not up to speed, is because I haven't done anything wrong."

"Give me the gun."

"I don't have it."

"Give it to me!" She was angry and determined and very focused. "I'll get rid of it for you."

This was a new Abby, with new capabilities. One of them an ability to dispose of a murder weapon.

"I don't have it," I told her.

"Give it to me anyway," she insisted.

I thought of the things sociopaths say on those occasions when, for pragmatic reasons, it suits them to tell the truth. I heard myself say, "Honestly, I don't have it."

"It's gone, then? Really gone for good somewhere?"

"I don't know."

"Oh, sweet Jesus!"

"I already reported it missing to the police."

"So we can assume that it's not going to turn up out of the blue. Good." She had a new, take-charge attitude. "We have to get our story straight."

"I don't have a story."

"Don't be naive. Of course you have a story. You were walking by the Charles. We were both walking along the Charles. We were together. From three o'clock. Then we went home in separate vehicles. You arrived home first. So you know the time I arrived home: six o'clock. That puts us both out of the danger zone."

"What are you worried about?"

"We're both suspects, Paul."

"Why would they suspect you?"

She was less than fluent and started slowly. "You know how they think," she said. But she recovered quickly, and I knew that with each repetition she'd be more and more compelling. "Anyone's a suspect who's been with the victim." She tossed off the reasons like a shopping list. "Because it ended. A crime of passion. The irrational woman. The lovers' fight. Anything's a motive." She hesitated, considering whether to tell me more. "Because a witness placed me there."

Of course she was recognized. She was a regular. As it had become routine, she'd gotten comfortable, she'd dropped the simple precautions. But then, what did she need to hide in going to Francone's place? Nothing from anyone, except me.

"The old lady who lives in the apartment downstairs. We'd had words before. She'd been upset about me parking in her space, so she'd written down my license plate. She saw me arrive. The problem is that she didn't see me leave."

"So you were there that afternoon."

She looked me in the eye. "Yes. I was."

"But, I mean, you were there right before he was murdered."

"Half an hour. Fifteen minutes."

"Pretty close."

"I guess it was. I left, and then—whoever—came in. He must have thought—Lou must have thought—it was me coming back for something I'd forgotten."

"That's why you need the alibi."

"I don't need it any more than you do!" She challenged me with her gaze. "If you want, we can go together and tell Detective Dempsey we made a mistake. We weren't together at all. We were driving around aimlessly, each one of us alone. But, what the heck, what have we got to hide?" She paused to see how I was reacting to her threat. "Look," she said, in a conciliatory tone, "it just makes things simpler, that's all. Otherwise . . ."

"Was it for you?" I asked. "The alibi?"

"For God's sake, Paul!"

"Just tell me yes or no."

She searched my eyes for the motivation for asking her this question, a faint smile of incredulity on her lips. It was the kind of expression you have when you know someone's faking it but you don't want to call him on it. I searched her face, too, but I didn't feel that I'd be able to tell whether she was telling the truth or not. I'd lost confidence in my intuition where Abby was concerned.

"Of course not." She sighed. "It was always for you."

The fact that each of us grasped hard at the lie of the alibi, was willing to elaborate and rehearse it, only confirmed our suspicions of one another. I ate supper with the woman I thought had killed her lover. Abby dined with the man she thought had killed her lover. We picked at our food and rearranged fragments of the meal around the plates to make it look like we were eating while we made trite, bizarre conversation, until I couldn't stand it anymore. I started to tell Abby that we should ditch the alibi and go to the police and lay it out, two separate accounts of where we'd been and what we'd done, and get a fresh start, but Abby told me not to tell her anything—she begged me—and ran from the room with her hands over her ears.

twenty

We watched the news on different channels on different TVs at opposite ends of our vast house. Francone's murder wasn't top of the news—the story was still too sketchy—but it was the second item on the program. There had been 'developments,' the reporter said, but the police were reluctant to say what these were, only that no arrest was imminent at this point in time. The newspapers the next morning were less reticent. I avoided them, but there was no escape. I was named as someone interviewed by police "in connection" with the fatal shooting of the state police officer.

Kovacs found a way to have a private word with me about my new notoriety. As if by accident, he happened to pass through the rear trap a little ahead of me, and he paused to hold the heavy steel door until I had caught up with him. From there it was natural for us to walk together to Admissions, and because the open space was almost deserted, it was as close as one came at Sanders to a private conversation.

"I wish you the best, Doc," he said. "We all do."

There was a gruff formality about the pronouncement that

made it sound like one of those ritual condolences that you say at funerals to family members of the deceased you don't know.

"Thanks," I said. I thought that indictments among the officers must have arisen often enough for there to be a need for such a formulaic form of speech to mark the occasion.

Now, beyond the formula, came the need for specifics, and Kovacs seemed embarrassed. He glanced behind to see if anyone might be within hearing distance.

"Look. If things don't go your way. They will. I'm not saying they won't. I have every confidence . . ." In his emotion, he seemed unable to remember how the cliché ended.

"I know," I said. I felt more concern on his behalf at that moment than I did for myself. There were times when I was numbed by what I took to be the absurdity of my situation. I didn't believe that this was the kind of thing that could happen to me. "I appreciate the thought," I told him.

"What I'm saying, Doc, is: If things don't go your way, there are worse places."

"I'm not sure . . ."

"I'm not saying you did it."

"I didn't."

"I know that."

"I haven't done anything."

"I know. But just in case. A word of advice."

"Sure."

He cleared his throat. "Don't be proud, Doc." He stared earnestly into my eyes. "Take the insanity plea. Then, when you get here, the guys will watch your back."

"It's not something I'd considered."

I choked down mad laughter that gathered in the back of my head. I felt myself losing contact with reality. At the same time, part of my brain ticked off the factors in my case that could be used to support an insanity defense.

But I came back to the serious expression on Kovacs's face. He was compromising himself in saying what he was telling me now; the moral abyss between correctional officer and inmate was the difference between the angels and Satan, and here he was offering to span that gap if it came down to it. It was a promise of great kindness that he was holding out to me. A mercy. This was a favor that I hadn't ever realized I'd earned, and now, in the correctional scheme of things, it was about to be paid back to me.

"I'll keep it in mind," I said.

A smile escaped me and it seemed to warm Kovacs and ease his formal stance.

"Jeez, Doc," he confided with a wolfish grin, "if anyone can pull off an insanity plea, you can."

He was going to say more. His lips opened slightly, and we both had a sense of the kind of thing it would be. He'd been about to take the scenario further, and I had the manic idea that he'd been on the brink of offering me, in my next incarnation, a plumb job—clearing tables, maybe, in the staff cafeteria. He looked down and away. It was a farewell of sorts. I thought of a father saying good-bye to a son who's about to enter the priesthood: The person he once was will disappear forever and be replaced by this other who cannot be spoken to in the same way, a new man who is both familiar and distant. Someone to be wondered at in stolen glances.

"Thank you," I told him.

I was touched. Truly. And in that moment of gratitude, I realized how lonely I had become.

Rounds were in full swing in the staff room at Admissions, but as I entered, a momentary silence fell, like a break in the sound-track of a movie. Maria Baldini, the unit director, got the process rolling again, but the clinicians were distracted and the energy had gone out of the room. I glimpsed their eyes on me, as if there might be some aspect of my predicament made visible on my face. I was undergoing a transformation: Before their very eyes, like a butterfly emerging from a cocoon, I was becoming a felon.

I interviewed the new admissions and then went to my office and called Brenda Gorn. I wasn't thinking of her as the assistant DA. I was thinking of her as I always do, as a lawyer on my side who'd give advice; if she didn't know the answer, she'd make a referral to someone she knew could be trusted.

I called a couple of times and got her administrative assistant. She was unavailable. It wasn't unusual. Brenda was busy. But the assistant didn't say she was in court or in a meeting, just unavailable. The third time, Brenda herself interrupted as the assistant said she'd be out for the rest of the day.

"Paul," she said, "I can't talk to you."

"It's that bad?"

"I shouldn't even be telling you I can't talk to you."

"Are you still on the case?"

"No. I had to recuse myself. I transferred it to another attorney."

"Not because of me?"

"Because of a potential conflict of interest. Let's leave it at that."

"If you're off the case now—"

"Don't even think about it."

"Brenda, I'm not asking for the crown jewels. There have been plenty of times when there's been give and take, off the record."

"This is a whole new ball game. Paul, you have to realize, we're on different sides of the fence. The old rules don't apply." She was choosing her words with extraordinary care. "We're still friends. But this is strictly professional. Until . . . you sort this out, I'm on this side, and you're on the other side."

She made it sound like I'd passed over into the spirit world. I'd become a ghost: sentient, observing, but unable to impinge on the realities of the world inhabited by human beings. Cut off from my friends, the living. I felt like I was going to disappear. Brenda was about to hang up, but there was something I needed, even if she didn't really want to give it to me. When you're hanging by your fingernails, you have no pride.

"What was the caliber of the gun?" I asked.

"You can't ask me that," she said.

But there had been the slightest hesitation, which told me that Brenda was withholding the answer reluctantly.

"Just this one thing," I pressed her. "That's all I want."

"They monitor these lines, you know."

Which let me know she'd tell me if I hung on. "What was it?"

I heard her sigh. I was sorry to put her in this position, but the regret lasted only a moment. When you're desperate, you're willing to override other people's feelings. There's a little bit of the sociopath in all of us, and under the right circumstances he comes out.

She whispered so low I almost didn't hear her: "A twenty-five."

It didn't have to be my gun. A thousand people in the greater Boston area owned .25-caliber handguns. Three hundred, at least. I felt a sinking sensation in the pit of my stomach.

"I'm sorry," she said. When I didn't say anything, she told me quietly, "Get a lawyer, Paul."

People who carried guns in their line of work—on both sides of the law—mostly went with 9 millimeters or .38s, but there were plenty of .25s in circulation. They weren't rare, but they weren't common. However I worked to convince myself, I knew, with a sense of the truth as persistent as the pull of gravity, that the gun that killed Lou Francone was my gun. The gun disappeared and the cop ended up dead: There was no getting away from it. And if that was the case, I'd entered the zone of nothing to lose.

I was sitting at my desk, putting this together in my head, look-ing for a way out, when the phone rang.

"All this stuff in the newspaper," Natalie said, slightly breathless. "I just wanted to call you and tell you that—I don't know—that I believe in you. And to give you support."

"Thank you," I said. I was glad to hear a friendly voice.

"Whatever you—whatever they say you did, I'm sure you didn't. And even if you did—is it okay if I say this?"

"Sure," I said. "What the hell."

"Even if you did, I'm sure you did it for a good reason."

My fate hung by two slim threads: a shaky alibi and a missing gun. Everybody wanted the gun. Even Abby asked me for it. If the police got their hands on it, if ballistics showed a match with the slug from Francone's body, I was cooked. If the gun turned up, I was going to jail for the rest of my natural life. Or maybe, in the least bad of all possible worlds, I'd end up at Sanders, a forensic curiosity, busing tables under the watchful eye of Lieutenant Ko-vacs. In an ironic twist, I reflected that the surveillance tape from the shopping mall, with me rushing like some crazy berserker after Craig, would play to my advantage if I went for an insanity plea. And if one of us had to go to prison, it was better me than Abby. Not that it looked like I would have much choice in the matter. But by this point I was pretty sure she'd shot Francone. Her adamant insistence on the alibi, her evasions, her preparedness in getting a lawyer, her anticipation of the questions the police would ask, all pointed to her. I prayed she'd done a thorough job getting rid of the gun. If the gun stayed lost, there was a good chance neither of us would have to do time.

There was a knock on my door. For security purposes, every office door at Sanders has a window, and I expected to see the face of the person who wanted to speak to me, but this person stayed to one side, out of view.

"Come in," I called.

The door opened promptly and Detective Wolpert took me at my word.

"I happened to be in the neighborhood," he said.

Sanders was a state institution, and I supposed he had a right to be there.

"I told you everything I know about Lieutenant Francone," I said. "I don't have anything more to say."

"As a matter of fact, I'm here about another crime."

"What crime is that?"

"Larceny of a handgun. A .25-caliber revolver. Unusual, a gun of that caliber."

"I reported it missing."

"Right. You did. You reported it stolen. But you were kind of slow in reporting it."

"I wanted to make sure it was gone."

"Oh, like you might have misplaced it?"

I hadn't asked him to sit down. He stood over me. It was a dominant posture, but because it placed him in a position where he had only a downward, oblique view of my face, it put him at a disadvantage.

"No. That isn't what I meant."

"Is a handgun the kind of thing you leave lying around?"

"No. It was locked up in a drawer in my desk."

He thought about this, or pretended to. "Was there anything else taken?"

"Not that I know of."

He started to speak, then seemed to hesitate as if checked by sudden puzzlement. "Well, you'd know, wouldn't you?"

"Not necessarily. He could have taken something insignificant. It could have been something I haven't noticed yet. It depends what kind of robbery this was."

"I didn't know there was more than one kind. I thought the only kind of robbery there was is when they steal stuff."

"There are different motives for stealing stuff."

"Why would someone steal your handgun?"

"To set me up."

His eyebrows expressed polite interest. "And this individual who was setting you up, he was doing this because . . ." Ostentatiously, he let the sentence lapse, and his distracted gaze around the office suggested he'd extended himself to his full range of politeness.

The next time I saw Detective Wolpert was when he came to my home with Detective Dempsey and a search warrant. They went through the house from top to bottom. Abby and I waited in the den; then, when they came to search that room, we moved to the kitchen. Outside, I saw officers with flashlights going through the garden with metal detectors. They finished with the house in the early hours of the morning and said they'd be back later to complete their survey of the yard.

We ended up slumped in chairs opposite one another in the library. We were washed out, too full of jangling nerves to go to bed.

"Are you sure they've gone?" Abby asked.

"You think they might have left someone behind?"

"Or some listening device."

"If they have, they can't use it."

"At the trial."

"There isn't going to be a trial," I said. "At least, not for one of us."

"It feels like they're closing in."

"There's nothing to close in on. Is there?"

"You're asking me?" she said.

"Yes, I am."

"You already know the answer."

"I know what you told me," I said.

"That isn't enough?"

"I wish it was. I really do."

"You think I did it?"

"Wolpert came to Sanders today. He just sort of dropped by."

"What did he want?"

"The gun."

"No one knows where the gun is. Isn't that right? It was stolen, and we don't know where it is."

"I told him a stalker took it."

"You think Craig took the gun?"

"No," I said.

"Neither do I," Abby said. "We both know who did it."

"Yes," I agreed. "We both know."

"And as long as we stick together, nothing's going to happen."

"They'll try to break the alibi."

"They can't, as long as we don't let them. We can't waver, Paul. We can't afford to give them an opening."

"No," I said. "I'm on board a hundred percent."

"I know you, though. You get sentimental. You get this urge to tell the truth."

"Not this time."

"It's a luxury we can't afford."

"Truth is a luxury we can't afford," I repeated, as if I was memorizing a new phrase in a foreign language, a phrase that would ease my way through paramilitary roadblocks I might encounter in this troubled land. "I'll keep that in mind."

"I have to be able to count on you, Paul!"

"You can. Completely."

"I can't have you going wishy-washy and philosophical on me. We've got to be practical!"

"You can count on me," I told her. "I'll do anything for you."

"Thank you," she said, with an odd formality.

"I mean it."

"I'm not asking you to do anything. Just keep to the plan."

"Look," I said. "I want you to know this."

I started to draw my chair closer to her. If I was going to have to run the risk of a murder conviction for her, I wanted it explicit. I wanted it out in the open so that at least she'd acknowledge me. I suppose, just as Abby had sought the magical father in her affair with Francone, I was making some fantastic gesture of my own. In extremis, with the world narrowed down to just a couple of issues, viewed with a tunnel vision that admitted no second thoughts, it seemed like a good deal: natural life in exchange for getting my marriage back. But Abby saw something coming and she wanted to put a stop to it before I started.

"No!" she insisted. "No! No crazy shit!"

"Listen," I told her, urgently, whispering. "Give me the gun."

"Stop it!"

"Just give it to me. I'll take it to the police. I'll tell them I did it. You're off the hook."

"What are you talking about?"

"I'll do this for you. Let's end the nightmare. I'll take the rap."

She stared at me speechless, wonderingly, for several moments. She scanned my face as mountaineers do a rock face, searching for handholds, purchase points, any line of approach that would give access. Then she recoiled in horror.

"Oh, God, you are a piece of work!" She brought her knees up into the armchair and crossed her arms over her chest for protection. "You cynical, devious bastard! I'm trying to help you. You killed—it doesn't matter. You know what you did. And I go out on a limb for you! My lawyer told me they could cite me as an accessory to murder. Do you know how many years that is? I did this for you! Because I love you!"

There is a certain comfort in hitting bottom. When you have

nothing left to lose, it's possible to achieve an icy, desperate clarity almost devoid of human need. But it's a hard-won vision. Against all instinct, I pushed aside the bitter sense of betrayal that she had brought me to. I struggled to see her clearly, now, in the present, without rancor. I've never made a greater emotional effort. It was like pushing against a massive, heavy door, at the very limits of my strength. I tried to focus all my experience of liars, all my clinical acumen, on the expression of horror and outrage on Abby's face. I had drawn blood from her. Her emotion had the sincerity of blood.

At the very instant in which I convinced her beyond a doubt that I was an evil manipulator who had murdered her lover, I saw with equal certainty that Abby didn't have the gun. She'd never had the gun. She hadn't a clue where it was.

twenty—one

The next morning Craig left a message with my answering service: one last session to tie things up. We'd sit across the desk from each other, but now I was the one facing prison. Or the Sanders Institute. It was a prospect that Craig couldn't resist.

I was glad we would meet. I wanted him to come within reach, felt no compunction about using our session to take him on. Therapy was revealed for what it had always been—a war of words. Now we both knew that. Larry Shapiro had told me I was off the case, but this was a session the patient himself had asked for; besides, it didn't matter any more what Larry wanted. None of the rules mattered.

I had thought Craig would gloat over my predicament, but I was underestimating him again. His thinking may have been disturbed around one issue with one person, but Craig was intact in everything else he turned his mind to. More than intact. He had honed the skills of the stalker. He was blind to what made Natalie tick, but he was as acute as any professional I knew in assessing any man who might come between him and the woman he loved. In assessing me.

Craig was far too disciplined to gloat. He was as I remembered him from our first meeting at Sanders: at once self-assured in the way of the world and diffident in the encounter, one-on-one. In other ways, he looked different, as though a phase of his life as an undergraduate had ended. He wore gray worsted slacks and a creamy white shirt open at the neck beneath a blue blazer—the uniform. But the blazer was a sleek, somewhat flashy item from an Italian designer—Gucci, perhaps, or someone with even more cachet. He looked like an emerging playboy.

"It was good of you to fit me in," he said, eyes down.

He'd made a joke for his own benefit that he saw no reason to share with me, no incentive to taunt me with. The joke was for an audience of one, but that was enough for him. I was impressed by his self-sufficiency; at the same time there was something monstrous in the absence of any need for validation from a source outside himself.

"I didn't have a choice," I said.

He sat hunched forward slightly, fingertips touching the edge of the desk, as a blind person might do, reminding himself where he was in relation to this important boundary in the room. When I spoke he looked up suddenly, as if the stark truth had startled him.

"I know." He gave a wry smile, as if to say, sympathetically, "Tough luck." "They made you do it."

"Yes."

The smile he gave me wasn't triumphant. This—making people do things they didn't want to do—was routine. It was part of being a Cavanaugh. He looked at me curiously for a moment, as people do when they're aware that a person's status has changed, like a strapping, strong man who's been diagnosed with cancer, for example, or an incumbent politician who's lost an election. Some power they'd had has begun to leak away. I sensed that in his eyes I wasn't the person I once was. I'd lost the power to harm him. Almost.

"But that's always been the story, hasn't it?" I said. "You got sent to Sanders and you had to meet with me whether you liked it or not. Then the positions were reversed."

"No hard feelings, I hope?" There wasn't a glimmer of irony in his face. He was playing it straight.

"Of course not." I was a good loser. "It goes with the territory."

"I wanted to say I was sorry to read about your recent problems."

"I thought there was only one of them."

"Well, yes. One. One big one."

"You're referring to the dead police officer?"

"Yes."

"The one who was murdered in his apartment."

"That one."

I see dozens of murderers a year. Each time I take my seat behind the battered green desk in Interview Room One and look into the man's face, I believe I ought to see some change there. Whether you like it or not, the act of murder, like the doctor's act of healing, is godlike. Against all reason, I feel you should be able to see some residue of that act in a man's face. And sometimes I do. Many of them are numbed by the enormity of what they've done. Others are overwhelmed by their future, or lack of it. But there are some who, despite their fear, regret, remorse, do feel the godlike glow of what they have done. This is why they break the second rule of murder; why, despite all the practical interests of survival, they can't resist boasting to another human being what they have done. They tell me, many of them. I don't ask, but they tell me anyway.

I've come to recognize a certain smirk; it's fleeting, and half-hidden, only halfheartedly concealed. The smirk says, "I've done The Big One." The person they've killed may have been their best friend or the woman they loved, and they may be looking at a life sentence. But human nature being what it is, they're overtaken by this irresistible flash of pride which emerges as a slight tightening at the corners of the mouth, accompanied by a covert glance, as if my face were a mirror in which they might see some aspect of their glory reflected.

Craig said, "I'm sure you didn't do it, by the way."

I was starting to recognize this form of expression. In social encounters with the potential murderer, apparently, it's considered polite to make a token expression of belief in his innocence. Nothing more than common courtesy. Except in Craig's case, he happened to know that I was innocent. He managed to twist even this social formula by making the remark in a tone that was intended to let me know it was only that—a convention, pro forma, null and void.

It was time to stir things up. So I asked him, "How do you know I didn't do it?"

He opened his mouth to speak, took a breath, blew out his cheeks in a gesture of being flummoxed. "Well," he said, "there are any number of ways."

And of course there were; there were so many ways in which he actually knew that I was innocent. His problem lay in selecting one that wouldn't show that he knew more than he was supposed to know. On my side, I wanted to avoid revealing that I knew he had killed Francone. Although he would suspect my knowledge, I'd maintain the uncertainty for as long as possible, because he wouldn't be satisfied until he knew I knew. I wondered if he'd been able to resist dropping by the garage—one of Craig's chance encounters—where Randall, the former Captain of the Guard, worked. If I was obtuse, if I didn't get it on my own, I was pretty sure he'd tell me, one way or another. And in telling me, he'd tell me something else.

He threw up his hands in a gesture of giving up. "Well, of course, I don't know for sure. But given who you are . . . it's inconceivable." There was a pause to indicate he'd run out of inspiration.

I was scrupulous in avoiding the slightest suggestion of irony. "Thanks for the vote of confidence," I said, my voice neutral, as if that were all there were to say and we would move on.

But Craig couldn't let it go, as I expected. "Either way," he said, "this will be our last session."

" 'Either way'?"

"I meant—I should have thought before I opened my big mouth. I meant, whether you're convicted or not. Sorry."

"I haven't even been indicted."

"No. Of course not."

"I think we ought to assume that I'll continue to be available as your psychiatrist."

"Sure."

"If that's what you want."

"If you're okay with it."

"I'm okay."

"The thing with your wife—the lunch setup—it was stupid. It was a stupid practical joke. And I apologize. I really do."

"It's over," I said.

"And the other thing, when I got the summer internship, I had no idea Abby worked there. Honest."

"I know that."

"You're sure?"

"That's what you're telling me, right? A coincidence."

"That's it. That's all it was."

"And the fact that you knew the state of the office chair in my home, that was a lucky guess."

"Well, not exactly." He let it out slowly—reluctantly it might have been.

I saw the shadow of the killer's smirk. He glanced at me; his eyes flicked over my face seeking to extract one thing only: whether I knew, whether I was sticking it to him. But there was no animosity for him to see. There was nothing much at all to read in my bland expression.

"Since this is our last session . . . ," he began, and let the implication grow.

"You mean . . . ?"

"I am what I am." He raised his hands in a gesture of resignation. "I couldn't help myself. I had to check it out."

"You went into my home?"

"Look, it's over. That's the only reason I'm telling you this."

"How did you get in?"

"Your house?" He scoffed. I had him going. "Your house is easy. You should do something about security, Paul. Especially if Abby's going to be there by herself for a while."

"But how did you get in?"

He waved me off. "Are you kidding? I do this kind of stuff—" He caught himself.

"You do this kind of stuff all the time."

"Your words."

"But this is the last time we'll ever speak to one another, isn't it? Why not tell it like it is?"

"Is that what you really want?" he asked.

"I do."

"Sure? You're sure you know where you're going with this?"

"If I knew where I was going, I wouldn't need to ask questions."

"You don't know what's been happening around you these last few weeks?"

"Tell me."

"No," he said. "You first."

Apparently, we each had a secret to disclose.

"What do you want to know?" I asked.

"You know what it is."

"No, I don't think I do," I lied. It was Natalie, of course. Everything led back to her. He had to know about the embrace. He couldn't leave it alone.

"You're trying to make me say it."

"No. I don't know."

"You're trying to make me ask. You want to humiliate me, but it's not going to happen. I'm the one in control now."

"Really," I told him mildly, "I don't know what it is that you want me to tell you."

The anger blazed up in his eyes as if I'd thrown a match. I watched his right hand twitch across his midline and stop short of the edge of his blazer. I wondered if he'd take the risk of carrying a handgun into the hospital. But it wouldn't be my gun. However arrogant, he wouldn't be so stupid as to carry a murder weapon around. That was stashed somewhere, to be made to appear at the worst possible moment for me, in the most compromising circumstances Craig could devise. If he was armed, it was the revolver he'd used to play Russian roulette that was hidden in the folds of his sleek Italian blazer.

"You motherfucker!"

He thought he'd put himself in charge, but I had him in a corner, and the only way out was for him to show what really mattered to him—the one thing he cared about in all the world—Natalie. And the only way he could hope for any peace from his jealousy was to humble himself. He had to ask me about that ill-fated hug in the coffee shop that had set all this in motion, and he couldn't lay that suspicion to rest without my cooperation.

"This is our last session," I said. "I'd hoped we'd be able to part on friendly terms."

He was seething. He gritted his teeth to restrain himself. And then, all of a sudden, he achieved mastery of his feelings.

"What were you doing while I was shut up in Sanders?" he asked.

"I was going about my business."

"Did that involve comforting the grieving widow?"

"Who are you talking about?"

"Who do you think? Natalie."

"She was hardly a grieving widow."

"You didn't answer my question."

"I'm not here to answer your questions."

"You are this time."

"What's your question?"

"While you had me locked up in Sanders, were you seeing Natalie?"

I could have denied this absurd accusation promptly. If I'd wanted to reassure him, if I'd wanted to dispose of the issue quickly and cleanly, I would have done so. But I'd already made him suspicious with my evasions during the last few exchanges. Now I compounded it with a pause and one of those ambiguous, openhanded gestures that suggests "It's obvious," as well as "Everything's possible." At this moment I became aware of what I was doing. I was already engaged in a strategy. Had been for several minutes. It hadn't been deliberate and it wasn't thought out. It had emerged of its own accord, as an instinctive revulsion against all the rules that I'd respected in my dealings with Craig, which I saw now would lead me to destruction.

"Tell me what you did with Natalie," he said, very quietly.

"You mean the time you saw the two of us in the mall?"

"Any time."

"You want to know, did I make love to her?"

I could have gotten the same effect by smacking him across the face. He actually flinched and turned his face aside. His cheek was flushed. He couldn't bring his eyes up to my face. I wasn't going to give him an inch. I waited him out.

"Did you?" he asked.

I could hear the dryness of his throat. He was shriveling inside. All the green was going out of him and he was curling like a dry leaf. I made him wait some more, and then a craziness of my own took hold.

"Yes," I told him.

He could hardly breathe. The blood had drained from his face so that even his lips looked pale. He gave a smile, a rictus. He looked me full in the face, but he couldn't speak for several seconds. He scanned my eyes, my lips, my brow, in that desperate, fruitless search that people who have had little use for the truth attempt when they suddenly find that they must have it.

"You're lying," he said grimly.

I couldn't believe what I'd done. But it was done, and now I had to go with it. I'd do everything in my power to ensure Natalie came to no harm.

"If you say so." I gave the sociopath's shrug. You find that all sorts of things come easily to you when you have nothing to lose. "You're free to believe whatever you want."

"You never touched her."

I stared at him and said nothing. We locked, eye to eye, like arm wrestling. I stubbornly held my gaze.

"Say it," he demanded.

"What is this—confession time?"

"Tell me the truth."

"Believe me," I told him, "it's not something I'm proud of."

He looked away first. "Your wife was cheating on you, so you thought you had a right . . ."

"You knew my wife was cheating on me, but you didn't know what Natalie was up to."

"I know her every move!"

"Maybe not."

"I know everything she does. Her every thought."

"Apparently you don't know everything about her. You missed a few things. You got distracted. Abby can do that. She has a certain way about her. I know."

"I don't give a shit about your wife. She's . . ." He gave a dismissive wave of his hand.

"A means to an end."

"Irrelevant."

"Really? I thought you were trying to get back at me."

"There are so many ways to get to you. You have no idea. You have no idea how vulnerable you are."

I tried to concentrate on the third rule of murder: Don't rush it. Don't be stampeded by the circumstances that present themselves; do it at a time and place of your own choosing. I settled back comfortably in my chair and contemplated him over interlaced fingers.

"Natalie's not a difficult person," I told him. "She's a very loving woman. She doesn't ask much. Just basic consideration, like privacy, a little personal space. And she gives her affection readily. If you'd played your cards right, all this could have turned out differently."

"You don't know jack shit."

"Oh, yes I do." I nodded significantly and even managed the barest trace of a smug smile. "You blew it."

He watched me, and I knew he was having a hard time not taking out the gun, there and then, and blowing me away.

"Which is too bad," I said.

I didn't know what I was doing or where I was going. I'd been trapped by a circle of events that Craig had contrived, and my only hope was to break out of them, in any direction. I had to jar him loose. Maybe he'd try to kill me. Better than waiting for Detective Dempsey to show up and take me away in cuffs. I did have some dim sense that I might drive Craig to suicide. It started out as a notion—at the back of my mind when I lied about having sex with Natalie—and it gathered force and definition as the interview went on. The only thing clear to me was that I wanted to fight back.

"It was too bad for you," I taunted him in measured tones. "Your pain, my gain. She came running to me."

"You're lying."

"This is our last session. Right? There's no point in holding back. Let's just tell it like it is. You thought you were getting back at me, but you were blindsided. I took Natalie right from under your nose."

"You're not her type."

"What would you know about it? You couldn't even get a date."

"She didn't care about you. She was just trying to help you out with your stupid report."

"Then why did she fuck me?"

He was dying from the inside out. He was still holding it together, but barely. He sat watching me with a supercilious grin that was slowly twisting out of alignment. His eyes darted about as he thought out permutations, reframed the problem, spun out possibilities, started over. I imagined what a PET scan of his brain would look like: like a house on fire.

"You didn't touch her," he said. He affected a relaxed confidence. "I watched over her. No one touched her. No one came close."

"You know, it wasn't even difficult. You got distracted, following Abby around. Trailing after her when she left the agency in the middle of the day. Scrolling through her e-mail. Checking her messages."

He didn't deny any of it. "Go on," he told me evenly.

He wasn't breaking up the way I hoped, and this made me uneasy. There was in his manner a condescension that suggested he was content to let me win a hand or two, secure in the knowledge that he held the trump.

"You followed Abby around, because you thought that was the way to get back at me," I said. "But you couldn't be in two places at once. So you lost track of Natalie. She was with me. While you were on your grudge quest, we were taking care of our own business. You've been through her underwear drawer—you're probably familiar with some of the little lacy things I had to tangle with."

I thought he flinched. An infinitesimal tensing of the lumbar muscles propelled him straighter and took his chest off the back of the chair. Then, slowly, he let himself sink back again and reassembled his expression of superiority.

Sooner rather than later, he would have to tell me what he had done to set me up. He was itching to tell me. I watched his lips. They were slightly apart, in the relaxed position of someone about to speak. He was very close to blurting it out. I'd humiliated him, and he wanted more than anything—almost—to tell me that he'd killed a cop. It was our last session, after all. Why hold back?

His lips tightened and closed shut. But I didn't care whether he told me or not. It wasn't going to do me any good now. I had as much of the truth as I needed.

Then Craig said, "Beethoven's Fifth."

He dangled the phrase like a bauble, waiting for me to snatch at it, to guess at its significance. I felt centered. I had nothing to lose and I'd wait him out.

"You don't know?" he asked. He was smiling, a sadistic grin, and his eyes were hard.

When I didn't respond, he rapped on the desk between us, three times quickly with the points of his knuckles, then once more with the flat of his hand, to play out the opening notes of the symphony.

"Sound familiar?"

"I'm a Mozart guy," I said.

"You never followed her?"

"No."

"But you knew about the cop, didn't you?"

"Of course." Lying didn't come as easily as I thought. I had an urge to swallow, blink, touch my lips. "She told me."

"That's nice. That shows trust. That's the way it ought to be between a husband and wife. Did she tell you about the secret signal?"

"No."

"She didn't?"

"I'm not like you. I don't have to know everything."

"But you'd have wanted to know this."

He tapped it out on the desk again, keeping the flat of his hand on the surface for several moments so that he was leaning forward, looking intently into my face. He was searching for some reaction. I think it was hard for him to believe that I hadn't followed Abby, as he would have done, and that I really didn't recognize the riff.

"That's how you ring the bell," he said. "And then the cop knows it's Abby returning for something in his apartment that she's forgotten—which is not an unusual occurrence, because Abby is kind of forgetful when it comes to small details, isn't she, careless about leaving things behind? That's Abby's signal, so he buzzes open the door—or, he used to—and you go straight up."

And there it was: the killer's smirk. He'd been leaning forward, closer to me, as though imparting his words in a false intimacy, and in the motion of sitting back he glanced at me, not to see me or to take information from my face, but for me to see into him, as though his eyes were portals through which, for a privileged instant, he would allow me to glimpse his soul and its secret triumph. He waited a long moment for me to process the implications. He knew already that people take time to assimilate such knowledge, to register a godlike act whose intensity dazzles the emotions.

With two slow, almost imperceptible nods, I conveyed my understanding. I knew that Craig would read more into this acknowledgment than was warranted: He would see respect there, too. I intended to disabuse him of this. I waited for my opening to break him down further.

But once Craig had started on this boasting, he couldn't resist going further. "Guess what?" he asked. He opened his hands, palms up in the no-brainer gesture. "When the cop was killed, there weren't any signs of forced entry."

"It's not easy to shoot a man," I said. "People think it's easy, but it's not."

He laughed spontaneously. "You better believe it." He was slightly giddy.

People break the second rule of murder with cops and psychiatrists because they've lived for days and weeks among people who don't know killing, and then, here's somebody who understands, someone who has the capacity to appreciate the enormity of the act. There was no holding him back now, so long as I didn't implicate him directly in what I said.

"It's not like they show it in the movies," he said.

"They make it look easy," I agreed. "And you'd think it would be easy: All you have to do is pull a trigger. It doesn't seem like much. But if you take your time, if you do it at a time and a place that you've chosen—there's no way to convey the huge amount of courage it takes."

He was listening to me closely and nodding his head in agreement. He wasn't grinning anymore. He was reliving the experience through my words.

"The door buzzes open," I suggested. "It's the last chance to turn around. This is the hardest part, because no crime's been committed. You walk away, free, and no one will know. Except you will. But if you go forward, if you go up the stairs with a gun in your hand—and it has to be in your hand, because you don't know if he thinks it's Abby, if he's still lounging in bed, maybe smoking that postcoital cigarette, or whether he's waiting for you. He's a cop. He's got a gun, too. So you have to have the gun ready in your hand, my gun, and you have to go quickly up the stairs, no hesitation, as if it was Abby. And then there's no going back—"

He balked. "You sound like you were there."

"No," I said, "it's just that I've heard the story a hundred times before."

"The police think you were there."

"Yes, they do."

"You can't prove you weren't there. Even if you weren't in the apartment, you don't have an alibi."

He was a thorough person and would have established my routine as soon as I became an adversary. He would have known I spent Tuesday afternoons working at home, alone. He would have figured out the blocks of time when I didn't have an alibi before he killed Francone. The line of reasoning gave him a feeling of security, and I let him move further along the chain of inference while I waited for my moment. I was becoming quite a good sociopath. I was the antipsychiatrist: lying, cheating, manipulating for all I was worth, driving my patient to suicide.

"You work at home every Tuesday. First, around two, two-thirty, you go running around some deserted beach. Not a soul in sight. No one to say you weren't at the cop's apartment, even if you weren't."

"Just because I haven't used an alibi doesn't mean I don't have one."

"Who's going to stand up for you? Abby? I don't think so. Abby was otherwise engaged."

"I spent the afternoon with Natalie."

He scoffed. I'd jolted him for an instant, but he regrouped.

"That's bullshit," he said.

"I was with Natalie," I said quietly. I was lying at ninety miles an hour, too fast to react to all the implications of what I said as they came at me. "We spent the afternoon in her bedroom." I paused as if to remember, as if taken unawares by the savor of the memory. "It's not the kind of thing you can be mistaken about."

twenty-two

The interview was over. He could have ranted. He could have shot me there and then. But at that instant I didn't matter to him. Craig's eyes passed over me without taking me in. He would turn his attention back to me later. At this moment, he was too caught up in a massive change of mind to have any computational capacity left over. He was thinking about Natalie. She was the center of his universe. He would go for her first.

It should have been a simple matter for me to warn her. I dialed her Harvard number as soon as the door closed behind Craig. She'd disappear for a couple of days, I thought, as I listened to the ringing tone. When Craig wasn't able to find her, he'd come for me with my gun.

But no one answered. I called her department, but no one would tell me where I could locate her. With rising anxiety, I called her cell phone, but she must have switched it off, because it was only taking messages. I called the number of her apartment. I left messages everywhere I could think of, some of them with her colleagues, who clearly thought I was crazy. But I made them write it down anyway.

"Get out," I said to her voice mail. "Craig's coming for you. Everything's changed. He's very dangerous. You have to go somewhere until the police pick him up. A couple of days at the most. Don't go home. Don't stay with friends he might know about. Just check into a motel and stay there."

I called the police. The station was only half a dozen blocks from where Natalie lived.

"Do we know you, Doctor?" the desk sergeant asked. "Your name sounds familiar." As he was talking to me I heard in the background the click of the keyboard as he typed my name into his database. When the sound of typing stopped his manner changed quite abruptly, in midsentence. His voice took on a tone of studied neutrality.

"Look," I said, "this isn't about me. There's a woman here who's in real danger from a stalker." I tried to explain to him the sound clinical reasons why Craig would hunt her down, never mind the restraining order.

He had his hand over the mouthpiece while he conducted a conversation with someone else. "Yes, Doctor," he said somewhat mechanically. I could hear another voice in the background coaching him on how to keep me talking.

"I have reason to believe," I began. But my voice sounded stilted, and then I thought that they would probably be tracing the call and that they'd come for me and put me out of circulation, and when I faltered I became even less plausible. I hung up in the middle of what I recognized was a hostage negotiation spiel.

I took off from the Methodist before they came for me. They would put out the license plate of my car, so I left it in the hospital garage. I didn't know if I was overreacting. I wasn't sure how paranoid I ought to be. The desk sergeant might report my emergency call to Detective Dempsey. But would that make her think I'd gone over the edge? Would it be enough to tip their hand, to arrest me on the circumstantial evidence the police had? I couldn't afford to take the chance. Once they had me, everyone would be frozen in place, and then, for me, it would all be over.

Once they had me, the gun would appear like magic.

I had to stay mobile, and that meant I needed a car. I called Abby's agency and Nan, the receptionist, told me she was with a client and couldn't be disturbed.

"This is her husband," I said.

"I know who you are," she said a little too quickly.

"Well, then, would you please interrupt her?"

"She doesn't like to be interrupted when she's with a client."

"This is an emergency," I said. "I think you'll find she'll want to be interrupted."

Reluctantly, Nan rang through to Abby, and when she came on the line, it was clear from her tone that Nan had been right.

"Okay, what?" Abby demanded in clipped tones.

"I need your SUV," I told her. "My car's broken down, and I have an emergency at Sanders. I have to get out there."

"What happened to yours?"

"I don't know. The timing belt, maybe. They had to tow it."

"I need mine. Why don't you rent one? You're going to have to do that anyway."

"Abby, help me out. I just have to have a vehicle now."

There was a pause at the other end. "Okay," she said. "I'll be done in half an hour."

"Great. Thanks. Leave the key under the driver's seat?"

"I'll drive you myself."

I took the subway. I hadn't noticed before how the rocking of the train coincides with changes in people's eye fixations. The girl opposite is looking at the ad over your head, then she's looking at you, then on to something else. The eye movements aren't random. If you start looking at someone, they start looking at you. It's a paranoid feedback loop. I wondered how many of the people in the train, now not quite minding their own business, had seen the photo of me that they'd shown on the TV news the night before. It was an old photo, blown up from a shot taken of a group of people, but all the same, a million viewers had seen it. I felt desperate and wild-eyed, and I was afraid it showed. At each stop, I waited to see if the car would empty.

I sat in the subway trying to avoid eye contact and wondered what would persuade Abby to give up her SUV. I'd set myself up as a target and I didn't want her anywhere near me. As I walked away from the subway stop on Mass Ave, I found myself scrutinizing the reflections in shop windows for signs of a shadowy figure on the street behind me. I started when a police cruiser overtook me. I was jumpy, and I used the rest of the walk to Abby's agency to talk myself down. I had to refocus: get a vehicle, find Natalie, take her somewhere safe. Then I'd figure out my next move.

I found Abby's SUV in the lot, but no Abby. The vehicle was locked. I turned at the sound of voices. A couple of women came out of the agency. They hesitated a moment when they saw me loitering.

"Hi," I called to them, and as they came closer, "I'm waiting for Abby."

They nodded and gave me stiff smiles. After they passed I saw them look back and then quickly get into a car together. It wasn't until they'd left that Abby appeared. She'd been there all the time, waiting behind a van for the right moment. It was a kind of ambush.

I started to come toward her, but she told me, "No!" louder than she'd intended and glanced about to see if anyone else was close enough to hear.

She made a pushing motion with her open hands for me to step back another car's width. Obediently, I kept two cars between us. It was only then that she felt comfortable enough to advance to her SUV. I was appalled that my own wife could be so frightened of me.

"Look," I said, "this was a bad idea. Let's forget it."

"I want to help you, Paul."

"Toss me the keys, and I'm gone."

"You know that's not what I mean."

"Do we have to yell at each other?"

She allowed me to reduce the separation to the width of one vehicle. We talked across the hood of her SUV.

"I don't want you to get caught up in this," I told her. "That's why you should give me your keys."

"No," she said. I recognized the tone. Once Abby made up her mind she could be stubborn, and then there was no moving her. "This is my fault," she said, "and I'm going to help you. I'm going to get you the help you need."

This sounded ominous. "Look," I told her, "this isn't what you think. This isn't about Lou Francone. This is about Craig."

She gave a hoarse laugh. "Come on, Paul."

"This is real."

She put her hands on the hood so that she could lean forward, and she whispered, "I'm your wife, for God's sake! For better or worse. And I know I have a lot to answer for. I'm not going to testify against you."

"So you're pretty sure I killed Lou?"

She nodded silently. I saw tears start in her eyes and suddenly they fell down the vertical drop of her cheeks. She was struggling to compose herself, and I waited until she was ready.

She spoke first. "You have to deal with this, Paul. You have to deal with the reality of what you're facing. There are things we can do. We'll take out a loan on the house. I don't mind. We'll get you a really good trial lawyer. You can turn yourself in. You'll get credit for that. You can make a deal. They're always looking to make deals. That's what you've told me. Why not you? Why don't we go now, together, and get you the best deal we can get?"

"Because I didn't do it."

"But you can't take off. You can't run from this. Wherever you go . . ."

"I'm not running. I'm not asking for the SUV because I'm running away. I've got a job to do."

"I wish you wouldn't say that."

"What?"

She looked away to choose her words, then sighed. "That you're on some . . . mission, or something."

"It's not a mission. No one said anything about being on a mission. It's something I have to do. I started something, and now I have to take care of it."

"But you don't know how crazy that sounds."

I stopped for a moment to look at this from Abby's point of view. I tried to hear the words I'd just spoken, the echo of them in my own mind. I said, "I don't think it sounds crazy at all."

"Listen to yourself, Paul. Can't you hear what you're saying? Larry called from the Methodist."

"Great."

"He was very nice. We had a long talk. They're worried about you. They're reaching out. They want to help you."

"Sure they do."

"Paul, they think you're impaired. They're not out to get you. They just want you to get help."

"Of course they do. It's all part of the same setup."

I stopped abruptly, but the words were out. They flew away and there was no getting them back. Abby turned her head quickly to hide the expression of shock. The trouble was—I had to admit it—I did sound pretty crazy.

I took a deep breath. This was my last shot. If Abby would still listen to what I was actually saying. "It has to do with Craig," I told her. "He's set up this whole thing."

I had to stay away from paranoid constructions like "this whole thing." Abby's eyes were on me, scrutinizing me in a way that could only be described as clinical. I was struggling to regain credibility, but only digging myself in deeper. Somehow, the truth just didn't work for me.

Abby looked down so that she wouldn't be distracted by the sight of me as she carefully selected her words. "I worked with Craig," she said. She was in professional mode, the tone kind but insistent. "I worked with him closely for weeks. He told me right off he'd been in Sanders over a love affair that ended badly."

"It never ended, as far as he's concerned."

"He regrets how he behaved. It was a very passionate time. We all act a little nutty when we're in love. Don't you remember?"

She turned a wan smile to me to evoke what she hoped was a better, older part. I recognized that her appeal—believing what she did about me—was an act of love and generosity, and I almost choked with gratitude, and with the anguish of regret that this gift had come too late.

"You're wrong about him," she said. She was talking quietly, directly, in a way she hadn't spoken to me in months. "You've got tunnel vision, Paul. You're in this criminal mind-set, and it doesn't apply to everyone who ends up at Sanders. Craig's a decent kid. He's personable, charming—"

"There you are." I felt the futility, the loneliness of the paranoid.

"Just because he's charming doesn't make him a sociopath."

"Believe me—he's a very highly evolved sociopath."

"He was also very caring, Paul. Whatever I asked him to do, he'd do it. He was everywhere. He was into everything."

"Craig killed Lou Francone."

"Why?" She opened her hands and held them wide in front of her to indicate the enormity of that improbability. "Why would he do that?"

"To get even with me. To put me in a place like Sanders."

"Why would he want to get even with you, Paul?" She asked her question in the flat, slightly weary tone that indicates the speaker's total absence of curiosity about the answer. It's the way laypeople ask psychotic people about their delusions.

"Because Natalie, the person he's been stalking, has a crush on me. Therefore, he thinks I'm having an affair with her."

"And are you?"

"Does it matter?"

Abby thought about this longer than I would have liked. Suddenly, I was afraid that it didn't matter at all. Maybe the emotional link that held us together, expanding over the last few weeks like a strand of gum, had snapped, and I had become nothing more to her than an individual to whom a debt was to be repaid.

"Yes," she said slowly. "It does."

"I never had an affair with her. I never touched her, except once, when I felt sorry for her and gave her a hug. I know—poor technique. And Craig saw it. Everything comes from that one impulsive act of kindness."

"I don't know what to believe anymore. You're telling me this and that. Words don't mean anything."

"I need the SUV, Abby. He's going after Natalie now." I held out my hand across the hood for her to toss me the keys. "Let me do this. Then I'll do whatever you want."

"I'm not getting in the truck with you."

"That's okay. Just give me the keys. Give me the keys, and I'll do what you want. We'll go to the police together, if that'll make you feel better."

She wasn't convinced, but Abby was already unhooking the ring that separated the vehicle keys from the huge bunch held together by a mountain climber's clip. I was going to get what I needed, but I wanted my wife to believe in me. Gingerly, she reached out and laid the keys on the center of the hood. I didn't like the sudden movement with which she pulled back her hand—as if I might make a grab at her wrist if she stayed within arm's reach. Above all, I hated to leave her thinking I was crazy. At that moment I had an idea that I was sure would convince her that Craig had killed Lou Francone.

I made my movements slow and measured, so that she could be sure I meant her no harm. I left the keys where they were for a moment. On the roof of the car I tapped out the opening notes of Beethoven's Fifth Symphony as Craig had done on my desk.

I'd hoped to startle her. I'd hoped the sound would jolt her with a flash of insight, make her recognize that everything I'd said was true.

Abby didn't react. I thought she'd been distracted, or hadn't heard it, or hadn't recognized, so I tapped it out again, leaving my hand flat on the car roof for the final drawn-out note.

"Sound familiar?" I asked her.

She shook her head with a puzzled frown. "No," she said warily. "What is it?"

"You don't remember?"

"No."

"The secret sign."

She looked at the car keys. I thought she might go for them. She was measuring the distance, calculating whether, if she pounced, I could snatch her hand and capture her. To what purpose? It didn't matter. That's what she thought I was capable of now.

"I don't know what you mean." She spoke slowly, enunciating each word carefully. She was frightened. She'd given up on the keys now; she'd lost that leverage. There were more important considerations. Now she looked like she might be preparing to turn, that my slightest move toward her would cause her to run, screaming for help from bystanders, across the parking lot.

"The secret sign you had with Lou Francone."

"We didn't have a secret sign. That wasn't . . . it wasn't his style."

"No," I insisted. Even with the sinking feeling in my stomach, I insisted I was reminding her of something that I knew more about than she did, that might just have slipped her mind. "When you rang the doorbell, to let him know it was you."

With one hand I reached across the hood for the keys; with the other I pressed an imaginary doorbell with my thumb and gave a rendering of the opening bar of Beethoven's Fifth.

As I hooked the keys on my finger and pulled them toward me, I heard footsteps, running, and when I looked around, Abby had disappeared between the next row of cars.

twenty—three

I drove randomly at first, circling through Cambridge and Somerville, with Crombie Street, where Natalie's apartment was, at the center. I called her home number and heard the familiar message of her answering machine. After the beep I kept talking in case she was there and might pick up, but the tape told me my time was up and cut me off. I called the cell phone number she'd given me, but all I got was a request to leave a message.

I was familiar with the general area where Natalie lived. Craig, who knew Crombie Street intimately from countless sleepless nights of surveillance, would have staked out the best position to watch for Natalie. And to watch for me. I figured I wouldn't be able to get away with more than one pass along the street. If I loitered, Craig would see me. In fact, even with the light fading as the sun set, I'd have to pass at speed, facedown over the wheel, and hope to locate him in one of the side mirrors as I passed.

I pulled over to the curb well back from the intersection with the main drag where Crombie Street began. Natalie's apartment was number fourteen. There was a liquor store on one corner and a laundromat on the other. Opposite the intersection was a gas station, and I thought I'd fill the tank.

I had a good view down Crombie as I pumped gas. It was a residential street of triple-deckers with short front yards. The street was partially gentrified, most of the houses converted to condos, freshly painted, with their front yards blacktopped for parking spaces. Here and there, holdouts of the original working-class neighborhood looked slightly down at heel. It wasn't the kind of place where you could sit in a car for long without drawing attention. Young families were out, pushing strollers, older children running ahead. A man carried bags of groceries from his car. People were in movement, going places, not hanging out.

I counted down and thought that Natalie lived in a house painted a brownish peach with white trim. The front yard was paved and a truck was parked in one of the three spaces. There were no trees or shrubs for Craig to hide in. As I watched, a man in a tank top came out the front door and got into the truck. I felt confident that Craig was not lurking in the hallway.

I decided to look at the rear of the house before I made my pass, and when I'd filled the tank I drove down the street parallel to Crombie, which was almost identical, triple-deckers back to back. No place there for Craig to watch from, either. I turned at the end and took the cross street back to the main drag.

I came down Crombie Street fast, with the sun visor blocking half the side window and a hand over my lower face, scanning the parked cars on either side. I saw no one. The only suspicious vehicle was an old van with smoked windows parked opposite Natalie's apartment. Somehow, it didn't seem like the kind of vehicle Craig would choose.

At the end of Crombie Street, though, the old character of the neighborhood reasserted itself, with a ramshackle variety store on one corner, and, on the other, an old-fashioned, ma-and-pa kind of donut shop, which had Natalie's apartment in direct line of sight.

I hunkered down as I went by the donut shop. I couldn't risk turning my head to see if Craig sat in the window, brooding as he nursed a cup of coffee. An instant later, I glimpsed in the mirror a figure with a newspaper. He was sitting in the right position for a view down the length of the street, but reflections on the glass hid his head and I didn't have time to make him out.

Craig would be watching for me, so I knew I couldn't pass twice. But I didn't want to park the car and get out on foot, because if Natalie showed up and it came to a race to our vehicles, he'd have his positioned close by and I'd be a step behind. I was back on the main street, in the process of thinking out my options, when a blue Corolla passed me traveling in the opposite direction with someone inside who looked like Natalie. I almost missed her.

I made a reckless U-turn into two lanes of oncoming traffic. At speed, I went by the donut shop. The figure reading the newspaper was gone. I made a right onto Crombie and saw the blue Corolla in front of a Passat. The Corolla was slowing. There was a single person in the Passat, but I couldn't make out if the driver was a man or a woman. The Corolla was pulling into a parking space across the street from Natalie's building. As the Corolla pulled in, I saw space behind it for the Passat to park, too, jamming the blue car in. But the Passat kept going and turned at the bottom of the street.

Natalie got out of her car. She was holding a briefcase and had stopped, looking to cross the road, waiting for my SUV to pass. When I came level with her I threw open the passenger door.

"Hey," I called to her, not loudly, trying not to startle her.

It was more of a friendly greeting than a warning. With Craig about to show up at any moment, armed most likely, I wanted her quick cooperation, but I didn't want to stampede her, either. I was searching every mirror to spot Craig before he came up on us.

"Hey," she called, recognizing me.

She was smiling, which I was glad of, but her smile contained the uncertainty and hesitation that I'd come to associate with my new notoriety. She was intrigued, all the same, by this sudden appearance. She came to the open door and leaned in tentatively with one hand resting on the top edge of the door.

"It was good of you to call," I said.

"Yes?" She was pleased.

"I really appreciated it."

"I wasn't sure what was the right thing to say. But I wanted you to know . . . that you're not alone."

It was one thing to talk to me on the phone, but in person I was a different proposition. She flirted with the threshold, an imaginary boundary that separated the inside of the SUV—a space that put her within reach of a man who might be dangerous, who could whisk her away—and the world outside. She ventured back and forth across this imaginary line as we talked, dipping her head and leaning into the vehicle, then straightening so that she stood outside. She was attracted and fearful. As the presumptive murderer of my wife's lover, I had a certain sexual status, a feral cachet. If she misunderstood what I was about, if some innuendo enticed her into the vehicle, I could clear it up later. The main thing was to get her away.

"You didn't get my message?" I asked.

"No." The disappointment was plain in her face. "I had my cell phone turned off." She reached for it in her pocket. She was distracted, turning it back on. "Otherwise . . ."

Her pleasure in the fact that I'd called her faded to puzzlement as she realized there were too many inconsistencies in my being here. If I'd encountered her by chance, why had I thrown open the door rather than lowered the window, if I'd only stopped to say hello?

In the right mirror, I glimpsed an elderly Cadillac lurching around the corner onto our street.

"But—wait a minute," Natalie said with a nervous laugh. "How did you know I'd be here now?"

I was watching the Cadillac in the rearview mirror. It was accelerating hard, bearing down on us. I wondered if Craig would risk a drive-by shooting. The Cadillac came level. It drifted by peacefully.

"This thing with Craig has entered a new phase." I felt myself in a bind: Very quickly, I had to get her to understand the urgency of the situation, but if I overplayed the fear factor, I'd lose her. "I think he's quite dangerous," I said, as if I were a doctor conveying a grave prognosis. "That's why, when I couldn't reach you to warn you, I felt I had to make sure you got to the police safely." I made a gallant sweep of the hand. "So I've been waiting for you."

She nodded uncertainly. There was a credibility problem, as I'd expected, but she was doing her best to overcome it. She was trying to reconcile the man on the newscasts with the doctor she'd impulsively embraced, the convergence of these two personas in the man before her now.

"Look," I told her, speaking in an even tone in order to keep my rising anxiety out of my voice. "We don't have a whole lot of time."

"For what?"

"To get you to the police."

"Then what?"

"You need to hide out for a couple of days."

She looked away, over the rooftops. "Then what?"

I began to tell her that Craig was entering a crisis, that the situation would blow up, and then it wouldn't matter anymore because he'd be in custody or dead, but she didn't wait for me to answer.

"You see what I'm saying?" she cut in. "There's no end to this. I've just come from a job interview in Connecticut. But even if I get the position, that isn't going to do it. Connecticut isn't far enough, is it? California isn't far enough. There isn't anywhere I can go to get away from him."

I hadn't noticed the smart, navy blue suit. That's why her cell phone had been turned off. She met my eyes in a feisty stare that defied me to sugarcoat the truth. She'd come to her edge. It was true; she really didn't have any options.

"If you want to come with me, I'll take you to the police," I told her. "Or go in your own car, and I'll follow you."

She looked down uncertainly at the briefcase in her hand. It was a substantial black bag, and I thought it must hold her thesis. "I don't want to leave it in the car," she said. It swung slightly at the end of her arm, like a pendulum of indecision.

"That's okay. Bring it with you. Put it in the backseat."

She looked across the road in the direction of her apartment. "Really, I'd like to freshen up."

"We don't have time." I tried to nudge her gently. "Craig is going to be along any moment."

"He's here already," she said. She could have been enunciating a philosophical position, an obscure proof of God's existence. "Just because you don't see him yet doesn't mean he isn't already here."

"Well, then we have to get moving."

She hesitated, then conceded. She swung the briefcase in and stepped up into the SUV after it. I took off even before she'd closed the door. In the mirror, I saw a black Honda Accord round the corner.

"Do you always go so fast?" she asked.

"What kind of car does Craig drive?"

"I don't know." She turned to look back. "Is that him?"

"I don't know."

"You see? Do you see how it's starting to affect you? You don't know if it's Craig. There's no reason why it should be him. But a car comes up behind you, and you assume it is him. After a while, you begin to suspect that every little thing is his doing. There aren't any accidents anymore. There aren't any coincidences. But really, it's you who makes him so powerful. You do this. You do it to yourself."

She seemed pleased by my reaction, as though she'd recruited me to a cause with few adherents. I wondered how much skepticism she'd had to endure in the face of a threat that had been all-but-invisible to those around her. Now that I was in her shoes, she was happy to let me carry the burden of paranoia.

I slowed momentarily to take a corner, then sped up again and took another. The Accord had disappeared from my mirror, and I thought I could afford to slow down a bit. I made some more turns, each one at the last moment, on a route that led nowhere. It did seem that we'd lost the Accord. If it had been Craig who was following us.

"So," Natalie asked, "do you want to tell me where exactly we're going?"

"I'm taking you to the police station."

"Been there. Done that."

"This is different. It isn't about just following and watching anymore. Craig's come to the end of the line."

She was looking at me, weighing what I said, trying to figure out the important part, the bit I wasn't telling her.

"There must have been something that happened," she said.

"He thinks you and I have been having an affair."

"And have we?"

"I don't think so."

"You're not sure?"

"You know we haven't."

"It seemed like there was some room for doubt there. A little bit of wiggle room."

I was facing forward, watching the road ahead of us, and Natalie had turned, one leg curled under her on the seat so that she sat looking sideways at me. I felt her scrutiny.

"Why aren't you sure?" she asked.

"No. I'm sure."

"Nothing happened?"

"Nothing."

She studied me silently. She might have been examining my face for signs of wavering. Maybe she was waiting me out, expecting that, eventually, I'd concede what she wished to hear.

Finally, she said softly, "Too bad," and the tone in which she said it indicated that it wasn't a conclusion reluctantly reached but a declaration given, another move in the game.

"We have to stay in the here and now," I reminded her. "I don't think you realize how dangerous he is."

"Oh, I realize. I don't react anymore because I've been living with it for so long."

"He's got a gun."

"Is that new, or is this something you're just finding out about?"

"What's new is that he wants to use it."

"On you?"

"All of us. You and me. Himself."

"So why don't you go to the police? Why don't you have him arrested? Or why don't you simply have him locked up? You can do that, can't you?" She waited half a beat for me to answer. "I know: Been there. Done that."

"It's complicated," I said. "I don't have a whole lot of credibility with the police right now. But you do. They'll protect you."

"What are you looking at in the mirror?"

The black Accord had reappeared, in spite of the sudden, arbitrary turns I'd made. At the last set of lights, the car had slipped into the stream of traffic and now followed discreetly, two vehicles back.

"I think it would be better if you didn't turn around."

"That's because you're new at this. Once you know about being stalked, you'll realize there's no point in trying to hide. If he's behind us, he already knows where you are."

She turned right around in her seat and took a good long look through the back window. She was still trying to peer around the truck that was directly behind us when her cell phone rang.

She was frozen for a moment. Even after she'd taken it out of her pocket, she stared at it in her hand as it rang again. Then she flipped it open, and, as she hit the button, she held it up between us so that we'd both be able to hear.

"Let's quit the cloak-and-dagger stuff," Craig said.

His voice came in diminished and unworldly, like the voice of an evil genie conjured from a lamp.

"You've shown me your best stuff," he said, "and I can see you're not much good at it."

"I'm taking Natalie to the Somerville police station," I said. "She's out of the mix."

"Then you should have made a right at the last intersection."

"I'm going to drop her off, and then you and I can talk."

"Or we can all go into the police station. Why don't we do that? I have something I want to discuss with them. Sooner or later I have to tell them where they can find a certain item. Now's as good a time as any. What do you think?"

"I think we should talk that over first."

"I think we should all get together to talk it over. The three of us."

"Just you and me."

"If you want to get that item, it'll be on my terms."

The gun was an object that conferred enormous power on the person who controlled it. But neither of us could be caught with the murder weapon in his possession. When the music stopped, no one wanted to be the one left holding the package.

"How long will it take you to get it?" I asked.

"No time at all. It's in a safe place. A place that's easily accessible to you. In fact, it's in a place where you might have stashed it yourself."

"In my house."

"Exactly."

The gun was a bomb that lay hidden somewhere between the attic and the basement. A single phone call to the police was all that was needed to detonate it.

"You put it back."

"It's always been there. Except—you know."

"All right," I said. "I'll meet you there."

"With Natalie."

"She's not part of the deal. She's out of this."

"Natalie *is* the deal. What's the point, without her? She's got nothing to worry about. No one's going to hurt Natalie. You're too suspicious, Paul. You expect the worst of people. I think all that time you spend in Sanders has made you dark. All I want is for us to talk. That's it. Then I'll give you what you want. And we're done."

"I can't do that."

"I want to hear what Natalie says."

I shook my head at her, but she took the phone away and held it to her ear so that I couldn't hear what Craig said.

"I agree," Natalie said, after listening for a moment.

I shook my head furiously to get her to change her mind.

"I think we should have one final, face-to-face meeting," she said, "so that you can understand that Paul and I love one another very much. I think this is the only way to convince you that what I have with Paul doesn't leave any room in my life for you."

With a flourish, she turned the phone off. Then she lowered the window and tossed it out of the vehicle. In the mirror, I saw it bounce on the road behind us and splinter.

"That should just about do it," she said.

"I'm not sure you know what you're doing."

"I want my life back."

The ramp to the highway north lay on the other side of the rotary we were now entering. We went up the ramp, and as I looked for a gap to merge with the other vehicles, I heard a surge of engine noise behind us and the Accord came past us at speed, threaded two lanes of traffic, and was quickly hidden from view by a tractor-trailer.

I let him go. He'd get to the house before us and he'd set his trap. I was resigned to taking my chances, but I still hoped to dissuade Natalie from joining what was to be my last interview with Craig.

"I understand your thinking," I told her. "But there's no reason for you to be there at the end."

"It won't come to an end if I'm not there."

"It's enough that he thinks you'll be there."

"That won't do it. You're forgetting who you're dealing with."

"Let me tell you what we are dealing with. He's melting down. He's going to self-destruct."

"That's the idea, isn't it? Isn't that what we want?"

"He's not just going to kill himself."

"Okay," she said, as if she stood corrected on a minor detail. "Murder-suicide, then."

"Right. He's going to kill himself right after he kills you. This is what we've done. The two of us have managed to convince him he has no hope of attaining his ideal. In life, anyway. So this is the other great reunion: together in death."

"And the plan is for you to come, too?"

"I'm first."

"How do you figure that?"

"Because when he comes to kill you, he'll want it to be a loving, tender moment of good-bye. He'll want the two of you to be alone for that."

"So, as long as you're alive, he won't kill me?"

"It's only a theory," I warned her. "I wouldn't bet your life on it."

"We kill him first. It's the only way."

"You don't just set out to murder someone. It's not that easy. It's not a simple thing."

"Come on! You killed a cop. This is nothing for you!"

I'd decided in the interview to drive Craig to suicide. On an impulse so slight, on little more than a whim, I'd tossed a rock that started a slide that caused the avalanche. I hadn't seen all the way to this final consequence. I was driving twenty miles with the clear and immediate intent—intent in the first degree—to kill a man. I wasn't ready. I didn't know how to sever the ties that bound me to humanity. I wasn't prepared for the reality of murder. The road in my headlights was coming up at me too fast. I wouldn't ever be ready.

"Okay," I agreed. "But we have to pick our spot. You can't rush this."

twenty-four

When we arrived, we found Craig's car parked in plain sight in the driveway. We were beyond deception. We had come to the end, and Craig wasn't concerned about what might happen afterward. For other people, life would go on. The car would be towed. Later, sold. His apartment cleaned out. Let things fall where they may. Someone else, a Cavanaugh staffer most likely, would gather up the loose ends.

We pulled in behind the Accord and I turned off the engine. It had grown dark, but the porch lights by the front door and the driveway lights, which were timed to switch on at dusk, weren't on. When we stepped out of the SUV, the light from the opened doors made pools of light on the gravel and illuminated the spectral shapes of trees. The lights inside hadn't come on, either, and the house was dark.

Natalie slammed her door defiantly. She was right: There was no hiding our arrival from him. We were out in the open. He was tracking us.

I couldn't assume the advantage of home territory. In essential ways, Craig knew my home better that I did. For me, the house was simply the place where I lived. For Craig it was enemy territory, and when he'd made his reconnaissance, it had been with an eye to ambushes, fallbacks, hiding places, escape routes. Somewhere inside, wedged in a corner, crouched in a closet, lurking behind a door, slung in the kitchen's false ceiling, at some place of his choosing, Craig waited for us.

I told Natalie, "He's pulled the fuses."

"Of course. He would." Her words were clipped, their articulation tight with the anxiety she was trying hard to disavow.

"You don't mind the dark?"

"What difference does it make?"

"You can still walk away."

"Forget it."

There was a note of rising irritation in her voice. She clung to the conviction that as long as I was alive, Craig wouldn't kill her; my questions undermined the very sense of invulnerability I had given her. As if to prevent any further discussion, she started toward the front door.

She waited for me there, but when I put my key in the lock, I found that the deadbolt had already been thrown from the inside, and when I gave the door a push, it swung open. He'd left the door unlocked as a message, not a convenience. Craig wasn't securing his lines of retreat; there would be no retreat. I paused a moment before I stepped across the threshold.

The house was silent. I took a deep breath, sniffing for gasoline, but the great Viking conflagration I had feared wouldn't be part of Craig's agenda. He wouldn't change his modus operandi now.

I started toward the kitchen so that we could arm ourselves with the knives there. The fire extinguisher would be useful, too. But before I could stop her, Natalie went ahead of me, striding boldly, loudly, into the hall.

"It's me, Craig," she shouted. "Here I am. Real flesh and blood."

She walked away from me toward the library, still shouting her challenges, while I went to the kitchen to find weapons. I needed a flashlight. The one I kept for emergencies was in the drawer, but Craig already knew that. He'd removed the batteries and left the useless casing for me to find. He'd brought his own. Groping under the sink for the fire extinguisher, I discovered that he'd taken that, too.

"You don't have to creep around," I heard Natalie declaim, her voice coming from the living room now.

I hoped I was right about Craig's order of business, because Natalie behaved as if she wore a psychological flak jacket.

"No more hiding in bushes," she taunted him.

Below, above, beside us, Craig bided his time.

She moved back in my direction. My hands closed around the kitchen knives in the block. He could have taken them, too, but he'd left them as an inducement. How well he read me! Without some weapon, I'd hesitate to come at him. His terms: my kitchen knife against his gun.

"Come out and deal with me!" Natalie yelled, with an intensity that I hadn't before seen in her.

I prayed that Natalie, for all her bravado, would steer clear of what Craig and I were set to do. A man was about to be killed, here, in my home—perhaps two—and I saw no reason for her to make a third body. Craig was my responsibility. I'd set myself free, or I'd be killed. Whatever happened, there could be no good outcome. I would sustain damage, either moral or mortal. The best outcome—the best—was that I would kill my patient.

Natalie stopped calling out, and I had no way of gauging where she was. Then, in the near-darkness, we almost collided as I came out of the kitchen. We paused to listen for the sounds of movement that her invocation might have provoked. In the silence, we heard the ticking of the living-room clock. Outside, as though on cue, the cicadas started up, and with their racket we couldn't hear anything else.

I offered her a long carving knife, almost a small machete, while I kept the eight-inch chef's knife for myself. Abby's fingers had curled where mine now clenched, and I was suddenly overcome with a pang of loneliness, the unbearable loneliness of dying.

"We have to split up," I whispered, my mouth almost touching her ear. "It's our only chance to jump him."

I could just make out her nod of understanding. She touched my shoulder.

"Stay up here," I told her. "I'm going down to the basement."

If I were in Craig's shoes, I'd have been hunkered down in the basement waiting for the enemy to come to me. It maximized all the advantages that he held over us. However quietly we stepped on the first floor, even on the rugs, he'd hear our footfalls below. However stealthily I approached the only set of stairs, he could track me. And at the bottom of the stairs, I'd blunder through the darkest place in the house, an obstacle course of cast-off furniture and sports equipment and packing cases, while he waited with a flashlight to illuminate me at his chosen moment.

I was thinking rationally, planning, calculating, but at the heart of all this activity was the knowledge that I had to kill a man. If I could. If, for one instant, I could overcome the ties of a lifetime that bound me to my fellow men. I stopped at the top of the stairs that led down to the basement and tried to control my trembling hands. I was worried I wouldn't be able to keep hold of the knife if I jarred it against something hard, like a rib. I repeated Kovacs's third rule to myself like a mantra: "Don't rush it. Don't rush it."

I forced myself to stay technical. If I was lucky, I'd slash his throat. Or I might get a chance, either coming across the chest and through the ribs or with an upward thrust, at the heart. But any one of these would be the second blow. Or the third. The last blow, anyway. I tried to think about the problem like a surgeon, but the problem wasn't just Craig. I was part of the surgical problem, too. Because I was going to get shot. That was what Craig would do as I closed in on him. If he fired at my head, that was it. There wasn't any point in gaming that possibility. When he fired, I had to keep going. You don't fall down just because you take a round. I told myself a .25 was not going to stop me. If the slugs didn't hit bone or a major artery, I might even survive two rounds. For a moment I got sidetracked calculating the rate of blood loss against the speed of the ambulance racing to resuscitate me.

As I took the first step down to the basement, I steeled myself to take a round as the price I'd pay to get close with the knife. Then: Disable the assailant. Acquire a stationary target. Cut tendons. Stab into a kidney. Thrust into gut. Put the point into a body cavity and lever it through an arc of viscus, vessels, bronchi. Then, before my own blood pressure dropped below the level necessary to sustain consciousness, deliver the death blow: to heart, or, through the left eye socket, busting through the skull into the substance of the brain, skewering the thalamus, then down to the mother lode, Kovacs's medulla oblongata.

I took the rest of the stairs, one at a time, down into the pitch-black basement.

Craig would have positioned himself on the opposite side from the stairs, near the only other entrance, the bulkhead doors. Between us lay a haphazard tumble of junk whose exact disposition I couldn't recall. From the bottom of the basement stairs, I went forward, crablike, with my left hand stretched before me, expecting at any moment to hear the crack of the gun and the blinding flash. Ready—if I found myself still on my feet—to spring forward. I put one foot out and then brought the other up to it and inched forward. It must have produced a furtive, shuffling sound, but I knew there was no hope of moving silently, even if I had known where Craig waited for me.

I stopped for a moment to listen to Natalie's footsteps above and to my right, moving back, through the front hallway, toward the kitchen. I could hear her voice quite clearly as she castigated Craig, trying to provoke him to show himself.

I stood stock-still. There was no point in moving if I didn't know where he was. I wondered if I'd be able to hear him breathing once Natalie decided she'd exhausted the first floor and went upstairs. I was seized by the sudden fear that Craig was upstairs in my office, sitting patiently in my chair, and that I'd left her defenseless; but there were fewer places up there from which Craig could have staged an ambush, and the light of the moon through the windows would have provided too much light for his purposes.

Natalie fell silent and stood still. At that moment, she was directly above me, and I could hear the faint creak of the floorboards as she made minute adjustments of posture of which she probably wasn't even aware. There is a strange intimacy to being directly below the wooden floor on which someone else is standing. You're close and invisible. The creeks of the floorboards were like the secret sounds of her body, the respiratory tide, the thud of the pulse, almost as if I were inside her. This was how it had been for Craig when we entered the house. This was the strange, elusive intimacy, at once near and yet consigned to complete, desolate anonymity, which constituted Craig's relationship with Natalie.

She was listening, too. I held my stance. We were all listening.

We three held ourselves tense and vigilant for a long time. We were a pyramid of awareness: Craig aware of Natalie and myself; I aware of Natalie; Natalie aware of nobody.

The moment stretched out, taut as wire. There was nothing to hear. Not in the physical sense. Yet we strained after the presence of another human. In darkness, in silence, you fancy you can sense emanations. In fear, you become a believer in a faculty that the hunters and cannibals who preceded us would have had, now shriveled and vestigial as the appendix, as our sense of smell. You hope this faculty will dilate, become sensible, as eyes adapt to gloom.

There was nothing to see in that black cellar. There was nothing to hear. But in some uncanny way, I knew that someone stood against the far wall, to the left of the bulkhead doors. I felt sure enough of this to take the kitchen knife in both hands, very slowly, to adjust the handle so that it sat in my palm with the most reliable grip.

Then five things happened all at once. A car's tires crunched the gravel of the front drive. Natalie started running. A flashlight came on directly in front of me. I dove in what I thought was Craig's direction. A shot was fired at close range.

I'd been right in my intuition but wrong on the distance, and I came up short, at Craig's feet. My shoulder jammed into one of his knees and toppled him. Deafened by the shot, blinded by the light, I tried to keep him from breaking free. I had to land a blow, any blow, before he got off a second shot, but he struggled so violently that I couldn't locate the bulk of his body.

I stabbed into darkness. At the extreme point of the arc, about to overbalance, I felt the momentary puncture of fabric, and then the satisfying, more solid resistance of flesh, the jarring deflection of bone. He let out a cry of shock and pain, and as I rolled away I heard the clatter of the gun falling to the concrete floor. Flat on my back, I saw the beam of the flashlight flicker crazily over the joists above, then illuminate the walls. Still rolling, I heard the rasp of the gun sliding across the floor, away from me.

I went after the flashlight. He went for the gun.

The flashlight rolled away from me, down a slight incline on the concrete floor. I scrambled after it, reached, missed, fell. He shot at the light. I rolled in the opposite direction and came up on one knee.

The flashlight came to rest against an old mattress frame. In the dim glow of its indirect light, I could make out Craig. He held the gun on me. He was kneeling. Through gritted teeth he let out a stifled grunt of pain as he struggled to his feet. I could see that he had a wound in the thigh. As he staggered back to find support against the wall, I took the opportunity to stand. I measured the distance to the flashlight.

Out of view, from the top of the stairs, Abby called my name.

"No!" I shouted. "Don't come down here!"

At the same time, Craig called, "Down here!"

"It's over," I told her. "Get the police."

"For God's sake," Craig called to her. "Don't leave me with him."

He sounded desperate. It was a good performance. The pain was real enough to inject a tremor of fear into his voice.

At the top of the stairs, Abby put her head round the wall to catch a glimpse and immediately drew back.

"Please, Abby!" Craig called. "He's going to kill me. I have the gun, but I can't hold out much longer. Take it from me, Abby. Keep it safe."

It was compelling enough for Abby to take another look. She didn't draw back this time. A dark stain, midthigh on Craig's chinos, was visible even in that dim light.

"I'll come up," I said.

"No," Abby said. "Better you stay where you are."

"Where's Natalie?" Craig asked.

He was very solicitous. A wounded hero, selflessly asking after the woman he loved. He was good. He was a piece of work.

"Is she all right?" he asked.

"The telephone's out," Abby said. "I sent her over to the neighbors' to call the police."

Her trust in him was growing. Now she stood in full view where the stairs made a turn, her body exposed to the weapon. He was winning her over.

"Thank God she's safe," Craig sighed.

He swayed slightly and seemed to be having difficulty staying on his feet, though I thought the stain on his pants belied any trouble from blood loss. Nevertheless, he played it up for Abby's benefit. The gun in his hand wasn't pointing at anyone. It hung at his side, his arm limp. He didn't look threatening at all.

I stood with bloodied hand and knife. And I wasn't relaxing my guard for an instant.

"Abby," I said, calmly and levelly, "listen to me: You don't know what's going on here. You may think you do, but you don't. Get out now."

"He's crazy," Craig said. "He's obsessed. If you leave, he's going to kill me. Look!"

He turned to show the wound in his thigh. The patch of blood had spread.

"Ask him why he has the gun," I told her. "How is it he has my gun?"

"Sure," Craig said. "I can tell you that. But I need medical attention."

"Did you do that?" Abby asked me.

"I had to," I explained. It was futile. "He shot at me."

"I'm feeling faint," Craig said. "I'm going to need some serious help."

"It's not as bad as it looks," I said.

"How can you say that, when you did it to him?" Abby said. She was close to outrage.

Craig took one limping step. He said, "Let's get the flashlight, at least."

"Wait a minute," Abby told him. "I'd like it better if you stayed where you were."

Craig took a step back against the wall. "I'm not a threat to you, Abby. I'd never harm you. You know that. Take the gun. How about that? Would that make you feel safe?"

He held it out to her, dangling it by the trigger guard on one hooked finger. Abby started down the stairs, one by one.

"This is a mistake," I warned her. "Don't come down here."

"I can't just leave him."

"Ask him how he got the gun," I said. "Before you take another step, ask him that."

"I took it from you, you crazy bastard!" Craig yelled. "Where else would I get it? He got me down here, Abby. He was going to kill me, kill Natalie, kill himself. If I hadn't jumped him, we'd all be dead." He held his hand above the wound as if it emanated pain. "Look at him! Look at the knife in his hand!"

I must have presented a lurid, terrifying picture to my wife in that half-light, in the long shadows cast by the half-forgotten detritus of our past lives: disheveled hair and torn shirt from the struggle; a long knife held poised in a bloodied hand; on my face the wild look of a man with all the odds stacked against him.

"That's the gun that killed Lou Francone," I said. It was almost impossible to talk calmly, to project the weight and balance of reason, when all I wanted was to scream and rant. "This is the gun that went missing. Craig took it from my desk. He killed Lou. Then he came back with the gun to incriminate me."

"Give it to me," Abby told Craig. She'd come all the way to the bottom of the stairs. "Slide it across the floor."

Craig made a show of weakness in bending to place the gun on the concrete floor, and when he gave it a push with his foot, it was a feeble effort, so that the weapon stopped halfway between us.

Abby started toward it, but when I also took a step, she froze. I had wanted to give it to her. A gesture of good intent. She saw the man with the bloody knife going for the gun.

"Okay." I backed off.

"If I have the gun," Abby said, "then everybody's safe."

"If that's the only gun," I said.

Abby took three quick steps, snatched up the handgun, and retreated to the foot of the stairs.

"All right," she said in a new, take-charge tone. "I want you both up against the wall on either side of the bulkhead."

Abby held the weapon in a businesslike way, as if she really would pull the trigger if we stepped out of line. Or, if I stepped out of line. Because although the barrel scanned back and forth from Craig to me, Abby kept the gun mostly on me.

"Now we're going to wait for the police to come," she said.

"Think about it, Abby," I protested. "Just think about the situation you came in on."

"Don't try to manipulate me, Paul."

"At least consider why he gave you the gun. Why give up his weapon? What's in it for him?"

Two blows from the flat of a hand slammed against the metal bulkhead doors reverberated through the cellar like thunder, startling us all, especially Craig, who reached into a pocket on the right side of his coat.

"The police," Abby said. She seemed to slump as the tension went out of her. "Let them in," she told Craig.

She didn't notice that he kept his hand in his pocket.

"I'm sorry, Paul," she said. The gun was down. She seemed to have forgotten it as her body went limp and her arms flopped to her sides. There were tears in her eyes, and she shook her head in incomprehension. "I'm really sorry!"

She started to raise her arms in a gesture of helplessness, or it may have been an attempt to embrace a murderer from a distance. She let her arms fall, as if the effort to save me was beyond her strength.

"It seemed like a small thing, with Lou. It really wasn't important. And now . . . it all turned out so badly!"

When the person on the other side of the bulkhead swung open the door, it wasn't a cop who stepped through, but Natalie.

She had taken a hand that reached out to help her over the high step of the threshold, and when she saw that it was Craig's, she recoiled.

I took her arm and pulled her away, out of his reach. And I kept up the tension on her arm so that she continued on toward the spot where the flashlight lay, so that it seemed the momentum of her stepping down from the bulkhead carried her further, and she was quick-witted enough to scoop up the flashlight that lay at her feet.

The beam jiggled as she shifted it in her hands, and it threw looming shadows on the walls of the cellar. For a moment, the light splayed on the ceiling, then ran the length of the side wall. I lost track of Craig in the mixture of shape and shadow. A second later, Natalie brought the beam onto him and caught him in the act of slinking away toward the cover of an upright piano.

He grinned into the light Natalie held on him. He might have been a playboy caught in the glare of a paparazzo's flash. If she'd scrambled away from the touch of his hand, it didn't seem to matter.

"I knew you'd come," he said.

"What are you doing here?" Abby demanded. "Where are the police?"

"Screw the police," Natalie said.

"Hold up the gun, Abby," I told her. "Keep it pointed."

Her arm straightened like an automaton, even as she looked, uncomprehending, from one person to the next. "Are you insane?" she asked Natalie. "You were meant to call the police."

"You should go for them," Natalie said. She talked calmly and levelly. "We have something to take care of here."

"Go, Abby," I urged her. "Get out now."

"It's okay, Abby," Craig said. "Go to your neighbors. Go to the police."

"But what's going to happen here?"

"Craig wants to shoot me," I told her. It came out flat and emotionless. I was done with words. All I had a mind for was distance, angles, rates of closure, reaction time. My gun in her hand.

"Why don't you come with me to the police?" Abby asked me. It was more a plea than a question.

"It's too late. The only thing that can make a difference now is what you do with the gun. If you take it with you, he's going to shoot me with the other one in his coat pocket."

"I can't give it up."

"You don't have to," I told her. "All you have to do is shoot the liar."

"You think I know who that is."

"Sure you do."

"I don't."

"Then give the gun to Natalie."

"I have to keep it."

"Give us something, for God's sake!"

I heard a furtive movement from Craig's direction, a movement hidden by the edge of the piano. A very faint sound: the rustle of an object moving through fabric. Then, though Craig shuffled his feet to hide the sound, I heard him cock the old gun, the gun that had started it all, the one he'd held in his hand as he struggled with the writing assignment Natalie had set him.

"Shoot him now," I told Abby. But I knew she couldn't do it.

He'd shifted further to the right. He stood in an odd posture with his right hand held behind his back. He sensed the emotion tipping, the advantage moving away from him.

As he began the uncoiling movement that would bring out the gun from behind his back, I yelled to Natalie, "No light!" and the cellar went black.

I hurled the knife in Craig's direction and took three quick steps toward Abby and my gun. The blade hit the wall, then clattered on the floor. It sounded like Natalie had heaved over a pile of chairs to block Craig. Someone tripped and a box of books fell from a shelf and burst on the floor. Everyone was changing positions in response to everyone else under cover of the noise. I tried to keep track of everyone from the sounds they made, but it was approximate at best. Only Abby stayed put at the foot of the stairs.

I touched her arm. She started in fear, and I lost her in the darkness again.

"It's me," I whispered.

She had one foot on the first stair. I put my mouth to her ear. She didn't shy away.

"Trust me," I murmured. "You know me. You know who I am. You know I'm not the liar."

She didn't pull away. She didn't shake her head. I listened to her breathing, deep and regular.

We heard Craig move. I was afraid for Natalie. He was in pursuit of her. A chair was thrown. I thought Natalie would have done that. I had to have the gun before he caught her.

"Trust yourself," I told Abby. "Trust me. Give me the gun."

With aching slowness, aware that Craig might fire at any moment but afraid that if I made any assertive move I'd scare Abby away, I reached out into the darkness. My fingertips touched metal. She would have felt the weight of my contact along the barrel. She could have snatched the weapon away from me, if she'd wanted to, but her hands stayed still. My hand came back along the barrel until my fingers touched hers. Abby was trembling. As my hand closed over the body of the gun and over her hand, I felt her fingers beneath my own loosen. It was not a passive relinquishment. My two hands closed over hers and melded to them, and in that touch I sensed her acceptance in the darkness, in silence. She delivered the weapon to me.

I stepped quickly away from her and crouched by the hot water tank. I heard movement on the other side of the cellar, but I couldn't be sure who it was. I hoped Natalie would keep free of Craig long enough for me to get off a shot. I waited. I told myself to be patient. I couldn't fire if he'd captured her, if he held her. I took deep breaths. I held the gun up, ready to shoot. I prepared to kill a man. I was as steady as I would ever be.

"Are you free, Natalie?"

"Yes!"

Craig fired at the sound of my voice.

I rose up, pulled around to his muzzle flash, and squeezed the trigger.

The crash of the guns was deafening in that confined space. My ears rang and my eyes were dazzled by the flashes. I was still standing. I didn't feel pain, but I knew that could be deceptive. I realized the sound I heard was a stream falling from the punctured water heater onto the concrete floor. Then, as the ringing in my ears gradually cleared, the slowing stream splashed in silence.

I strained to catch the slightest noise that would give me Craig's position. No one moved. I heard no cry of pain, no moan.

We waited a long time, without speaking, without moving,

while the water from the tank diminished to a trickle and, finally, like sand run through an hourglass, emptied. Then we waited longer.

Finally, I said, "Nobody move."

When he didn't fire in the direction of my voice, I took a step in the direction in which I'd shot. I kept the gun stretched far in front of me, ready to pull the trigger on the slightest sound. I took one more step, and then one more. In darkness, distances are deceptive. With each step, I experienced the illusion I was about to bump against Craig.

I drew closer, hearing no sound, meeting no resistance. And then my gun did come up against something. I reached out with my other hand and found his shoulder, then his head which rested on it. The chest was wet and sticky from the wound, and when I ran my fingers up past the landmarks of the sternal notch, along the edge of the sternomastoid to the carotid artery, I could detect no pulse.

twenty—five

Detective Dempsey didn't let go of me easily. She didn't want to let me go at all. Now that they had my gun, ballistics had shown that it was the .25 that had been used to kill Lou Francone. It did turn up in my home. And, when the music stopped, I was the person holding the weapon. To her way of thinking, if I had the guts to kill Craig with a single shot, in pitch darkness, while being fired on, then I was capable of dispatching Lou in cold blood.

Abby had seen Craig holding the gun. But as Dempsey was quick to point out, she was my wife, and she might be inclined to say anything that would get me off the hook. Then, also, she'd only seen it by the unreliable illumination of a flashlight. And even Abby had to report that Craig said he'd wrestled it from me. The thigh wound was consistent with that story. My case was shaky, no doubt about it. Once you've seen an experienced prosecutor in action, you know that any opening can be leveraged to raise doubt about a witness's testimony.

In the end, they've had to let me go on with my life. "Lack of evidence," Dempsey grudgingly acknowledges. This doesn't make me innocent in the police's eyes. On the contrary. They "know" I did it, but they can't prove it. They have a number of cases like mine in their files. They can't go forward against me because they'll lose at trial and they can only try you once; but there is no statute of limitations for murder, and they vow they will never close the case. They'll wait, so Dempsey hopes, until I slip up, or someone with new evidence comes forward. Meaning Natalie, or Abby.

At the Methodist, Larry Shapiro has taken the tack that I'm innocent until proven guilty. In spite of his protests, Old Man Cavanaugh still sits on the hospital's board of trustees, and this would suggest that my continuing membership on the medical staff has caused no lasting damage to the hospital's relationship with its most important donor. Still, Larry would like me to go away. But in a society that doesn't know the difference between celebrity and notoriety, I'm in demand. When I gave Grand Rounds last month, the auditorium was packed, though I'm not sure everybody was paying close attention to some of the finer points in my lecture on declarative deception. My telephone rings off the hook with lawyers who want me as a defense expert; apparently they think, being a killer myself, I can relate to their clients. By and large, my colleagues treat me with kid gloves. Some of this is because they feel a bit sheepish after condemning me before all the evidence was in. And paradoxically, part of their new consideration arises from the uncertainty that still surrounds me: Do you really want to risk pissing off a guy who's already killed a man or—who knows?—maybe two?

At Sanders, my reception is less ambivalent. I have the unabashed respect of all staff and patients. Indeed, sometimes I catch a glint of frank admiration in the eye of a correctional officer. Apparently, I have earned my spot in the best of all possible worlds: I am both a killer and innocent. When I arrive at the front gate first thing in the morning, I rarely have to wait more than a few seconds before they buzz it open for me. As I pass through the front trap, though I feel the steely gaze of Lieutenant Kovacs on me, if I turn my head suddenly and catch him as he lolls in the chair rocked back to its farthest extent, there is a puzzled, reflective look on his face as he studies me.

I reflect, too, on what I have done. On the whole, I was more shaken up by my first lumbar puncture than by my first homicide. I know this sounds facile, but when you're really ready to kill another man, if you sincerely mean it, it doesn't take as much out of you as you might think. The first rule—Do it yourself—is much more than an injunction against hiring a hit man. Doing it yourself means being there, taking responsibility for your action. That's why it flows naturally into the third rule: You don't rush something you do mindfully, with all your faculties engaged. There can be no regrets when you do something this way. I have none. I sleep soundly at night, untroubled by dreams.

Mercifully, Abby and Natalie didn't have to see the violence. I hustled them out of the cellar and made sure they stayed upstairs until the police arrived. For them, Craig's death, in darkness, had an abstract quality. He disappeared. Even the body's exit from the house occurred through the bulkhead, out of view.

But for Natalie, the sense of Craig's presence lingered for a while. She told me that she would sometimes wake suddenly from deep sleep with the conviction that he was waiting for her in his black Accord parked in the street outside her apartment. She has pulled more into herself and remains distrustful of the kindness of strangers, chance encounters, blind dates. But there's a lot to be said for the geographic cure: She successfully defended her thesis and sent me a card from the city on the West Coast where she is an assistant professor at a private liberal arts college.

Time has not healed Abby of her grief over Adrian. Nor has the probing therapy of Ellen Hollenburg, however well-meaning and theoretically correct. Nor did her out-of-character fling with Lou Francone. For all our knowledge of serotonin receptors and evoked brain potentials, we still don't know what heals a broken heart. But I sense her sadness ebbing. Clouds remain, but our days together are dappled sunlight. I feel we are moving closer. I don't know the reason for this. Perhaps you have to be put at risk to feel more keenly what you do have. The reason why doesn't matter. The main thing is that our two lives are linked once more. I feel her presence. I feel her affection, like green shoots, tender, tentative, easily bruised. It's not so much what she says as the subtle background of her speech. I see the spontaneity of her pleasure in the gaps between words, when Abby may pause in mid-sentence, looking for the right phrase, only to abandon the search as her eyes come up to mine and she allows a secret smile to take possession of her lips. The contraction of the zygomatic major muscles is asymmetric, and there's a slight hunching and letting go of the shoulders, and . . . you get the picture.